Mitzi of the Ritz

by

Lee René

This is a work of fiction. Names, characters, places, and incidents are either the product of the author's imagination or are used fictitiously, and any resemblance to actual persons living or dead, business establishments, events, or locales, is entirely coincidental.

Mitzi of the Ritz

Cover Art by *Tina Lynn Stout*

The Wild Rose Press, Inc.
PO Box 708
Adams Basin, NY 14410-0708
Visit us at www.thewildrosepress.com

Publishing History:
Previously published by Solstice Publishing, 2016
First Vintage Rose Edition, 2020
Trade Paperback ISBN 978-1-5092-3199-7
Digital ISBN 978-1-5092-3200-0

Published in the United States of America

We descended the grand staircase. The flash of teeth, eyes, and diamonds nearly blinded us. The maître d'hôtel led us through a grove of papier-mâché palm trees everyone swore were leftover props from Valentino's *The Sheik*. The scent of perfume mingled with plumes of smoke from a thousand cigarettes. The gods and goddesses deserted Mount Olympus that night—hair coiffed to perfection, skin suntanned, teeth perfect, they had descended into the Cocoanut Grove.

A baritone crooned "Prisoner of Love" and caressed the microphone as if it were his lover, while a throng of extra girls stood at the foot of the bandstand in silent adoration. Mr. Factor had personally supervised the girls' transformations, and watched as an army of cosmetologists plucked, powdered, and rouged them. Hairdressers had lacquered every lock of hair, whether lemonade yellow or flaming red, into submission. They wore gowns of cerise, chartreuse, teal, and pale pink, blossoms of a giant bouquet cast at the singer's feet.

Votive candles illuminated every table, along with the tiny flares from cigarette tips. That night everyone drank "coffee" mixed with ginger ale or Coca-Cola. Omar smiled mischievously. "A cup of joe here is at least a hundred proof."

Stars flickered on the blue ceiling, but I kept my gazing to the celestial bodies crowding the dance floor.

Dedication

To my parents, William and Thora,
who planted the love of film and Hollywood in me.
Thank you to my late friend Steven Whitfield,
who is always close to my heart.

Chapter One
New York, New York

October 1930

Jews will tell you grief brings on a ferocious appetite. After Pops died, my older sisters and I buried him the next afternoon. Shiva, our week of mourning, began that evening. Most of our neighbors could barely feed themselves, yet food came in by the minute. By the second day, the tables in our tiny apartment groaned from the weight of fruit baskets and bowls of chopped liver. Plates of prune Danish blanketed our piano, and the starving mourners fell on the offerings like a pack of hungry lions.

Gloomy predictions lurked behind condolences, and some offered veiled prophecies of our inevitable downfall along with dishes of food. "Such a wonderful man to pass away so young. We heard he lost all his money in the horrible mess in '29."

One old biddy put it bluntly. "You poor girls, unmarried and with so much debt, how can you survive? Your father is dead. What will you do without husbands?"

I wanted to tell the nosey parker to buzz off, but kept my lips buttoned. Even in those desperate times, I knew I'd find a job. Nothing, except mourning my father, would stop me from looking.

My older sisters, Leah and Zisel, ignored the doomsayers and took comfort in the words of Pops' musician friends from Harlem. Times were tough, especially for performers, but the fellows had managed to scrape together fifteen bucks as a funeral offering. Between sips of coffee and nibbles of babka, a trombone player named Sneaky Pete regaled us with stories about Pops.

"No one played jazz fiddle like your pops. One night he gigged with Louis Armstrong and Bix Beiderbecke, and the three of them blew the roof off the joint. Isaac Schector, Benny Goodman, and George Gershwin were the hippest white cats in New York!"

By the third day of Shiva our apartment reeked of boiled eggs, stale grub, and humanity. Some of the ancient grandmothers and grandfathers suffered from flatulence that added to the stench. After each wave of visitors, I'd open the windows to air out the rooms and spritz our flat with Arpege perfume. It didn't help.

The seven days of Shiva ended, and my job search began the next morning. Leah had once earned a pittance teaching piano to pampered brats, but she'd changed occupations. She'd found work as a taxi dancer at Roseland, the biggest dance hall in New York. Leah shielded me from her dime-a-dance chums, yet she remained philosophical about her new occupation. "Being a nickel hopper isn't my dream job, but it sure beats starving."

The idea of tangoing with men reeking of tobacco and hair oil, sweaty fellows stepping on her feet while trying to cop a feel, made me want to puke. How could I expect my twenty-year-old sister to support me? I felt like a moocher every time I asked her for a quarter.

After all, hadn't I turned eighteen in August? Although it nearly killed me, I'd said farewell to college, dropped out of Barnard, put my dream of teaching music aside. Somewhere a job awaited me.

Before I left on my hunt that morning, our next-door neighbor caught me at the stairwell. The old fellow made a ritual of reading *The New York Times* cover to cover every day. He handed me the Help Wanted pages. Amidst somber advertisements for experienced stenographers, waitresses, and telephone operators, he'd circled the one bright light.

"The ad says, 'The famed Broadway Ritz Theater seeks an usherette. No experience required. Applicants must be willing to work multiple shifts. Only attractive young ladies need apply. Ask for Mr. Stein.' " He turned to me, a bright smile on his face. "This would be a perfect job for a pretty girl like you."

Only attractive young ladies need apply. I checked my face in my compact mirror, powdered my nose, and then applied lipstick and rouge. I'd heard makeup clogged the pores, but Leah pooh-poohed it. "As long as you pile on the Pond's cold cream to take it off, you can roll in it."

Not that my looks were so bad to begin with. Perhaps nature hadn't blessed me with the sultry beauty of my two older sisters, Leah and Zisel, but no one would call me a dog, either. With my round face, dark eyes, and dimpled cheeks, people swore I resembled the movie star Clara Bow, minus the red hair and penciled-in eyebrows. Folks, especially Gentiles, said I had very "American" features, which I guess meant I didn't look Jewish.

Zisel's new beau worked in the garment industry

and had given me a *très* chic black-and-scarlet woolen dress. The frock looked very professional, yet the bodice showed off my bosoms to full advantage. The new, longer length would set the ideal tone for my job search. I turned my red beret at a jaunty angle and marched off to the subway station, my nickel the ticket to the great White Way.

I stared up at a steel-and-concrete forest of skyscrapers that reached all the way to the heavens, where a sliver of blue sky peeked out. A fashionable belle in a fox fur smiled in my direction as I hurried down Broadway, and the jazzy trumpet of my favorite musician, Louis Armstrong, blared from the entrance to a music store. I took a precious minute to pop my fingers and tap my toes to the hot rhythm, but then remembered the time, and off I went.

As I rushed past the beautiful movie palaces and theaters dotting the street, an agent tipped his hat in my direction. The air smelled crisper than the first bite of a McIntosh apple, birds chirped, and despite the chilly weather, the sun cut through the concrete forest and beamed down on me. All at once, life was peachy keen again. It would be my red-letter day. Then I reached the Broadway Ritz. The queue of girls wanting the usherette job reached the end of the block. Some red-letter day.

I walked through a maze of cheap perfume to the back of the line. A few of the candidates glared at the additional competition. Some of the girls weren't exactly what I would call attractive, but what did I know? Several went heavy on the makeup with mascara and penciled brows. A couple even wore eye shadow, a product my late, lamented Aunt Sylvia swore only floozies used. I noticed a profusion of bottle blondes and henna-heads and felt a pang of jealousy because some had the money for finger waves. I possessed a shoulder-length mane of black, curly hair, longer than most, but longer hair was back in fashion, or so I hoped.

A muscular young man in a dark gray overcoat and Homburg hat, probably a lackey for Mr. Stein, walked past, sizing up the talent. He stopped before one, then another, and dismissed the flashier girls with a scowl. By the time he reached me, his mood hadn't improved, and he looked as if he'd swallowed a green persimmon.

From a distance, the fellow had a chiseled, Arrow-shirt air about him, and with his baby face, looked to be in his early twenties. Up close, I noticed the cut of his jaw, the full lips. He possessed the looks and arrogance of a movie actor, along with brilliant come-hither eyes, the most beautiful I'd ever seen. Tall, elegantly dressed, he smelled of Pinaud Clubman aftershave.

Mr. Handsome gave me a quick once-over, then turned away. My career as an usherette had ended before it began. But then, without warning, he doubled back, why I don't know, and took a second look. I'd never seen such a gorgeous guy before, and my heart almost beat out of my chest.

His eyes narrowed, he smirked like some wisenheimer fraternity boy, crooked a finger, and said, "Hey, girlie, follow me."

We walked past the losers, their bitter faces glaring in my direction. I glared back. I wanted to shout, "Don't blame me because he picked me. The guy knows what he wants and I need a job."

I forgot the sourpusses the moment I crossed the Broadway Ritz's threshold.

Stepping into the lobby could have been a stroll in Versailles. I followed Mr. Handsome through gargantuan marble columns flanked with giant mirrors shot through with gold. The reflection of the crystal chandeliers on the glass nearly blinded me. I almost collided with an usher in a scarlet uniform, who stood at attention like a palace guard.

My guide removed his hat and overcoat, then tossed them to his lackey. He had "debonair" written all over him, right down to his polished oxfords and the black suit that fit his tall frame to a T. He ran a hand through his dark hair, glanced back, and signaled for me to follow him. "Walk this way, sister."

We passed a Louis XIV-style fountain with perfumed water and dancing cherubs. I looked up at a massive bronze-and-mahogany staircase, the steps covered with the finest crimson carpet. The young fellow opened a door with a sign affixed to it reading "David Stein." He motioned me into Mr. Stein's office, pulled up a chair, and beckoned to me to sit.

"Take a load off those tootsies, little lady. What have you got for me?"

I didn't know what game he was playing, but I took the seat as ordered. He looked at my bosoms and smirked once again. I wanted to wipe the leer off his face, but I needed the job. Instead of telling him off, I handed over my high school diploma along with letters of recommendation from our rabbi and two of my Barnard professors.

"Will you please give these to Mr. Stein?"

He took a seat behind the desk and leaned back in his chair like the cock of the walk. "Mr. Stein? I'm David Stein."

Just what I needed, a spoiled playboy acting like a hotshot. He kept looking from my face to my bosoms. Perhaps I should have picked another frock. I was on the verge of walking out when I noticed the wedding band flashing on his left hand. A married man wouldn't try to put the moves on me, would he?

While Mr. Stein examined my papers, I glanced around his office. The place matched the theater for elegance and smelled of furniture wax and lemon soap. A paperweight embossed with the Harvard insignia sat on a highly polished desk with every scrap of paper, fountain pen, and inkwell perfectly positioned. Paper flags dotted a huge map affixed to the wall behind him, marking his theaters around the country. Mr. Stein finished his perusal and sat back in his chair, a big grin plastered across his kisser.

"These are very nice letters. So you're from the Washington Heights and a 'Barnyard' girl to boot? Swell."

"Yes, Mr. Stein, but my father just died, so I'll have to pack college away for a while."

He gazed at me so intently I averted my face. "So when did your old man pass away?"

The fact that Pops was no longer with us struck me once again, his death still so fresh it took a moment to answer. "Last week, sir. Shiva ended yesterday."

He folded his manicured hands into a pyramid. From the look of them, he'd never lifted anything heavier than a fountain pen in his whole life. "Sorry, doll."

His condolences seemed hollow, but he looked up at me, and the pain in his eyes took me aback. Could I have been mistaken? Was he sincere?

"Life's hard, isn't it? I'm a Harvard man myself, even graduated at the top of my class just to make those goy schlemiels choke on their own bile."

I'd heard about the trials and tribulations of Jewish boys at Ivy League schools. The outright hostility sometimes escalated into fistfights, much worse than the genteel anti-Semitism I'd experienced at Barnard. His mouth tightened.

"Mama wanted me to go on to law school, but my dad had other ideas. When he died last year, I had to take over the family business. Things fell apart. Pardon my French, but it was pure hell."

He stopped speaking. For a moment, we were two kids who'd had the rug pulled out from under us. Then the smirking started all over again.

"What the heck, I'm sure talking shop is boring to a charming young thing like you. So tell me, Miss Mitzi Schector, what can you offer the Ritz?"

I hadn't expected the question. "Uh, oh, uh, well, Mr. Stein, as you know, America is in a dreadful jam, and it's getting worse by the day. Maybe the bankers have stopped jumping out of windows, but businesses are still failing right and left. Folks don't have much joy in their lives except for the movies. I can show a little kindness, make them comfortable, help them forget the wolf at the door."

He seemed interested, so I kept talking. "I know things are tough, Mr. Stein, and I'll do anything you need—sell popcorn, mop floors, anything you throw my way. By the way, I can sing and play the piano, too."

His mouth tightened once again, and his eyes turned to green ice. I could tell the job had gone down the drain and rose from the chair. "Well, thank you for your time, sir."

Mr. Stein suddenly jumped up from his desk and stepped in front of me. He stood so close I could see the gold flecks in his eyes. "What's your hurry, baby? I wouldn't have brought you in if you didn't have the job. Go get your uniform and show up tomorrow at ten. You can work the matinee."

He took my hand in his. "How about we shake on it?"

After we shook, Mr. Stein stared into my face for a long moment without releasing my hand. I don't know what he was looking for, but the guy unnerved me. It seemed forever before he released me. I rushed out of his office as quickly as my legs would carry me.

Mr. Stein followed me, flagged over the head usher, and whispered something into the fellow's ear. Whatever he said brought a leer to the chump's pimply face. The usher signaled to me with his forefinger, and I followed him down a dimly lit corridor to the staff dressing rooms. He handed me my uniform and a key. "Your locker is number 301, toots."

The fellow smirked and licked his lips. "Mr. Stein figured you'd wear a small. Since you're starting tomorrow, he thought it would be a good idea if you caught a movie to see how we run the place."

I followed him into the auditorium. The fragrance of fresh popcorn perfumed the enormous room. Exquisite murals covered the walls and crimson-colored velvet covered the chairs, but the orchestra pit sat deserted. In the days of silent dramas, the Broadway Ritz had had a full orchestra and presented saucy musical prologues before screening the movie.

Unfortunately, after they wired the place for talkies, the Ritz had switched to canned music. The days of live music floating through the auditorium into the sumptuous lobby had ended.

The auditorium went black, the stage curtains opened as if by magic, and the famed Regal Pictures logo, a gloved hand shooting an arrow from a bow, the arrow propelled around the globe, appeared on the screen. Metro might have Leo the Lion, but everyone in the world recognized the Regal Pictures arrow circling the globe.

The newsreel echoed what everyone in America knew—the times stank and America had plopped into the crapper. They finished and the screen went dark once again. The Regal logo flashed on the screen, followed by the words *The Devil Dancer*, the new offering from Regal Pictures, starring my favorite actor, Rex Dallas, as Detective Harry Paige, and the colored comedian Buster Sweet as his partner.

I knew *The Devil Dancer* wouldn't be a masterpiece. Regal Pictures didn't make masterpieces, but in my humble opinion, no one in moving pictures had the charm of the dashing Rex Dallas. He hailed from Georgia and, despite the lousy sound, Miss Louella Parson's description of his Southern drawl rang true. "Rex Dallas has a voice like molten honey." Mr. Dallas uttered his signature phrase, "Time's a' wasting, Buster!" and the audience broke into applause. When the movie ended, I didn't walk out of the Ritz, I floated.

Chapter Two
Mr. Nussbaum

I arrived home barely able to catch my breath but called out, "Leah, I have a job!" Before she could answer, I heard a knock at the door. When I opened it, Mr. Nussbaum, the owner of our brownstone, stood in the doorway.

I guess you'd call Mr. Nussbaum a sharp dresser. A wiry man in his thirties, he had an affinity for pinstriped suits, spats, and fedoras. Still, one look at his angry mug would give anyone the heebie-jeebies. Words like "thug" and "gangster" stuck to him like chewing gum on a shoe sole. Grown men made way when he walked down Fort Washington Avenue, and some even crossed to the other side of the street. He rarely spoke above a whisper, but the air of menace surrounding him escalated the moment he opened his mouth.

"Hello, Leah. Hello, Mitzi."

My stomach knotted when he took my face in his hands and gave me a pained look like the movie star John Gilbert mooning over Greta Garbo. Leah twisted her handkerchief, and I knew her nerves were on end. She smiled weakly, then pointed to a parlor chair.

"Mr. Nussbaum, please sit down. Mitzi, why don't you put on a kettle for tea? You're welcome to join us. Would you care for a slice of apple cake?"

His face contorted into something resembling a

smile. "Yes, that would be lovely."

Nussbaum turned to Leah with what some might call a soulful expression on his mug. Maybe he wanted to show he shared our grief, but to me he looked as if he needed to pass gas. He settled back in our best chair as if he owned the place, which of course he did. Leah pointed me toward the kitchen.

"Mitzi, please, make the tea."

I hated leaving my sister alone with the likes of Joseph Nussbaum and planted my ear firmly to the door. Nussbaum spoke so softly I strained to hear.

"Leah, please accept my condolences on the death of your father, such a fine gentleman. Everyone will miss him. I understand your pain since I lost my own dear wife."

What a load of hooey. Everyone swore he'd bumped off his "dear wife" then made it look like an accident. I kept my ear on the door, but conversation stopped and the flat went silent. I peeked into the living room praying he'd left, but no such luck. They faced each other, Leah twisting her napkin, Mr. Nussbaum's lips stretched in an angry smile.

"Leah, don't think me insensitive, but there are practical matters to discuss. You see, I made allowances for your family. I prefer cultured tenants, and since Mr. Schector worked as a violinist for the New York Philharmonic—"

Leah interrupted. "First violinist. My father was first violinist."

"Of course, first violinist, and because of that, I asked for half the rent I could have charged."

Leah jumped up from the wooden crate, and I hoped she'd give the bum the old heave-ho, only she didn't. "Mr. Nussbaum, this isn't the time to discuss money, especially with my younger sister in the next room. Yes, the Crash killed my father, and we'll never get over his loss. It's as bad as when Mama died in 1918, during the influenza epidemic, but don't worry about the rent, Mr. Nussbaum. I have a job and Mitzi has just found employment. We don't like to think of life without Pops, but at least we have each other."

When Leah walked into the dining room and hauled down my photos, I knew what would happen next—the kvelling. Leah took pride in my smallest accomplishment and praised me to the hilt.

"I wasn't much of a scholar, but let me show you how accomplished my little sister is. Here she is playing the Wurlitzer organ at the Capitol Theater, only ten years old. Look, Mr. Nussbaum, our little genius at her high school graduation, not quite fourteen yet president of her class. Did you know about the quota on Jews at Barnard? They wanted my little sister anyway. Imagine, our Mitzi, fourteen years old and already a college girl."

Oh, the humiliation, but thankfully she didn't pull out my baby pictures. Nussbaum took the photographs and caressed them for what seemed an eternity.

"Yes indeed, Mitzi is a beautiful, cultured girl."

After he left, I'd scrub the picture frames down with bleach. The kettle whistled and I arranged the tea, pastry, lemon slices and lumps of sugar on a tray. How easily I could have spooned strychnine into his cup, but it would have been inhospitable, even for him. I slapped a phony smile on my face, waltzed into the living room, and placed the refreshments on the ottoman.

"Mitzi, why don't you go to your room? Mr.

Lee René

Nussbaum and I have things to discuss."

I managed another approximation of a smile and stepped out of the room. Suddenly, I thought better and snuck back into the hallway. If Leah needed help throwing the bum out on his ear, I'd be near.

"Mr. Nussbaum, did you come to share in our grief? If not, may I be so bold as to ask why you're here?"

Nussbaum didn't answer right away since he was busy stuffing his face with pastry. He slurped his tea, rattled the plate onto our coffee table, and resettled his rump in the chair.

"Very tasty, thank you." Nussbaum smacked his lips, then dropped the bombshell. "Leah, I'm here to make an offer of marriage."

Pops had died six short days ago and the skunk proposed to my sister? Yes, he was a rotten egg all right, but this took the cake. "What you ask is impossible, Mr. Nussbaum. Pops isn't even cold in his grave, and we barely know each other."

Nussbaum picked up the teapot and poured, seemingly transfixed as the amber liquid trickled into his cup. He threw in four lumps of sugar and sucked down his tea like the toad he was. I hoped he'd get diabetes or at least choke to death.

"Leah, you're a woman of great charm and beauty, but I couldn't propose marriage to a dancehall gal."

The room went silent. Nussbaum slurped more tea, then began chortling. "You didn't think I knew about you working at Roseland, did you? Girlie, I have eyes and ears around the city. No, it's Mitzi that I want to talk to you about. I want to marry her."

Me? Suddenly, I couldn't breathe. Leah sat

14

speechless, and Mr. Nussbaum appeared to enjoy her confusion. He wore a triumphant grin on his ugly puss, one I would have loved to wipe away with a punch in the nose.

It took a moment for Leah to find her tongue. "Mr. Nussbaum, Mitzi is a young lady of eighteen and has no plans to be a wife. As I said before, she has a new job and hopefully will be able to return to her studies shortly. I'm afraid we must decline your offer."

My stomach rumbled, and I regretted breakfasting on lentil soup and bagels. I leaned against the wall to keep from slipping to the floor. Scum that he was, Nussbaum appeared to relish Leah's discomfort.

"Look, sister, I'm putting my cards on the table. Everyone knows your father speculated in the stock market and left you penniless. Let's be honest—you have no money, or else you wouldn't be prancing around for dimes in a dance hall. I have lots of long green and can afford to be generous. Mitzi is a cultivated young lady, a real looker, and I have the means to take care of her."

Wasn't the year 1930? Did this dolt think I'd wander around Manhattan dressed in rags, with a pushcart? Weren't the days of arranged marriages over?

My sister stared at Nussbaum, her look one of complete shock, but it didn't stop him from flapping his jaws. "As for you, Leah, your pain can be avoided. I'll pay any debts plus give you enough money for you to be free of Roseland and dancing until your feet drop. Mitzi will want for nothing, and you can stay in this beautiful apartment, free of any obligation. All I ask is for your sister."

Leah rose, grabbed his hat, and walked to the door.

"You've given me a great deal to think about, Mr. Nussbaum."

Nussbaum chugged down the rest of his tea and jumped up from the chair, a victorious grin on his face. "I'm a very patient man, Leah. By the way, since we'll be relations, please call me Joe. Shalom."

Leah shut the door behind him. "I know you were listening, Mitzi. Come here."

I entered the room, took one look at her face, and bawled like a baby. "Leah, I'll work my fingers to the bone, but don't make me marry that horrible man. Please."

My tears were infectious, and she sobbed as she pulled me close. "Silly baby, do you think I'd let that animal touch you? I'll speak to Zisel before I kill him."

****

Zisel showed up the next morning, dressed to the nines as usual. She wore a woolen frock with a capelet rimmed in mink, a matching cloche, and elbow-length gloves. Although she was only a few years older than Leah and me, she'd already been widowed twice, and always wore black.

People celebrated the beauty of the Schector girls, yet our styles were quite different. People referred to me as cute and pert, while they labeled Leah the seductress. Zisel had mastered the European hauteur look. Her style was as au courant as a page of *Vogue Magazine*. She'd bobbed her dark hair and become a devotee of Elizabeth Arden's face powder, rouge, scarlet lipstick, and nail polish.

Zisel, the very picture of elegance, removed her gloves and began drumming her Chinese-red nails on the tabletop. "The nerve of that schmuck. Let me at that lecher. What are we? Polish trash who pimp their daughters for a few shekels?"

Leah looked at me and turned crimson. "Please, you can't use that kind of language in front of Mitzi."

Zisel scowled at her and kept ranting. "Mitzi better learn that kind of language if she's going to live in this world. If that crumb thinks he can stick his schlong in our baby sister, he's got another think coming. I'll cut it off first."

She collapsed onto the chaise, but I knew her second wind was imminent. "Nussbaum is a crook and a chiseler. In the old days, they would have strung the bastard up. He shot his wife when he got tired of her, and his police cronies helped him get away with it. Suicide, my ass! I heard when he left New York a few years ago, all of Washington Heights danced in the streets. Unfortunately, the louse came back. If he wants Mitzi, he'll never give up."

Those weren't the words I wanted to hear. Leah began sobbing with the same bitter intensity as she had when Pops died. Zisel blabbed away, undaunted. "He'll make your lives a living hell if you refuse him. Even if we found another place in the city, he'd have his hoodlums search you out, and the police won't help. Leah, you have to take Mitzi away."

Zisel's words spurred Leah to find her voice. "Zisel, do you want us to surrender to that monster? Isn't this 1930 New York City, not 1830 Russia? We should fight, shouldn't we? What about Mitzi and her new job?"

"Forget about the stupid job, Leah. We've got to save our baby."

When Papa became ill, I had to drop out of

Barnard. Now, I'd have to give up the Broadway Ritz, Zisel, and New York. I might as well jump off the Brooklyn Bridge. Zisel raised my chin and looked me square in the eyes. "Mitzi, we'll have to get you far away."

Leah chimed in. "What about New Jersey?"

Zisel nixed her suggestion. "No, Jersey is too close, and so is Chicago. What about Los Angeles?" Leah stared at our older sister as if not comprehending. She repeated the words. "Los Angeles? Where poor Baron burned to death?"

The two siblings looked at each other in silence for a painful moment, then Zisel nodded. "Yes, Leah, Los Angeles. I know Uncle Baron died there, how could I not remember? It cut our family in two. Our grandmother died a broken woman because of that spoiled boy."

Leah glared at Zisel. "You shouldn't speak ill of the dead."

Zisel returned her nasty look with one of her own. "You can't stop me from telling the truth, Leah. Baron caused our family nothing but pain. Do you remember when Papa rushed across the country to search for Baron? He left Bubbe alone to fend for three girls. She had to turn to friends for the money to feed us and keep a roof over our heads."

When Zisel jumped from her chair, I knew only an Act of Congress would shut her up. "Nineteen years old, the path as a scholar already mapped out for him, but Baron abandoned everything. He finagled a job at Regal Pictures and burned to death before Pops found him. No one should have died like that."

Zisel slumped into a chair, winded and sobbing.

The room became hushed. Then the grandfather clock struck nine, puncturing the silence.

After a few minutes, Leah spoke. "Yes, Zisel, it's a sad story, and you're right, Los Angeles is where we should go. It's far away from Nussbaum." She steeled her shoulders. "We never learned where they buried poor Uncle Baron. That sweet boy is lying somewhere with no family to tend to his grave. Perhaps we can finish Pops' search."

I looked around our living room with its saffron walls covered with paintings, and the New York sky shining through the bay window. This had been my home since I could remember, but we'd have to leave it. May God forgive me, but at that moment, I hated Joseph Nussbaum more than anyone in the world.

Chapter Three
The Fuller Brush Man

The next morning I arrived at the Broadway Ritz with a throbbing headache. A confrontation with a furious David Stein didn't lessen my pain. He'd dressed in a natty pinstriped suit with spectator shoes, smelled like paradise, and looked even more handsome than the day before. I hadn't prepared myself for his anger, and his irate response to me quitting took me aback.

"What the hell do you mean you've got to quit? You haven't even started yet."

I told him as much as I dared. "Please, Mr. Stein, I'm so sorry. You have every right to be sore. I don't want to leave, but there's this fellow, and well, Leah and I have to get away from New York."

His beautiful eyes blazed with so much fury, I stepped back from him. "Fellow? Did you get yourself in trouble or something?"

How dare he ask such a question! "I'm not having a baby, if that's what you're thinking. The guy's a thug, and I hate his guts, but he's twisting my sister's arm because he wants to marry me."

His eyes softened. "A thug? I have friends on the police force."

"Yes, and so does he. The police looked the other way when he shot his wife."

When he took my hand, I didn't pull away. "Mitzi,

I'm a man of means. I can help you."

I had a vision of the Broadway Ritz in flames. "I can't talk about it, Mr. Stein. Believe me, you don't want to get involved. Let's just say it's a family matter, and Leah and I have to leave New York, pronto."

"Where are you going, Mitzi?"

"To Los Angeles. You see, this fellow is after us, and we have to vamoose. My sisters decided we should go there. My uncle died in Los Angeles years ago, and we're going to find his grave. I haven't told anyone but you because the louse might find out. He's a real stinker and could make plenty of trouble."

Mr. Stein gazed into my eyes for an uncomfortable moment, his handsome face unreadable. He picked up an embossed card from the holder on his desk and handed it to me. "Sounds like you've been through the wringer, doll, but maybe your luck is changing. I own a theater in Los Angeles. It's not grand like the Broadway Ritz, but I always can use an extra usherette. I'm leaving for Los Angeles tomorrow. Call me as soon as you arrive."

He looked at me with such intensity I felt a blush coming to my face. "Yes, Mr. Stein."

His mouth spread into a wide, Cheshire-cat grin. "I know you're a woman of your word, Dollface, but how about we shake on it?"

He held my hand in his for a moment, then turned it over and kissed my palm.

"Goodbye, Mitzi. We'll meet soon."

I looked down at his card as soon as I left his office.

David Lincoln Stein, Stein International Theatre Company.

Perhaps I should have been turning cartwheels at the prospect of steady work in a new town with a young, handsome boss. Still, something dark and troubling gnawed at my psyche, and stopped me from jumping for joy.

****

We left New York on the twelfth of November. That morning I ignored Nussbaum's threat and strolled through our neighborhood. I said farewell to everyone and everything I knew. Although Pops adored the highbrow stuff, Chopin and Debussy, he loved popular music too. We'd while away the hours listening to Louis Armstrong and Duke Ellington on our Victrola. Al Jolson's jazzy baritone became my father's favorite, and he often swore, "Nobody sings like Jolson."

Pops had delighted our friends and neighbors by belting out "I'm Sitting on Top of the World," "April Showers," "Swanee," and his number-one favorite, "Blue Skies."

No matter how lousy life became, while the world sank deeper in the crapper, Pops had a perpetual smile on his face, even after the Crash took everything and finally killed him.

Images, smells, and sounds flooded my senses: the soulful clarinets of klezmer music, Yiddish radio, and strolls down Fifth Avenue, while taxi drivers honked their horns for no reason.

That evening, Leah, Zisel, and I walked under one of Penn Station's monumental arches. Leaded glass windows released ribbons of light in every direction. I stopped in my tracks, awed by acres of stone, concrete, and steel. Zisel's voice soon brought me back to earth. "Mitzi, stop dawdling. You have a train to catch!"

The three of us marched through the station, constantly looking over our shoulders in case Nussbaum and his goons had tracked us there. For the past two weeks, Leah and I had been in hiding at Zisel's brownstone and couldn't even mourn my father properly. We didn't have an ounce of courage left between the two of us, and the frenetic pace of the station only added to our anxiety.

Our enemy had sworn to set fire to everything we owned, but Leah and Zisel had the last laugh. We'd slipped out of his clutches and the crumb could bay at the moon for all we cared. Perhaps the rabbi of the grand new temple in Los Angeles would find us lodgings and, most importantly, jobs. After we settled, we vowed to search for Uncle Baron's grave.

Heads turned at Leah in navy serge and Mrs. Zisel Goldberg looking hoity-toity in her signature black. People swore my eldest sister resembled the movie actress Kay Francis, but in my humble opinion Zisel surpassed her in every way. Leah possessed a quality that turned on men's motors. Folks described me as cute as a bug's ear, but everyone swore I had the best figure. I walked behind my two sisters and got a few whistles myself.

Zisel dropped a roll of cash into Leah's pocketbook.

"Guard this with your life. It should keep you going for a while. I'll be expecting a telegram as soon as you arrive in Los Angeles. Leah, I expect you to take care of our baby." She turned to me, a concerned expression on her beautiful face.

"Mitzi, you listen to your big sister. Don't either of you worry about Pops—I'll look after his grave. You guys concentrate on Baron. With a little luck, some thug will shoot Nussbaum between the eyes and you'll come back to me."

When Zisel began sobbing into her handkerchief, the bawling started in earnest. Leah transformed from seductive vamp into a red-nosed ball of snot, and I could barely contain myself. "Zisel, it's bad enough that Leah's blubbering, and now you're a big creampuff too. We'll never make our train."

Zisel took my face in her hands. "Promise you'll both write as soon as you're settled. If I don't hear from you two, I swear, I'll call the cops."

With that, she pointed her Kodak camera at me. "I have lots of pictures of Leah, Pops, and Mama, but I want something to remember you by. Say cheese, my little Mitzi."

I failed miserably in fighting off my tears, but tried to flash a smile. The camera clicked, Zisel took one last look, then walked away. I started bawling like a crybaby, then dried my tears. Leah and I had practical matters to consider. Zisel had heard lurid tales of crossing the country by Greyhound, so she'd refused to let us take the bus to Los Angeles.

"Do you know what happens to pretty girls at those bus stops? Pimps kidnap them and sell them into white slavery!"

Everyone knew folks exaggerated stories of life on the road, but Zisel refused to listen. She'd spent an arm and a leg on train tickets, and I wondered how Leah and I could ever repay her.

Leah and I would leave New York on the Broadway Limited, then transfer in Chicago to travel in the lap of luxury on the famed Santa Fe Chief. I looked around the vast waiting room. The aroma of freshly percolated coffee mingled with the scent of desperation permeating the place. Although everyone had put on a brave face and dressed in their Sunday best, few had the money for anything other than a cup of joe.

A thin woman with dark circles under her eyes spent the long hours crying into a soggy handkerchief, ignoring her two monstrous children as they wreaked havoc throughout the terminal. The couple sitting across from us held each other, whispering as they looked at photos of a smiling child. They'd just buried their son, and their grief compounded the general feeling of hopelessness. Only a pair of newlyweds on their honeymoon appeared immune to the misery that surrounded them. They spent every moment staring into each other's eyes, oblivious to everyone else.

Could things get any worse? It would be hard to top the Crash unless all of Penn Station came down with bubonic plague. Then I heard a voice through the din, a salesman hawking his wares.

"Lovely ladies, this is your lucky day. I'm selling a lot more than brushes. How about stockings that feel like silk, the best face powder on the market, all at a big discount. For the gents, I have talc and shaving cream to make your skin as soft as a baby's bottom."

A group of Fuller Brush men made their way through the terminal, their suitcases packed with goodies. The fellows bustled with youthful energy as they strolled through the waiting room flashing ear-to-ear grins. I admired their gumption, peddling their wares in these desperate times, and even the guards looked away.

One guy in particular stood out. He wore a snazzy

serge suit, had pomaded his blond hair in place, and his blue eyes blazed like a million klieg lights. I'd read the Fuller Brush Company hired fellows right out of college, and this handsome dude couldn't have been over twenty.

The gloom lifted, people forgot their troubles, and the Depression blues vanished. The fellow charmed every woman in the place, refusing to take no for an answer. After he sold his goods, Mr. Fuller Brush Man dipped further into his bag of tricks.

He signaled to the other fellows, and they opened music cases in unison. One pulled a harmonica from his pocket, another a clarinet from his brush case, and one more an accordion from who knows where. A fourth fellow tapped out a downbeat on a small drum, and the makeshift band went to town.

The gorgeous leader walked around the waiting room strumming a ukulele as he serenaded everyone with a snappy rendition of "When You're Smiling." The Fuller Brush man sang out in such a resonant baritone that I nearly jumped out of my shoes.

Leah shoved me over in his direction. "Go on, sing with them. They might pass the hat." My skin turned to gooseflesh when the blond fellow looked me up and down and said, "What's cooking, good looking?"

Good looking? I felt a blush moving up from the bottom of my feet to the top of my head. "How about I sing with you? I'm good, I swear I am."

His eyes twinkled, and he whispered, "Heck, if you sing half as good as you look, we're aces." He called out to passengers and passersby alike, "The little lady wants to sing. Should we let her?"

People applauded, and he whispered, "What tune,

baby?"

Wow, he called me "baby" as if I were his girlfriend. "How about "Singing in the Rain"? In E flat?"

He nodded to his fellow buskers, played the opening vamp, and I belted the song out like Sophie Tucker. The guy seemed awfully impressed and flashed his million-dollar smile my way. "You got a great set of pipes."

I didn't have time for false modesty. "My father always said I could warble with the best of 'em. You ought to hear me tickling the ivories."

He grinned that whiter-than-snow Fuller Brush smile again, and my heart soared. "Maybe I will one day. Hey, little lady, how about "It Don't Mean a Thing If You Ain't Got that Swing"?"

I gave him a nod and boy, did we wow them. Our audience spurred us on, shouting out their favorites. Even the guards patrolling the station got on board and popped their fingers along with everyone else. I sang with all the passion I could muster, and the guy harmonized like a pro.

"Hey, Mr. Fuller Brush Man, you've been holding out on me!"

I matched him lyric by lyric, song by song. Our voices blended so perfectly that folks from all over the station found their way to our impromptu nightclub. By the time we finished our little concert, even the sourest apple applauded. He passed the hat, and we split twenty-four dollars and forty-eight cents!

Leah had planted her face in a book and didn't notice when the Fuller Brush man crammed a paper bag into my hands. I could barely contain myself when I saw the lipsticks in shiny steel tubes, tiny pots of rouge, silver compacts, and face powder.

He gave me a Fuller Brush grin. "I know you're a natural beauty, baby, but every girl likes a little help."

I felt heat on my face. Guess I was a blushing fool as well as a natural beauty. I stuffed the treasure into my pocketbook.

"We're going to Los Angeles, and I'll need this with all the glamour girls there. This is a real mitzvah."

His blank look told me he definitely wasn't Jewish. " 'Mitzvah' means an act of kindness."

The Fuller Brush man kept smiling but didn't say a word. I felt my face warming, my knees shaking. You might as well call me Nervous Nelly, but I managed to extend my hand. "My name is Mitzi, Mitzi Schector, S-C-H-E-C-T-O-R."

He laughed and his eyes crinkled in the corners. I thought I'd plotz right there on the spot, blow up into a million pieces that would scatter all over the terminal.

"The name's Chick Hagan, H-A-G-A-N, of the Fuller Brush Company, but that's just temporary. I have a good feeling about you, Mitzi S-C-H-E-C-T-O-R. Kid, you've got talent in spades. I envy you going to Los Angeles. I sing with these fellows, the Society Crooners, and we've played gigs all over the state. Heck, we're making my way to Los Angeles one step at a time."

He stopped talking for a moment and grinned. "Aw, enough about me, baby. We'll meet again, Good Looking. I can feel it."

Then Chick stroked my cheek, his hand as gentle as velvet. Forget about plotzing. My heart would explode and I'd probably keel over and die right there in Penn Station. He took my hand for a moment, brought it to his lips, then went on his way with a tip of his hat.

How could our paths ever cross once more? Leah and I were on our way to sunny Los Angeles, while Mr. Chick Hagan and the Society Crooners would be stuck here in New York with the Fuller Brush Company. Maybe we wouldn't see each other again, but I knew I'd never forget him.

When I brought Leah the riches from my singing adventure, she practically did a backflip. "And I thought we'd be stuck eating the liverwurst sandwiches I brought."

We locked arms as we walked to the underground concourse where the Broadway Limited awaited us, and on the way we passed a magazine kiosk. Rex Dallas, my idol, grinned at every passerby from the cover of *Photoplay*. Seeing his smiling face made me feel a million times better.

****

That night, I thought of Uncle Baron, so beautiful, so reckless. I remembered how he'd cradle me in his arms and whisper, "You hold my heart in your hands, little Mitzi."

The rhythm of the train lulled me into dreamland. I lay glued to the mattress, unable to move as a handsome Fuller Brush man blew hot breath on the side of my face. My dream man took my chin in one hand and warmth spread between my legs. His beautiful mouth caressed my cheek, and then he whispered, "Mitzi, baby, kiss me, please."

His lips moved to my mouth, closer, closer, then— I woke up. Maybe I should have felt guilty about my wicked dream, but I didn't, not in the least. In fact, I'd never had a better one.

Chapter Four
The Santa Fe Chief

The next morning Leah and I took our place in the elegantly appointed dining car with all the swells going to Chicago. The Broadway Limited attracted the carriage trade, regal matrons, sober businessmen, and a few cigar-chomping fuddy-duddies who treated the porters like slaves.

With everyone acting so hoity-toity and living high off the hog, you'd never know there had been a Crash. What fakes we were, two Jews facing the poor house, but since the other passengers dressed to the nines, we did too. I wore a Kelly green frock; Leah dressed in black gabardine, with faux pearls at her throat, the epitome of European chic. Who would have guessed we'd been born in Flatbush?

Sixteen hours after Leah and I had left New York, the Broadway Limited rolled into Chicago, where we'd change trains. We looked around the spanking new Chicago Union Station, only five years old, a stunning mass of steel arches and concrete. Folks called its main concourse the portal to the Midwest, yet the massive driveways built for taxis and automobiles offered no protection from the murderous weather. An icy squall dispatched newspaper pages higgledy-piggledy, reached under the ladies' skirts and gentlemen's collars, encircled heads, tossed hats into the air.

A porter, observing the mayhem, yelled out to me, "Watch out, little lady. There's a reason they call the Chicago wind the Hawk."

Yes, the wind reminded me of a bird of prey, grasping everything in its frigid claws. Only the newlyweds I'd seen in Penn Station took no notice of the freezing gale. They wrapped themselves in the young man's greatcoat and floated away into their future.

The elegant Santa Fe Chief stood in wait for us, her sleek chrome lines majestic in the bright light.

A crowd of photographers swarmed over the platform, flashbulbs popping, the whole place scented with burnt glass and flash powder. Leah and I pushed through a mass of newsmen, none of whom paid us an ounce of attention. The air crackled with electricity as reporters jostled past the two of us. Suddenly, a cry went up, and a crowd blocked our way. "It's Jill Carpenter!"

Every orb focused on a beautiful girl with silvery blonde hair perched atop a mountain of luggage. Another explosion of a million flash bulbs, and a photographer called out, "Hey, Jill, give us a smile."

I heard a collective intake of breath when the young woman turned to face the cameras. Venus had just risen from the sea. Hollywood had named the goddess Jill Carpenter, the *Movie Mirror*'s cover girl and Regal Pictures' rising star. Her skin looked as though it had been fired from the finest porcelain. She had plucked her eyebrows into near nonexistence, then penciled them back in, rouged her lips, and lacquered her platinum hair. Miss Carpenter smiled, revealing a set of dazzling white teeth. She finally spoke, her polished tones that of an actress trained in elocution.

"Ladies and gentlemen of the press, I'm overjoyed to be here with you, and thrilled with the critical praise of my motion picture, *Honeymoon Hijinks*. I want to thank Mr. Ben Roth, President of Regal Pictures, for giving me this wonderful opportunity."

Miss Carpenter blew a kiss at a powerfully built man watching from the sidelines. Mr. Ben Roth looked to be in his late thirties, and although he missed being handsome by a hair, he possessed something more compelling than simply good looks. Mr. Roth exuded power all the way from his polished oxfords to his homburg hat. He never averted his pale blue gaze from the actress.

At the mention of Ben Roth, something icy zipped up my spine, and it wasn't the Hawk. Leah squeezed my hand, her eyes misted, and she looked away. We'd known his name since our childhood, when Pops' younger brother, Baron, a handsome youth as wild as a whirlwind, ran away from home to get in the movies. My father left New York and searched all over Los Angeles before discovering Baron worked as an extra at Regal Pictures. Leah whispered in my ear, and I heard the catch in her voice.

"Pops had planned to bring Uncle Baron home by hook or by crook, but fate intervened. Poor Uncle Baron. He died on the Regal Pictures lot in a horrible fire that also killed the movie actress Clarice Dumont."

Although Leah spoke under her breath, I heard the anger simmering beneath her calm façade.

"The world mourned Clarice, the golden-haired shiksa, but no one outside of our family knew about our Uncle Baron. The movie people sent blood money, a check signed by the president of Regal Pictures, Mr. Ben Roth himself. Remember how our poor grandmother shriveled up and died from grief? It was then I learned the difference between money and happiness. To hell with Ben Roth and all his gold."

Without warning, Miss Carpenter turned her back on the reporters and dropped her fur cloak, revealing a winter-white sheath dress that accentuated every curve. The sleek lines were a dead giveaway. It had to be a creation of Regal Picture's great couturier. "Look at that beautiful dress, Leah. Alexandre of Paris must have designed it just for her."

Before Leah could reply, a lady standing near us harrumphed like an old yenta. She glared at the platinum goddess. "That Jill Carpenter is nothing but a common tart, and everybody knows she's Ben Roth's mistress. When she dumped her husband, the actor Bobby Fayette, the poor man tried to kill himself. She's just another Hollywood hussy. Movie people are a bunch of floozies and lechers." The dame elbowed her way through the crowd, probably to get a closer look at the floozies and lechers.

A roar from the newsmen and the throng separated as if Moses had parted the Red Sea. A tall fellow in a full-length beaver coat, a Trilby hat covering his dark hair, walked through the opened path. The theatrical makeup slapped on his face didn't detract from his chiseled features. I recognized him immediately, the "dashing devil from Atlanta," Rex Dallas, in the flesh.

"Look, Leah, it's him. It's Rex Dallas!"

Leading men cropped up in movies all the time, but my heart belonged to just one. I called out to my idol, yelling at the top of my lungs. "Yoo-hoo, Mr. Dallas!"

Miracle of miracles, he heard me and turned his regal head in my direction. When I waved at him, somehow, someway, he saw me through the crowd. It must have been destiny. Mr. Dallas stared at me for the longest time, a huge smile on his face. How fabulous, my favorite actor noticed me. Then, from my periphery, I saw Mr. Roth had turned from Mr. Dallas to me, displeasure written across his face.

Mr. Roth bounded over to Mr. Dallas, pointed at me, then shook his finger in Mr. Dallas's face. Mr. Dallas looked as if he wanted to slug Mr. Roth. A mass of reporters surrounded them, and the two men pulled apart. Suddenly, Miss Carpenter stepped forward. The crowd lurched, everyone converging around the two stars, and I feared we'd never get on the train. Suddenly, a man's voice called out, booming above the hubbub, "Ladies, over here, please!"

A Pullman porter waved to us, and we rushed over to him. Once we climbed aboard, a comforting blanket of warmth embraced us, vanquishing the Hawk. The youthful fellow couldn't have been over twenty-one and didn't look like the other porters scurrying around the railway terminal. Passengers called those hardworking men of color in their snappy black uniforms "George," and treated them like servants.

Though the Southern conviviality of the other Pullman porters charmed everyone, this young man seemed very much the Continental gentleman, with European features, and beautiful gray eyes.

"Ladies, I'm sorry, but there's always confusion when movie people are on board. The stars from the big studios—MGM, Warner Brothers, and Paramount— often ride with us, but for some reason, the folks from little ol' Regal Pictures get the most ballyhoo."

Leah showed him our tickets, and he pointed toward the front of the car. "Follow me, please. It's a long walk to your compartment, but at least you'll be away from the crowd."

He looked out the window at the mass of reporters. "Miss Carpenter caused quite the commotion, didn't she?"

I still basked in the glow of my first celebrity encounter. "We saw Mr. Rex Dallas, too, and can you believe it? He smiled at me."

The porter's jaw dropped, so I guessed I'd impressed him. "Mr. Dallas saw you?"

No matter how much I thought about it, I couldn't believe my good luck.

"Yes, he did. I've always heard that actors are snooty, but he wasn't, not the least bit. He waved at me, and it was thrilling, but for some reason Mr. Ben Roth seemed peeved with Mr. Dallas. I guess he's one of those fellows who're always in a perpetual funk."

The baggage handler looked around the car as if someone might be listening, then whispered, "I really shouldn't say anything, but to put it bluntly, Mr. Dallas likes young ladies, the younger the better. He's a real Romeo, and chases after anything in a skirt."

I couldn't believe that of my idol. "But that can't be true. It just can't."

Leah gave me the Look, a gaze passed down from the Mongolian hordes by the Cossacks to my grandmother. Bubbe never spanked or slapped me when I misbehaved. The Look was always enough. Now that fate made Leah my guardian, she'd picked it up. "Mitzi, if the gentleman says Rex Dallas is a lecher, then I'm sure he is."

She turned to the porter and handed him a whole dollar. "Thank you, for your help and the information. We were afraid we'd be stuck out in the cold."

The porter grinned, his cheeks blushing red. Leah returned his smile with a laugh as he added, "If you ladies need anything, anything at all, please call on me. My name is Omar."

"Omar? What a lovely name. I'm Leah, and this is my sister, Mitzi."

Omar looked down at his feet, his embarrassment obvious. "I'm afraid I can't call you by your first names. The railroad won't allow it."

Leah steeled her shoulders. "Well, to heck with them. If you can't call us by our first names, we won't call you by yours. It would be impolite, Mister—?"

The porter didn't say a word, just gazed into Leah's face for the longest time. He finally whispered, "Fournier. My family name is Fournier, madam."

Leah extended her hand. "Fournier? That's French, isn't it?"

He answered with a nod. "Yes, ma'am, I'm from New Orleans."

"Our last name is Schector. We're honored to make your acquaintance, Mr. Fournier."

Omar looked down the hallway. Once he was sure no other riders were nearby, he shook our hands. "The honor is all mine, Miss Leah Schector. I'm pleased to make your acquaintance, Miss Mitzi Schector."

Except for Chick Hagan's, I hadn't seen a smile like his since the Crash. Omar still had the grin on his face when he signaled to us to follow him.

He led us through a labyrinth of elegant

staterooms, sleeping compartments, and lavish suites. "Ladies, you'll be very comfortable. The Chief has all the amenities—running water, electric lights, and a system that keeps the compartments cool in the summer and warm in the winter."

The white-walled dining car gleamed with fine cutlery, bone china, and crystal vases overflowing with fresh flowers. The heavenly aroma of hot coffee, cinnamon toast, and griddlecakes scented the air.

Mr. Fournier led us to our sleeper. "Good evening, Miss Leah Schector and Mitzi." He tipped his hat, then strolled off.

Minutes later, we entered the white and chrome Ladies' Lounge, where a pretty attendant waited for us. "My name is Betty, like Betty Boop. I'll see to your needs."

She couldn't have been more than sixteen, with sparkling eyes and skin the color of cocoa. Betty flashed a hundred-watt smile, then handed us fluffy towels and terrycloth bathrobes before directing us to the shower baths.

"Omar stopped by and said to take good care of you ladies. The water's hot, the towels are clean, and you can wash your hair. I got Lux Soap, Queen Helene Shampoo, and Pond's Cold Cream." She looked around the lounge before lowering her voice. "I even have pads if it's your time of the month. I can press your dresses if you want, seventy-five cents apiece."

Leah and I whooped for joy at the thought of a shower bath. A few minutes later, I sloshed in hot, sudsy water, feeling quite decadent all the while. After our baths, Leah lined her eyes in black pencil and painted her lips deep carmine. I wondered who she wanted to impress.

My newly shampooed locks fell into loose waves. I changed into a stylish frock of crimson gabardine that Zisel had provided for the trip, and we were ready to find the dining car.

A grinning porter in a white jacket passed us, dinner chimes in hand. My stomach growled, and so did Leah's. "Hey, kiddo, it's time to eat. How's about we put on the dog again and pretend we're two swells?"

We locked arms and followed the porter.

Chapter Five
Beyond the Blue Horizon

The dining car tables blazed with candles, brilliant white tablecloths, and gleaming silverware. A steward ushered us to a corner table, where we dined on an iceberg lettuce salad and braised duck Cumberland, washed down with fresh lemonade. For two wonderful hours, we put our grief and Mr. Nussbaum behind us.

After our meal, we made our way to the berth that would be our bedroom for the next four days. A porter had turned down the beds and left neatly folded green blankets atop the narrow beds. I took the upper bunk while Leah napped in the lower. As I stared out the window at the bleak panorama, I wondered if my Fuller Brush man spent his days in the freezing cold schlepping his wares. He probably passed his evenings wrapped in some high hat babe's embrace. Time to forget about the guy.

I cracked open the book I'd brought for my journey, *The Bridge of San Luis Rey*—interesting, but not exactly fascinating. All of a sudden, I remembered the actors onboard the train. The prospect of meeting movie stars held more attraction than a fictional bridge collapse in eighteenth-century Peru. I dug out a mirror and applied a coat of Fuller Brush lipstick in a flattering rose shade. My old copybook would be dandy for autographs. I slipped from our berth and made my way to the supercar. Plumes of cigarette smoke wafted from open state rooms full of drunken reporters. I ignored the catcalls and wolf whistles from the soused newsmen and made my way down the narrow corridors, finding my train legs with the rhythmic movement of the Chief.

I'd just turned onto a quiet, reporter-free passageway when I heard the honeyed tones of a son of the South.

"Well, hello, little lady."

Rex Dallas sauntered toward me, dressed in a natty dinner jacket and tuxedo trousers. He looked quite dashing minus the heavy theatrical makeup he'd worn in the station. His dark eyes twinkled and his teeth glinted in the light. My heart boomed at my good fortune, but I tried to act cool and nonchalant.

"Hello to you too, Mr. Dallas."

Mr. Dallas appeared at my side so quickly I wondered if he wore seven-league boots. He bowed like a cavalier of old and kissed my hand.

"Sweet Pea, I noticed you in the crowd and I thought to myself, 'That little darling is out in the cold, freezing to death because of ol' Rex.' I wanted to show that pretty little gal how a real Southern gent treats a lady."

How lucky can a girl be? I found his attention thrilling.

Then he moved closer and blew into my ear, which wasn't so thrilling.

"Mr. Dallas—"

"Call me Rex, darling."

"Oh, well, uh, Rex, would you believe that I've seen all your movies? Is your partner, Mr. Buster Sweet, traveling with you?"

He tossed back his head and laughed. "That coon? They don't let them on the trains except to clean toilets. Why would I want to tour with a jigaboo anyway?"

Coon? Jigaboo? No one I knew used such horrible language.

"Mr. Dallas, you can't—"

He cut me off with a laugh. "You are just the prettiest little thing. By the way, how old did you say you were?"

I didn't remember mentioning my age. "I'm eighteen."

Mr. Dallas lifted me in the air. "Eighteen? Can you believe it? Eighteen is my lucky number."

Rex Dallas's face suddenly took on the same salacious expression I'd seen on Nussbaum, Mr. Stein, some of the reporters, and one particularly ardent Columbia student. "Mr. Dallas, please put me down!"

He threw his head back and laughed again. "I bet a pretty little thing like you must have beaus a-plenty."

I went from dizzy to queasy. It would serve the guy right if I puked all over his face. "I don't have any beaus. Please put me down and sign my book."

"Aw, honey, ol' Rex has got something a lot better than any autograph book. Gimme some sugar, baby."

Mr. Dallas opened his mouth and moved his tongue to my lips. Up close he looked really old, at least thirty-five, and he smelled of liquor. I thought I'd retch, and I certainly wasn't going to kiss him. When I turned my face away, the bum had the nerve to pull it back. I whacked him as hard as I could. "Let me go, you louse. I don't want to kiss you."

Horror of horrors, Mr. Dallas grinned as if he found my resistance exciting. From the bulge poking inside his trousers, I figured yes, he did.

"You little minx. So you want to play rough, do you? Rex likes gals with spirit."

A voice boomed from the corridor. "Hey, put the girl down, you son-of-a-bitch. Put her down right now."

Ben Roth rushed over with Omar at his heels. Mr. Roth's face blazed as red as a tomato. He gave me a quick once-over, then went nose to nose with Dallas. "I've had it with you, you cracker schmuck. You always pull this bullshit on me the moment I turn my back. I knew I couldn't trust you. I'm not spending another nickel to keep you out of jail. Do you know what the Mann Act is, you putz? No? Let me refresh your memory. Taking a female across state lines for nookie is a Federal offense. It gets worse when the female in question is underage."

Mr. Dallas screamed back, the veneer of southern chivalry gone. "Underage? With those tits and that ass? The girlie said she's eighteen. That's legal, isn't it? Besides, the little chippie gave me the come-on."

I couldn't believe my ears. "But that's not true."

Mr. Roth turned and glared at me. "Can it, toots. I'll take care of this."

His lips curled when he turned to Dallas. "Listen, you son of a bitch, I know you think you've got me by the short hairs because we have a contract. Well, you're wrong. Guys like you are a dime a dozen, and besides, it's Buster Sweet people come to see, not you."

Dallas glared back at him with such savagery I thought they might come to blows.

"Don't throw that Sambo up to me. I'm tired of you treating me like a darky, you Jew bastard."

Mr. Roth absorbed the insult in silence. How could

Rex Dallas, a man I'd adored since childhood, say such horrible things? Mr. Roth mumbled something to Omar before slipping him what looked like a wad of bills. He grabbed Dallas by his lapels. "Get back to your stateroom. We'll rustle up someone who's interested."

Dallas shot him a poisonous look, gave me a curt bow, and stormed off with Omar following. When Mr. Roth turned back to me, his demeanor softened. "Look, baby, I want the truth. Did he touch you?" He looked me dead in the face.

"No, sir, I mean, Mr. Roth. You see, I know your name. You're the president of Regal Pictures."

I finally had an opportunity to ask him about Uncle Baron, but unfortunately, he seemed quite agitated. "Oh, so you know my name. What else do you know?"

My smile didn't improve his mood, so I dropped it. "Everything, Mr. Roth. Anyway, I was walking down the corridor when I met Mr. Dallas."

"You walked down the corridor and met that schlub?"

"Yes, sir, and he said, 'Hello, little lady,' and I said, 'Hello,' right back and told him that I'd seen all his movies. He seemed so pleased. Then he asked how old I was. When I told him I'm eighteen, he seemed even more pleased."

Mr. Roth slapped his forehead. "What the hell, I'll kill that schmuck!" His eyes narrowed when he looked back at me. "Is this a shakedown, girlie?"

"A shakedown? No!"

Mr. Roth stopped glaring, so I guess he liked my answer. He pulled out his wallet. "Well, honey, since you say nothing happened, how's about twenty bucks to make it all go away?"

"Twenty dollars? Did you say twenty dollars?"

He raised an eyebrow and handed me another sawbuck. "Okay, okay, girlie. I'll make it thirty."

He shoved the money into my hand. "How about I throw in a few pairs of silk stockings, too? You've got to promise you won't let anyone know what happened, especially any of those nice men from the press, the ones crawling around the train like cockroaches. By the way, if anyone asks, say Christmas came early this year. You seem like a sweet kid, so let's forget it ever happened."

Mr. Roth handed me the cash. Perhaps he waited for me to faint in appreciation, but Mr. Dallas' words still rang in my ears and I could barely muster a smile.

"Thank you very much, sir."

I walked away. He followed, took hold of my shoulders, and turned me around.

"Hey, what's wrong? Thirty smackers ain't chopped liver, especially nowadays. Sorry, little lady, that's all you're going to get."

"Rex Dallas called you a 'Jew bastard.' "

I saw the confusion in his face. "Yeah, so what else is new?"

"Mr. Roth, I'm Jewish, and that man insulted everyone who is Jewish. What kind of fellow is he? It's an affront to the gentleman who puts a roof over his head. My father used to say, 'I sing the song of he who puts bread on my table.' You put bread on his table, but he dishonored you. I hate Rex Dallas, and I'll never go to any of his movies again!"

After all the strain of the previous month, I started blubbering. I'm sure I looked like the world's biggest softie. Mr. Roth didn't say a word, but the strangest

45

thing happened—he sobbed too. He handed me his handkerchief and wiped his own eyes on his sleeve.

"Forget it, kid, he's not worth tears. What does a goy know anyway? Thanks for the kind words, girlie."

With that, he turned. I couldn't let him go without asking him the most important question of all. "Mr. Roth, please, my uncle died in that fire, the one in 1923. My sister and I are going to Los Angeles to search for his grave. Can you please help us, sir?"

Mr. Roth stopped in his tracks. He turned, his face as white as starch.

"What did you say?"

"My uncle died in the fire, the fire that killed Clarice Dumont. His name was Baron, Baron Schector. Please, Mr. Roth, we want to know where they buried Uncle Baron."

He opened his mouth, closed it again, shook his head, and walked away.

Chapter Six
The Smoke Clears

Before I returned to Leah, I scrubbed away every trace of Rex Dallas from my body. I decided to keep my encounter with the dreadful man a secret. When I arrived at the sleeping car, I found Omar waiting in front of our berth.

"Mitzi, Mr. Roth asked me to keep a special eye on you. Remember, keep quiet about Dallas."

I nodded. "I'll remember."

A few minutes later, Leah awoke from her nap. I managed to keep my lips buttoned during dinner, and chatted away about the luxury of the train. "This is sure a lot better than living on some old rickety bus for a week." I knew if my older sister found out about Dallas making the moves on me, there'd be holy heck to pay.

When we returned to the berth, I found a box wrapped in white tissue propped on my cot. I didn't open it until Leah went to the ladies' lounge. When I unwrapped it, I found four pairs of silk stockings, courtesy of Mr. Ben Roth. The hose created another conundrum. How would I explain silk stockings and the extra thirty dollars I'd tucked under Leah's pillow? I decided to forget my worries until morning.

That night, I dreamed of walking down Park Avenue in autumn, the street awash in gowns of hunter green and burnt sienna. Society beauties in their swankiest autumn frocks promenaded arm in arm with their sweethearts. I floated toward a dashing young man from the Fuller Brush Company. He wore a pinstriped suit, spats, and a million-dollar smile. Chick took me in his arms and whispered, "I love you, baby."

What a swell dream.

****

On our second day on the Santa Fe Chief, I discovered Betty, the ladies' lounge attendant, would spill the beans about Miss Jill Carpenter for a fifty-cent piece.

"Miss Carpenter's maid told me they use peroxide, ammonia, and soap flakes to bleach her hair out. The stuff stings like the devil, and sometimes when her hair don't look right, she wears a wig. All those ladies in the movies are lightening their hair. I once heard they use Clorox, but her maid said that's a lot of hooey. Problem is, now there's a bunch of sick women around the country with burned-out hair."

She looked around to make sure we were alone, and moved a bit closer, her voice a whisper. "White hair and white skin—I've seen a whole lot of ladies before, but nothing like her. Yesterday, Miss Carpenter stood over there…" Betty pointed to the center of the tiny lounge. "…stark naked, without a care in the world." She looked around the lounge once more before murmuring, "And there was no hair, nowhere, except on her head."

What woman doesn't have hair on her nether parts? "But, Betty, every woman has hair, uh, down there."

"No, miss, not her."

The image disturbed me, but a trip to the shower-bath soon erased Jill Carpenter and her lack of pubic hair from my thoughts. When I emerged, Betty offered me a sanitary pad. "Just in case."

It wasn't my time of the month, but I told her about one of our rituals. "Did you know that when a Jewish girl first starts her cycle, her mother slaps her?"

She blinked her eyes in disbelief. "Why?"

"Don't know. It's an old custom, a lousy one at that. My mother died in the influenza epidemic, so she never slapped me, but I knew a girl whose mother hauled off and smacked her really hard."

Betty arched an eyebrow, a cagey grin on her face. "Aren't your monthlies bad enough without someone beating you up over them?"

The doors opened before I could reply. Jill Carpenter slithered into the lounge, her hapless maid in tow. She wore a white chenille robe, her hair wrapped in a silken turban. Minus her heavy makeup, Miss Carpenter seemed more like a sullen child than the seductive beauty I'd seen at the station.

Miss Carpenter didn't utter a sound, simply looked me up and down before turning away. Perhaps no one had taught her manners, so I introduced myself.

"Hello, Miss Carpenter. My name is Mitzi Schector, and I'm honored to meet you."

I extended my hand and she ignored it, dismissing me with an absentminded, "Hello."

Miss Carpenter walked to the shower, stood as still as a statue, then dropped her robe to the floor. There she posed, naked as a jaybird, for her audience of three. I tried to avert my eyes but couldn't. Betty hadn't exaggerated one bit. Jill Carpenter had the skin of a cadaver. She looked as if someone had carved her from a block of marble, and yes, she was completely hairless.

Miss Carpenter stepped into the shower bath and called out to her servant, "Mary, don't dawdle. I need you to wash my back."

Her maid rolled her eyes but scurried off to attend to her. I couldn't stop myself from smirking. Jill Carpenter might be a famous movie actress with diamonds and furs, but my bosoms were bigger than hers. I wasn't bragging, simply stating facts.

She turned away. I got a view of her rump, and I couldn't stop from chortling. I had a rounder tush and a smaller waist too. Take that, Jill Carpenter. Then I stopped gloating. She possessed flawless skin, while I was as hairy as a great ape. Most of my Barnard sisters shaved their legs and underarms, but Zisel wouldn't let me near a safety razor. I made up my mind, then and there, that one day I'd rid myself of my excess hair. Still, I drew the line at shaving my pubic area. Looking like a five-year-old from the waist down held no appeal for this girl.

I slipped on a navy blue sweater and dark gray skirt, left the ladies' lounge, and Jill Carpenter and her bald privates. I had to figure out a way to explain four pairs of silk stockings and thirty dollars. As luck would have it, I came up with the perfect story to tell Leah: Mr. Roth and I met by chance and I told him of our plight; he remembered the Schector family and Uncle Baron's tragic death; though he couldn't tell me where Uncle Baron had been laid to rest, Mr. Roth took pity on two poor refugees from New York, yet wanted no thanks for his charity. Leah would be pleased by my concoction, a heartwarming tale of Jewish camaraderie. I thought it best to leave out the Rex Dallas part.

I returned to an empty compartment, the bed made

and a note on the pillow. "My darling sister, I am waiting for you in the dining car."

The scent of fresh coffee lured me to the dining room where Leah sat. She looked every inch the stylish traveler in her woolen suit as she signaled to a waiter, who laid out the grub.

"Mitzi dear, eat it while it's hot."

I devoured a bowl of Cream of Wheat, plus stewed prunes to keep me regular, then washed it all down with a cup of the Santa Fe's famous hot cocoa. Leah smiled so sweetly I knew something was percolating besides the coffee.

"Darling, I had the best sleep I've had in months. You were already gone when I awoke. On my way to the shower bath, I passed some newspaper fellows who were following Jill Carpenter. Did you hear about the nasty business last night with Rex Dallas?"

The jig was up. She knew. I felt the color working its way up to my face.

Leah continued torturing me. "I met a reporter, a rather angry fellow, who'd run into Rex Dallas when he was as drunk as a skunk. Mr. Dallas complained to him about a 'little tart' who had caught his eye. He planned to have his way with her, but Ben Roth rescued the poor little thing and told off the big, nasty man. Mr. Roth sent her on her way, and paid for her silence." She gave me the Look. "Why didn't you tell me about that gorilla?"

"Because I knew if I did, you'd probably punch the chump in the nose."

Leah threw down her napkin. "You're right, I would have. We escaped Joseph Nussbaum's lechery only to have another degenerate pursue you. Lucky for us, the newsman didn't catch the girl's name. The guy hates Rex Dallas's guts and was miffed when he couldn't report the story."

I stared into the remnants of my cocoa, wishing I could squeeze into the cup and drown in a wave of liquid chocolate.

Leah picked up her tossed napkin and fiddled with it. "Omar said you just wanted Rex Dallas's autograph."

I had to fess up. "Yes, it's true. Omar told the truth about Dallas—he's a real jerk. Mr. Roth gave me the thirty dollars along with some silk stockings to keep quiet. Maybe we should give it back."

She didn't say a word. A thrashing would have been preferable to her silence. I started sobbing. "Please, Leah, say something. I'm so sorry, but Rex Dallas is a horrible man. He called Mr. Roth a 'Jew bastard' and Buster Sweet a 'jigaboo.' I hate him."

Leah rifled through her pocketbook and handed me a handkerchief. She watched in silence while I dabbed my eyes and blew my nose.

"There's something else. I asked Mr. Roth about Uncle Baron."

She gazed at me, and I read the anticipation on her face. "I'm sorry, Leah, but he wouldn't answer. I don't think we'll find out anything from Mr. Roth."

Her lovely face fell to the floor. "Oh, how disappointing. Mitzi, except for Zisel, you're all I have in the world, and I get a little overprotective. They call the Chief 'the rolling boudoir,' and it sure lived up to its name. Well, we're not giving back the thirty dollars, or the silk stockings either. You earned it after that jerk put his filthy paws on you." When she took my hand in hers, I knew things were all right again.

"Mitzi, the Schector girls need a little comfort right now. It's still early, but how would you like to share a banana split with your older sister?"

Who could say no to an offer like that?

****

The Santa Fe chugged on through Colorado, the land of pine trees, mountains, blue skies, and green earth that shimmered in the late autumn light. We rolled past Utah and made our way to Nevada. A porter said the conductor pushed the speed and we'd arrive in Los Angeles before dusk. Unfortunately, I'd finished *The Bridge of San Luis Rey* and had nothing else to read. I was itching to explore the train. "Please, Leah, I'm bored."

She hesitated for a moment but thankfully didn't give me the Look. "Promise me you'll be back in ten minutes. Remember, no autographs, and no Rex Dallas."

Off I went. I followed the narrow corridors and passed the train's barbershop. The place buzzed with male energy and smelled of Bay Rum and talcum powder. Mr. Roth sat there. A pert manicurist buffed his nails while an obsequious barber shaved him. I tapped on the glass and waved to him. He looked up at me with such a plaintive expression I feared he might break down again. After staring at me for a long moment, he averted his eyes. Perhaps I should have waited to ask him about Uncle Baron, but it was too late. I continued my trek.

Light spilled from Jill Carpenter's regal stateroom. The place reeked of fine perfume and movie star hauteur. Miss Carpenter looked over a bunch of photos

that were sitting on a small table. One of the
photographs so upset her that she flung it across the
chamber with a bejeweled hand, then tossed the
remaining images to the floor. What a charmer.

When I arrived at the entrance to the ladies'
lounge, I found Omar sharing a laugh with Betty at Rex
Dallas's expense. "He said he needed his 'medicine'
brought to him from the baggage car, the one-hundred-
proof kind of medicine."

I decided to join in the frivolities. "Golly, in all the
excitement, I haven't seen Buster Sweet. I'd love to
meet him. Where is he?"

Omar stopped smiling, a sheepish expression on
his handsome face. He gave Betty a sideways look.
"I'm afraid Mr. Sweet doesn't come on these jaunts.
You see, the railroads don't allow some people to ride
in the sleeping berths or staterooms. They have separate
accommodations."

"Buster Sweet is a movie star, isn't he?"

He sighed before answering. "Yes, Mitzi, but not a
white movie star. Mr. Roth rents a private car for him,
so he won't have to mix with the other passengers."

We looked away, embarrassed; then Omar sighed
and changed the conversation. "Do you and your sister
have a place to stay in Los Angeles?"

I answered with a shrug. "No, not yet. We got in a
real pickle in New York and left so quickly we didn't
have time to rustle up a place. I guess we'll find a cheap
hotel. There's a place in Los Angeles called Boyle
Heights where a lot of Jews live, but who knows where
we'll end up? Leah thinks we should live closer to
downtown for jobs."

I suddenly thought of Mr. Stein's handsome mug.

How could I forget? "I have a job, at least I think I do, at the Broadway Ritz."

His eyes twinkled, and he grinned as if he'd thought of something. "Then downtown would be the perfect location, especially if you're working there. Perhaps I might—"

Before he could complete his sentence, Leah rushed down the corridor. She and Omar stared at each other for an uncomfortable moment. Leah nodded to Betty, then acknowledged him with a shy smile before glancing my way. "Young lady, I said ten minutes."

She turned back to Omar, a grin dancing across her lips. "I'm sorry to disturb you all, but Mitzi and I have to finish packing before we reach Los Angeles. The conductor says the train will arrive ahead of schedule."

Omar's face had turned a bright shade of red. "Ladies, please excuse me. I better be on my way."

He left the lounge before I discovered what he'd wanted to tell me.

Chapter Seven
The Dorchester

By late afternoon, Leah and I had packed up our luggage in preparation for our new lives in a strange city. Before we departed, I went searching for Omar. He'd been a real brick and I wanted to thank him for all his help. Unfortunately, I couldn't find him.

I bid adieu to Betty in the ladies' lounge and gave her a farewell gift, a Flaming Crimson lipstick from my Fuller Brush man. "Maybe our paths will cross again, Betty."

She gave me a sad little smile. "Maybe, who knows?"

We hugged our goodbyes, and then I left to help Leah with our luggage.

Fifteen minutes later, Leah and I stepped off the Santa Fe and immediately shed our winter coats. The calendar said November, but even the night air warmed us. We found ourselves in a Mesopotamian palace straight out of *A Thousand and One Arabian Nights*, La Grande Station, Los Angeles's portal to the rest of the country. A massive dome that resembled a mammoth golden onion crowned the gargantuan terminal. The design mingled Moorish, Russian, and Arabic architecture, with flourishes from who knows where. Palm trees lined the walkways, and oranges and lemons scented the air. We'd left New York behind us.

We passed a magazine kiosk where Jill Carpenter's face pouted from every cover. The Mischief Makers, the premier child performers in Hollywood, smirked like imps from the cover of *Movie Classic*. Zisel's favorite actor, Bobby Fayette, America's favorite juvenile, struck a pensive pose for *Gentleman's Quarterly*.

The frantic pace exhausted me. Porters zoomed around the station moving mountains of luggage. Ladies tossed fox stoles about their shoulders, gentlemen positioned their fedoras, and those who could afford it made their way to the rows of waiting taxis and limousines. The less affluent carried their bags to the Alameda Street trolley.

Rex Dallas left the station under a canopy of flashes from popping camera bulbs. A pack of speeding newsmen almost knocked me over. Mr. Roth paced up and down on the platform as a mass of photographers stood in wait for Jill Carpenter. Leah stared at him for a moment before wringing her hands. "Mitzi, do you think if I made my way to him, I could ask about Baron?"

I shook my head. "You could ask, but I don't think he'll answer. So many years have passed. Perhaps he's forgotten Uncle Baron, if he even knew him in the first place. I'm afraid he won't be of help."

A porter rolled down a set of stairs, and the Chief's doors opened as if by magic. Jill Carpenter emerged, looking more glamorous than any mortal had a right to be. Her heavy silk frock clung to her like molten silver. From the smoothness of her silhouette, I doubted she wore undergarments. The reporters whistled in unison, and she smiled triumphantly.

An alien perfume, tantalizing and spicy, wafted throughout the station. My stomach growled. The enticing fragrance held my nose captive. I followed it to a young boy in a striped serape, hawking his wares in front of a steaming clay pot. "Get your fresh tamales here!"

Leah and I were starving, but I picked up a Red Car schedule instead of sampling the local cuisine. We collected our bags, and a porter helped us with our trunk as we made our way toward a taxi. Then, the honk of a motorcar and a masculine voice shouting our names stopped us.

"Leah! Mitzi!"

Omar sat behind the wheel of a sleek limousine. He jumped out and opened the back door. "Ladies, I have the loan of this vehicle and can take you to a vacant flat that might interest you. It's even within walking distance of Broadway."

Who could decline such an offer? He deposited our luggage in the motorcar's trunk, and at his insistence, we sat in the back seat like two swells. Omar took his place behind the wheel, stuck a chauffeur's cap on his head, and laughed at our shocked faces. "It's just a precaution. The Los Angeles police aren't the friendliest lot and might look askance at two lovely white ladies driving with a fellow of color, even a light-skinned one."

He turned onto residential streets, many full of signs offering vacant apartments, but all featured the same coda in bold print: "No Coloreds, No Mexicans." Others proclaimed, "No Dogs, No Jews."

Golly, we didn't even get top billing.

Mr. Fournier made a jaunt down Los Angeles's

Broadway, the theater district, the highlight of the tour. Streetcars and automobiles packed the narrow boulevards. The Edwardian-style buildings lining the street were dwarfs compared to New York skyscrapers.

At the start of our little trek, we passed a garish marquee with the words "Broadway Ritz" spelled out in neon. I noted a sign on the kiosk, "Organist wanted." Omar pointed to it.

"Mitzi mentioned the Broadway Ritz. It's the only movie house on the street not wired for sound. Who knows how long it will stay in business."

Mr. Stein hadn't lied about the place; it wasn't grand like the New York Ritz, but my heart began pounding a fast tempo.

I pulled his business card from my pocketbook and remembered I hadn't mentioned that I'd once played the Wurlitzer on Youth Night at the Capitol Theater in New York. A job as an organist had to pay more than working as a mere usherette. If I could land that job, Leah and I could repay everyone who helped us flee from New York. I'd visit the joint as soon as we found a place to live.

We drove past movie palaces with façades so ornate they rivaled those in New York. I'd read film attendance had dropped around the country, but not in Los Angeles. Well-dressed folks stood in line, queuing for the picture shows. Omar pointed out the Million Dollar Theater, the most opulent place on the street.

"Even New Yorkers are impressed when they walk up the grand staircase. The restrooms have gilded toilets with golden flush handles. Dreams are made from less."

We traveled farther down Broadway, then turned

onto the steep drive to our destination. When Omar drove up 3rd Street, he pointed to two electric trolleys chugging up and down a track. "They call those the Angels Flight. For a penny you can take one up the hill."

I looked up the steep walkway. "We'll need our pennies, Omar. The exercise will do us good."

He pointed to a collection of elegant mansions in the distance. "That's Bunker Hill, once the swanky part of town, but I'm afraid those days are gone."

He hadn't lied. Although a few of the mansions were beautifully maintained, many had lapsed into disrepair. The paver stones covering the streets hinted at its once swanky past. They led to a rather decrepit rooming house, nestled alongside other Victorian-era mansions that also had seen better times. Leah's shoulders slumped the moment she saw it. Omar drove us up the path to the ruined beauty, its paint faded and peeling.

"That's her, the Dorchester Arms. I know she doesn't look like much now, but in the years before the Great War, she was quite grand. Unfortunately, the swells abandoned Bunker Hill for choicer pickings, and the Dorchester became a boarding house. Still, the old gal is like a plain woman of great virtue, a lot prettier inside."

The Dorchester had gone to seed, but even in dusk's dim light I could see someone had given a great deal of attention to her flowerbeds and filled them with night-blooming jasmine and petunias. A trio of ancient pensioners sat on the veranda listening to Russ Colombo crooning from the radio as they rocked away their fragile lives. I'd never seen old ladies so highly rouged, with hair dyed in colors ranging from lemon yellow to jet black. They weren't at all like the bubbes back home.

Mr. Fournier signaled to a middle-aged woman watering the potted plants on the veranda. "That's Mrs. LaRue, the landlady. She worked in the movie business and is quite open-minded. She'll rent to anyone, unless they're a souse or a chippie."

He called out, "Mrs. LaRue, your new tenants are here!"

She put down her watering can and sauntered over. "Hi-ho, ladies!"

Mrs. LaRue wore a floral housedress, had finger-waved her hennaed locks, and replaced her shaved eyebrows with thin black arcs. Omar kissed her extended hand in the European manner. "May I present Miss Leah Schector and her lovely sister, Mitzi? I'll handle their luggage and leave you ladies in Mrs. LaRue's capable hands."

Omar bowed, touched the brim of his cap, and turned away. Mrs. LaRue smiled as he strolled to the auto. "High class fellow, ain't he? My other guests are show folks from vaudeville and the nickelodeons, a broadminded lot, but to be on the safe side I tell them he's Egyptian. They're such rubes, none of them knows the difference anyway."

She spoke with a Boston accent and gestured with grand flourishes. "Since you gals are looking for a place, how about joining me for the grand tour?"

We clambered up the steps and crossed the threshold. Omar hadn't exaggerated a bit. With her stairwell of highly polished wood and vaulted ceilings, the Dorchester was beautiful. Someone had gone through pains to preserve the leaded glass windows, mahogany doors, and gleaming chandeliers. Mrs. LaRue pointed up the stairs.

"Mr. Fournier lives up there, in the attic. Sometimes he plays the saxophone at night. It's kind of sad, like him."

I'd never thought of Omar as sad but, yes, he had a melancholy air about him, the rootless loneliness of a young man perpetually on the road. Leah called out to me, rousing me from my reverie, "Mitzi, come to the parlor."

I moved into an enormous room packed with heavy furniture that almost obscured the hardwood floors. Leah pointed to the sumptuous touches throughout the vast chamber. "Look at these wall sconces and that marble fireplace. One of the tenants says there's even steam heat in the winter."

Leah and I exchanged a look. The moment Mrs. LaRue opened the door to the vacant flat we knew it would be our new home. "Old Lady Hopkins kicked the bucket, so I have a vacancy."

She gave us a sideways glance and chortled. "She didn't die in the Dorchester, if that's what's worrying you."

The room looked a tad threadbare, but we thanked our lucky stars Omar had brought us here. Mrs. LaRue took a puff on her cigarette. "Girls, I know it's not high-class, but don't look a gift horse in the mouth. The rent's cheap, and you won't find a roach or mouse." She scrutinized our faces. "Your name is Schector, ain't it? Are you ladies Jewish?"

Uh-oh, perhaps this wouldn't be home. Maybe Mrs. LaRue wasn't as open-minded as Mr. Fournier thought. What a quandary; do we tell the truth and lose out on this place or lie and feel like phonies? I soon discovered Mrs. LaRue had mind-reading on her curriculum vitae as well as running a rooming house. "I like Jews, very cultured people. They've been good to me all my life. If you want it, you've got the place, girls."

Mrs. LaRue flicked away her cigarette ash and it was a fait accompli. We dined on her pot roast that evening. Later, I bunked down on a small cot in the corner of the room. Within minutes, I lay dreaming of a smiling Fuller Brush man who waltzed toward me and took me in his arms.

Chapter Eight
The "Other" Broadway Ritz

Two mornings after our arrival in Los Angeles, I trekked down Broadway to the Ritz Theater. I'd decked myself out in a navy frock that set a very professional tone, meaning it didn't show off too much of my bosoms. Since I now resided in the land of glamour, I powdered my face, globbed my lashes with mascara, and rouged my mouth with one of Chick Hagan's lipsticks.

Trees I'd only seen in the Botanical Gardens and the *National Geographic* magazine bordered the streets. It may have been autumn, but palms, magnolias, jacarandas, and eucalyptus flourished in the California sun.

Daylight revealed downtown Los Angeles as a lovely place with scrubbed sidewalks and nattily dressed people. I passed the Million Dollar, the most stunning movie palace on Broadway. I'd once read Sid Grauman spent a million bucks building the place. It certainly looked like he had, at least from the sidewalk. Gigantic chandeliers in the lobby glittered like a universe of diamonds hanging from a gilded sky.

More opulence surely awaited inside, but I couldn't spare a quarter to take a look. A huge poster showed a smiling Gaylord Carter, the King of the Wurlitzer, sitting at an organ keyboard. If someone gave me a chance, I could give that Carter fellow a run for his money.

I walked a few more blocks and reached my destination. From the outside, I knew this Broadway Ritz was a far cry from her beautiful New York sister. The marble exterior façade might have been stunning a decade ago, but it needed a good scouring. Grime dulled the terrazzo floors, and the glass on the marquee demanded polishing. The billboard heralded two films, *Sunrise* and *A Woman of Affairs*, both silent dramas. Fortunately, the Help Wanted sign remained taped to the kiosk window: "The famed Broadway Ritz Theater is looking for a skilled musician to accompany silent dramas on the Mighty Wurlitzer organ. References required. Ask for Mr. Stein."

I strolled in and eyeballed the place. Three chandeliers, with dim crystal prisms, hung from the lobby ceiling. Washed-out murals of the English countryside covered the walls. The ratty carpet with dingy fleur-de-lis accents had faded to a pale red.

Identical twin boys clad in faded usher uniforms were at work in the lobby. One labored behind the concession counter; the other stood at the entrance to the auditorium, flashlight in hand. An usherette in an outfit as frayed and threadbare as the Ritz itself approached me. She couldn't have been over seventeen and had the same auburn hair and open brown eyes as the twins.

"I'm sorry, miss, you'll have to come back later. We ain't open yet."

I pointed to the sign on the kiosk. "I'm here about the position."

She gave me the once-over. "Kind of young, ain't

you?"

I threw my head back and cocked my right eyebrow like Joan Crawford. "Well, the sign said, 'skilled musician.' I'm a skilled musician, I'm not as young as I look, and I need a job."

The girl signaled for me to follow. "Okay, sister, I'll take you to Mr. Stein. He owns the joint, but he's almost never here. He's got a bunch of nicer theaters all over the country, so I guess you'd call the Ritz his redheaded stepchild."

She looked around the joint, then spoke in a whisper. "Between you and me, Mr. Stein is one cool hombre. For Pete's sake, don't get too close to him—he doesn't like to be touched."

Doesn't like to be touched? Could this Mr. Stein be the Lothario I knew? "I'm acquainted with Mr. Stein from New York."

The girl looked perplexed. "You know him and you still want to work for him? Honest?" She extended her hand. "The name's Edna, and those ushers are my brothers, Andy and Randy. What's your name?"

"Mitzi, Mitzi Schector."

We shook hands, and then Edna knocked on the office door. "Miss Schector is here to see you, Mr. Stein." She gave my arm a pinch and whispered, "Good luck, Mitzi."

The door opened and my heart surged. Mr. Stein stood in the doorway, a smirk slapped on his handsome kisser. "Ah, Miss Schector. Please, come in."

He looked spiffy as usual in his black woolen suit and black-and-tan spectator shoes, his dark hair combed in place. His eyes narrowed. "Glad to see you're a woman of your word, Miss Schector. May I say you look as charming as ever?"

I felt the color coming to my face and averted my head. I hoped he couldn't see that I'd turned as red as a tomato. "Thanks, Mr. Stein."

His Los Angeles office didn't have the swank of the one in New York, but it certainly was an improvement on the lobby. He'd filled the place with fine mahogany furnishings and kept it as spit-and-polish as his other office.

Mr. Stein pulled out a chair for me before taking a place behind his desk. His eyes remained on me, but he didn't say a word. I decided to lay my cards on the table.

"Sir, when we were in New York, you mentioned an usherette job, but I noticed you're looking for someone to play the Wurlitzer. I'm your girl."

He didn't respond, so I took the sincere approach. "I performed on a Wurlitzer on Youth Night at the Capitol Theater. I'm not boasting, Mr. Stein, but folks liked my music. Sir, as you know, lots of moving picture fans still love silent dramas. With the help of the Wurlitzer, I can help them forget their troubles and give them a good time. They'll come back for more. I know I can do it, Mr. Stein. You don't have to interview anyone else. I was destined to work at the Ritz. It's my fate."

After a moment of silence, he laughed, and not a chuckle either. His head fell back and he slapped his knee as if he'd just listened to a particularly hilarious episode of *Amos n' Andy*. The nerve of the crumb. The fate part might have been baloney, but I meant the rest of it. He looked at me and continued snickering. "That's a lot of words for a little girl. Just how old did you say you are?"

I'd promised myself he wasn't going to say no. "I'm eighteen, with a high school diploma and three years of college."

While he digested that bit of information, I tried another angle. "I come from a cultured family, a very cultured family. My father was the first violinist of the New York Philharmonic and my sister trained at Julliard."

Mr. Stein looked at me as if I had two heads. I guess the Wurlitzer at the Ritz wasn't in the cards. "Well, I'm more than happy with an usherette job, Mr. Stein, that is, if the offer still stands."

"Hold your horses, little lady. I haven't heard you play yet."

Wonderful. I'd have a chance. When I rose, he jumped up from the desk and bounded over so quickly I plopped back down, chair bound. The guy was in such close proximity, our faces almost met. I'm sure he could hear my heart pummeling my chest. What had I gotten myself into? It seemed like an eternity before he stepped back.

"Why don't we visit the Mighty Wurlitzer?"

****

We stepped into a dreary auditorium with worn carpets, faded wall paintings, and seats in need of new upholstery; then, Mr. Stein flicked a switch near the old orchestra pit, and the magic began. A Wurlitzer organ ascended through a trap door in the orchestra pit, lit up and waiting for a skilled pair of hands. Perhaps the Ritz Theater lay in tatters, but the Wurlitzer Company had created that baby from the finest polished mahogany and gilded her with Florentine accents. Every sound effect known to man would be at my disposal.

"She's wonderful, Mr. Stein."

When I sat down to play, I could feel him behind me, his eyes drilling through my skull. I refused to let the guy frazzle me and started with improvisations on classical themes, a little Bach, some Schuman, and lots of Chopin.

"Mr. Stein, the organist at the Capitol Theater said I'd have to create my own melodies. The big movie houses with orchestras had full scores, but I guess I'm on my own."

He placed a manicured hand on my shoulder, and I had to stifle a scream. "Nah, you won't have to wing it, baby. The projectionist will give you sheets cued the way the music fits into the film. Maybe you'll have to fly by the seat of your panties for the first show, but you'll know what to do by the second."

By the seat of my panties? If I hadn't been desperate for work, I'd have given the crumb a piece of my mind. "Mr. Stein, does that mean I have the job?"

He grinned like a smug toad, and I wanted to clobber him.

"Of course, doll. We show the classics with Valentino, Gloria Swanson, and Chaney, and the studios are cranking out silent prints of talking pictures. We'll be screening the silent version of the new Clara Bow talkie, and I'm expecting a couple of Joan Crawford movies too, but I have to warn you, it won't last forever."

"What won't last forever?"

He moved in a bit closer. "Everybody's wiring their theaters for sound. Silent dramas are on their last legs. I don't know how long I can keep the Ritz open."

Hearing the truth didn't make it any easier to swallow, especially when I'd just gotten a job there. "But you're keeping it open for now, aren't you, Mr. Stein?"

He must have heard the desperation in my voice because he softened.

"Yeah, sure I am. Don't worry, Dollface, you've got the job. I've already paid a fellow for tonight, but I'll expect you here tomorrow morning at eleven sharp." He pressed his cheek to mine. "Now, how about us having lunch to celebrate?"

The thought of sitting across a table from that goon made me nauseous. "Thanks for the offer, Mr. Stein, but I have to get home."

He seemed a bit disappointed. "Oh, well, since you're in a hurry, I'll drive you."

I opened my mouth to refuse, but from the look in his eyes, I couldn't say no. "The limo is waiting, doll."

Five minutes later, I'd parked my tush on the buttery leather seats of the most beautiful automobile I'd ever seen. He sat behind the wheel of a Cadillac sedan, the exterior ivory enamel with gleaming chrome. "You really don't have to drive me, Mr. Stein. I'm from New York, I'm used to walking."

Mr. Stein turned over the engine. "But I insist." I slid next to him and he turned to me, an annoying leer on his face. "Ever been in a Cadillac, baby?"

Except for Omar chauffeuring us down Broadway, I'd never ridden in anything fancier than a Model-T before. "No, sir, I can't say I have."

He laughed, but it sounded more like a crow of triumph. "Well, maybe you'll get used to it."

In a pig's eye, I would. Although I didn't intend to

ride in his car again, I kept quiet while he blabbed away about life in Los Angeles.

"The weather here is swell, but they roll up the sidewalks at dusk. There's no football, theater, opera, ballet, or anything else, for that matter, except for a few after-hour joints on Sunset Boulevard. I guess Los Angeles must be quite a letdown for a New York girl like you."

I never mastered small talk, but tried to be cordial. "I'm sure my sister and I will acclimatize in no time. I hear the central library is quite grand, and I plan to spend a lot of time there."

Mr. Stein patted my knee and I nearly jumped from the seat. "So you like to read, huh? I've always had a soft spot for brainy girls."

After what seemed like endless minutes of banter about the city, I finally mustered up the nerve to ask about his wife.

"And how does Mrs. Stein like Los Angeles?"

Mr. Blabby suddenly went silent. He stared ahead, then whispered a reply. "Mrs. Stein has never been to Los Angeles."

I turned to ask him why not but clammed up the moment I looked into his face. His mouth had tightened and the smirk had disappeared. The temperature inside the Cadillac dropped to freezing. Mr. Stein drove up 3rd Street and parked in front of the Dorchester. I wanted to bolt from the car, but he stopped me before I could. "Wait, baby, let me get the door."

Mr. Stein took my hand in his and walked me to the porch. "Mitzi, it's my sincere hope that we become better acquainted in the next few weeks."

Not if I could help it.

****

When I entered the parlor, Mrs. LaRue and three old ladies were in the midst of a brisk game of pinochle. I tiptoed past the merrymakers toward our empty flat. Leah had nixed pounding the pavement to look for a job and found work as a hostess at a place called the Roseland Roof, on Spring Street.

She'd lied about her age, claiming to be twenty-one. I asked her about it, and she chortled, her laughter cynical and empty. "They're all the same, cigarette smoke, smelly hair tonic, cheap aftershave, sweaty hands. The only difference is that in Los Angeles, the customers are lonely Filipinos, and in New York, they were lonely Italians."

I looked around our apartment. We couldn't do anything about the chipped molding, but the paper roses pasted over the peeled wallpaper were a nice touch. A braided rug covered the scarred floors. We normally kept the flat shipshape, but the wooden floor needed a good sweeping, so I grabbed a broom and set to work. I stepped on one of the planks and heard the disquieting squeak of a loose floorboard. I tiptoed around the spot and heard the sound again. I knelt, examined the floor, and discovered the culprit, a plank that didn't quite fit.

When I pried the board up, I found an old Astor Coffee tin. I opened it and discovered Leah used it as a safe. I found a small role of bills and a cache of letters in Pops' hand. From the postmarks, he'd written them when he was courting Mama. Leah must have found them among Pops' things. My mother had perfumed them with rose petals and bound them with red ribbons. I slid one from the envelope and read the purple prose of an ardent suitor:

My darling, you are in my thoughts every waking hour. I can't sleep without dreaming of your beautiful face. Please tell me you think of me too.

Obviously Pops had fallen for my mother the moment he set eyes on her. What a romance they'd had. His love for her cascaded from every sentence. Every word dripped with adoration. After I'd perused every letter, I replaced them in their envelopes and re-tied the ribbons. I dug around and found a cigar box holding more letters, ones addressed to my grandmother, all postmarked California 1923, the year Uncle Baron died. Nosy parker that I was, I couldn't stop reading.

Dearest Mama,

It's been another day of sunshine and forced gaiety. Lethargy permeates this place, a lazy civility so different from the frenetic pace of home. Still, I'd gladly give up the sun and serenity for a glimpse of your face. How I miss you, Zisel, and our darling Leah and Mitzi. The people here are kind and have been gracious, but the town is a sapling, everything green and new and devoid of the rich flavors of a real city. The constant sun forces everyone to wear dark glasses as if it is a city of the blind. Each night, I dream of skyscrapers and a giant moon framed by steel and concrete.

I'm fast on Baron's trail. He's managed to charm half of Los Angeles and has been an extra in a number of moving pictures. One of his chums told me that he has found regular work at Regal Pictures and has a flat at the Hotel Hollywood. I plan to drop by unannounced and will bring him back to New York by hook or by crook. All I can think about is returning to you, and my beautiful girls.

Isaac

So Uncle Baron had once lived at the Hotel Hollywood. My visit to the famed place would have to wait until Monday, the only day the Broadway Ritz closed for business. If there was something to find, I'd find it.

Chapter Nine
The Hollywood Hotel

Everyone swore red flattered me, so on my first day at the Ritz, I became a scarlet woman. I carted a portfolio of sheet music along with the nutritious lunch Leah had made for me. She'd also forced a nickel into my hand. "This is for milk; you're still a growing girl."

Yes, she'd promised Zisel she'd take care of me, but acting as if it were my first day of kindergarten went too far. "Leah, I stopped growing when I turned twelve. I'm too old for milk money."

She gave me the Look. I took the nickel, and gave thanks she didn't make me carry a Teddy bear too.

Mr. Stein stood in the lobby flipping a twenty-dollar gold piece like some dime store Romeo. He stopped the coin toss the moment I crossed the threshold and looked at his wristwatch. "Aren't we punctual? I like that in an employee."

I managed a sunny, "Thank you, Mr. Stein," then walked past the goon. The gods must have been with me, because he didn't follow when I entered the auditorium. The Mighty Wurlitzer sat in wait for me, looking quite welcoming. I pressed every tab, delighted in the arsenal of sound effects at my disposal. Mr. Stein had finagled a silent copy of the Clara Bow talkie *My Heart Belongs to the Navy*, along with the music cues.

Edna sidled up next to me and whispered, "We're

letting the audience in, Mitzi. Mr. Stein asked that you play something cheery while they take their seats."

The man said "cheery," so I gave them cheery. The crowd needed a respite from the bleak times. I switched on the Bingo Night microphone and ripped into one of my favorites, "Makin' Whoopee." Some might think the song a bit saucy, but my voice soared, and the folks in the auditorium broke into wild applause. "Embraceable You" went over even bigger.

When the lights dimmed, and the newsreel started, my real work began. I played a rousing melody improvised from British martial music. For the comic shorts, I slid into bright snatches of Broadway tunes. The childish antics of the Mischief Makers were favorites with our audience, and I used every bell and whistle. Little Jill Carpenter started her usual on-screen havoc, and the audience's laughter nearly drowned out the Wurlitzer. By the time the short ended, the audience rolled in the aisles. I wondered how such a talented darling could have grown into a platinum-blonde witch.

The title card announced *My Heart Belongs to the Navy*, a lively comedy about a counter girl with too many boyfriends for her own good. The crowd went nuts over the antics of my doppelganger, Clara Bow, and cheered when she kissed her sailor boyfriend to my favorite Gershwin tune, "How Long Has This Been Going On."

The show ended. I rose from my chair and bowed as if I'd played at Carnegie Hall. Folks rushed up to the Wurlitzer and some even asked to shake my hand. Who could ask for a better debut? I made an even bigger smash at the next show.

That evening I floated out of the Ritz, past Edna

and the twins. Suddenly life seemed wonderful again, as if I were still in New York playing for Pops and his musician friends. I felt like a million smackers—that is, until I walked out onto the street. Mr. Stein stood at the curb in front of his Cadillac, flipping his gold piece. The moment he saw me, he pocketed the coin and began applauding.

"Doll, you claimed you could sing in New York, but I haven't heard a voice like yours since Ethel Merman. This calls for a celebration."

He flung open the front door of his motorcar. "Here's our magic carpet, baby. Get in and I'll take you to dinner."

How could I escape? "Gee thanks, Mr. Stein, but my sister is expecting me. She'll be worried if I'm late. I really have to get home."

His lips contorted into a boyish pout. "Oh, yeah, okay, I get it. I'm heading back east tomorrow and won't be around until after New Year's. I guess I was hoping maybe you'd cheer up a fellow New Yorker, but I keep forgetting about your sister. Let me drive you home."

I knew by his expression refusal wasn't an option, so I planted myself next to him, smiling the entire time, overjoyed I wouldn't see his smirking mug for the next three weeks. He nattered on about some sort of deal with a movie studio involving the theaters he owned around the country.

"I don't want to jinx it. It'll take time, but if it goes through I'll be starting a new line of work. Just you wait, baby. I'll be a big man in this town."

It didn't matter to me how big he'd be, just as long as I didn't have to deal with his unwanted attentions.

He might have been a handsome devil with money to burn, but I remembered he wore a wedding band, even if he didn't.

The streetlights suddenly flashed on, revealing broad avenues flooded with pedestrians. When we finally arrived at the Dorchester, he insisted on walking me to the front door.

"You haven't had many gentleman callers, have you, Mitzi?"

I averted my head. He didn't have to know about my lack of gentlemen callers. Mr. Stein took my chin in his hand, moved my face back to his, then gazed at me through those beautiful peepers. Despite the fact I knew what a stinker he was, I went weak at the knees. "Baby, I have a feeling this is just the beginning."

Beginning of what?

****

That Monday, I boarded the Red Car and headed for the Hotel Hollywood. Talk about a bad case of the jitters. My hands shook so much I barely got the token into the coin box. The streetcar took its time as it glided through the sun-kissed boulevards. It seemed an eternity before the trolley turned onto Hollywood Boulevard. Boy, what a letdown!

I had expected a fantasy highway lined with black marble façades on skyscrapers. Where were the glamorous actresses strutting up and down the street in furs and jewels as they walked Russian wolfhounds with diamond collars on their slender necks?

To my great disappointment, Hollywood Boulevard looked like the rest of Los Angeles: flat, clean, a ritzy shop here, a restaurant there, swaying palms everywhere, but with none of the hoped-for magic. Out of the blue, an ivory-colored Cadillac whizzed by and set my heart to pumping. I peered through the window to see if I knew the driver. Thankfully, an older fellow in a plaid suit sat behind the wheel. I must be going nuts. For a week I'd dreamed about a beautiful Fuller Brush man, but now I had that rat David Stein on the brain.

The trolley passed the Roosevelt Hotel, the place where I'd read the stars met. It failed to excite me. Since Christmas was less than two weeks away, they'd festooned the street lamps with evergreen wreaths encircling dramatic images of movie actors. The constellation of Regal's stars twinkled from the opposite side of the street. A beautiful image of Jill Carpenter, swathed in white fur, almost made me forget what a sourpuss she was.

Finally, the streetcar arrived at the famed Hotel Hollywood, a sprawling Spanish colonial adjoining a forest of palms and a grove of lemon trees. A grand veranda ran the entire length of the entrance. I imagined Uncle Baron wearing his favorite Panama hat as he saluted the ladies who passed him on the Boulevard.

The hotel sat next door to Grauman's Chinese Theater, a movie palace designed to capture the magic of the Forbidden City but instead looked like a brassy Oriental temple. Grauman's gaudy touch showed up across the street in the date palms and stuffed camels of the garish shrine to faux Egyptology, the Egyptian Theater.

I threw back my shoulders and strolled into the Hotel Hollywood's lobby just as a string quartet ripped into a hot-blooded tango. Wrought iron chandeliers hung from the beams and illuminated the heavy

Castilian furnishings. I maneuvered my way to the front desk through a platoon of bellmen in snazzy black uniforms trimmed with gold braid.

The front desk manager had garbed himself in a topcoat and striped pants. The fellow made a deep bow and addressed me in an English accent, probably phony.

"May I assist you, young lady?"

I'd dressed to the nines, but I could tell my duds didn't impress him, so I decided to let the debutante come out. I placed my copybook on the desk and tightened my jaw like a rich shiksa from Barnard.

"Yes, you may, my man. The name is, uh, Miss Vanderbilt. My family is wintering in Los Angeles, and I decided your establishment would be a splendid subject for my school newspaper."

He looked at me and smirked. "Well, Miss, uh, Vanderbilt, may I ask the name of your school?"

I didn't like his attitude and flared my nostrils like Gloria Swanson. "Yes, of course you may. It's Barnard, Barnard College, in New York City. All the Vanderbilt girls attend Barnard."

The mention of Barnard didn't wipe the smirk off his face. He just grinned at me like I was a lox. Maybe I hadn't taken the crumb in, but I kept the act up anyway. "If it can be arranged, I'd like to talk to someone in a senior position who has been working here since 1920 and is well acquainted with the hotel's history. A few colorful stories would be nice, but, uh, not too colorful. After all, I am writing for young ladies."

The desk clerk motioned to a bellhop. "Please escort Miss, uh, Vanderbilt to Clyde's, uh, office."

He turned back to me, his wicked smile still in place. "Clyde has been part of the staff longer than anyone and can answer any questions, or so he assures me. I'm sure he'd be overjoyed to be of aid to such a charming young lady—especially a Vanderbilt."

Clyde, a scrawny old bird in a shiny black suit, sat behind a desk affixed with a brass plate that read "Concierge." He smiled, flashing a mouth of full brown choppers. "The name's just Clyde. I've been working here since nineteen hundred and fifteen."

The guy didn't look a day under eighty. A milky film covered his eyes, and he used a walking stick to maneuver around the hotel. Still, despite his infirmities, Clyde had a full head of gray hair, sharp hearing, and most importantly, all of his marbles.

"You had to deal with the Limey at the front desk, did you? Can't stand the fellow myself. He's always so snooty. He would have thrown me out on my ear, but the former owner wrote in her will that I'd always have a job here. I swear, since she died, this place has gone to hell in a handbasket."

He took a deep drag and coughed. "I came to Los Angeles from New York to be in the movies, only the lights gave me klieg eye, so I got a job here. You should have seen the place in '26, before they opened the Roosevelt. What a time we had."

Clyde took another puff on his cigarette and waxed poetic. "I guess it would've been too much for a little lady like you. Those were wild days. Millionaires used to smuggle in cases of champagne. The extra girls would do the shimmy until dawn. Valentino danced in the lobby with Mae Murray. Rudy always said tile floors were the best for the tango. Oh, the glamour, the stars, the hooch. The poor owner was a teetotaler and frowned on gin and hanky-panky, so she had her hands full watching over the girls."

Clyde had another coughing spasm, and I figured he'd probably be joining the deceased owner soon. But he'd given me an opening, so I asked, "Girls? What about the boys?"

"There were some young fellows living here. Most were sterling young men, but a few would bring in bootlegged booze and even narcotics. It caused a big stink."

"Did you know a young gentleman named Baron?"

Clyde stared at me through half-blind eyes. "Baron, do you mean Baron Schector? What a dashing youngster, charmed every gal he met. He used to play the piano at the Thursday dances, and boy, he could tickle those ivories to beat the band. Such a shame he died that way. Poor kid. Say, how would you know his name anyway, you being a Vanderbilt and all?"

I dropped the high-hat accent. "He was my uncle."

He sat back in his chair, digesting my words. "Well, what do you know? So Baron's real name was Vanderbilt? What a classy fellow."

I had gone this far so I continued the charade. "Father made a visit here once."

He thought for a moment, tapped his right temple and smiled. "I might be old, but my noodle is still as sharp as a tack. I remember him. Your father is a classy fellow too, him being a Vanderbilt and all. He came here after Baron died, but they'd already cleaned out the kid's room and taken everything."

In his last letter to Leah, Pops bemoaned the fact that someone had gotten hold of my uncle's property and the sheriff's department refused to discuss what happened to his body.

"Did the police take Uncle Baron's things?"

The old guy coughed up a load of phlegm into his handkerchief. I averted my head, praying I wouldn't puke on his desk. Clyde didn't seem to notice my face had turned green.

"Nah. The flatfoots were worse than the Keystone Cops, a bunch of crooks and chiselers, but they had nothing to do with it. The bigwigs at Regal Pictures handled everything."

So Mr. Roth had been involved. Claude turned his milky eyes toward me and spoke in a low murmur. "You might not know this, Miss Vanderbilt, but they were going to make a leading man out of him, sign him to a contract and everything."

"Golly, being a movie actor was Uncle Baron's dream. Do you have any idea what they did with his body?"

The old fellow shook his head. "Don't know, Miss Vanderbilt. No one ever talked about it." He paused for a moment, trapped by his memories. "There was something else. Your uncle had a lady love, Clarice Dumont."

Clarice Dumont? My head began throbbing. "I'm sorry, please excuse me, I'm not feeling well. I think I should leave now."

He looked at me through dim eyes. "Was it what I said about your uncle and Clarice?"

I found it almost impossible to keep up the masquerade. "Yes, it's a bit of a shock. I'm afraid I should be on my way."

Clyde flashed a grimy smile. "Miss Vanderbilt, I know you'll only be in town for a short time, but can you leave a telephone number? There are papers in the vault that no one knows about."

I scribbled down Mrs. LaRue's phone number. "Please call the moment you find anything."

During the return ride home, I decided that perhaps it would be wise to keep my lips buttoned about Uncle Baron's love affair with Clarice. It wouldn't hurt to learn more before I involved Leah. When I arrived home, I read through Pops' California letters once more. Pops mentioned Clarice Dumont died in the same fire as Uncle Baron, but wrote nothing more. I doubted he knew they were sweethearts. I thought about bringing it up to Mr. Stein but immediately nixed the idea. He might want something in return for helping me, something I wasn't willing to give.

****

Working at the Broadway Ritz was aces. I'd become pals with Edna and her twin brothers, and we made a jolly foursome. I had friends and a regular paycheck; however, Edna presented a teensy problem. My parents had taught me to respect other people's beliefs, but I had to bite my tongue every time Edna brought up Jesus.

"Gosh, Mitzi, you've got everything a girl could want, looks, talent, brains, but if you don't mind me saying, you need to find Jesus. If you don't, you won't be saved, and your soul will burn throughout eternity in the fires of Hell."

What an unpleasant thought.

Edna would corner me between shows to talk about Jesus or give me Bible tracts courtesy of a radio preacher named Aimee Semple McPherson. Mrs. McPherson fed the poor and extolled the benefits of Christianity while she ranted against movies, dancing, jazz music, and Charles Darwin. Despite her religious mumbo jumbo, I couldn't stay angry with Edna. We were friends, and I sure needed one.

When I arrived home on Sunday evening after working at the Ritz for a week, Leah sat in the front room, soaking her aching tootsies in Epsom salts. Mrs. LaRue handed me a message. "Some old guy called from the Hotel Hollywood looking for a Miss Vanderbilt."

I'm sure my expression told all. She laughed at my concern. "Don't worry, kiddo, I didn't give you away. The poor fellow coughed something awful, like he had pneumonia. He said to tell you that Clyde found a paper you'd want."

Hallelujah!

The smarmy English fellow worked behind the front desk when I strolled into the hotel's lobby the next morning. He smiled, banana oil dripping from the corners of his mouth. "It's Miss Vanderbilt from Barnard, is it not?"

I threw back my shoulders and put on my hoity-toity accent. "Yes, it is. My social secretary received a message from Clyde. It seems he has a few more stories to share with me."

The Englishman paled. "Oh, my goodness, you don't know, do you? Miss Vanderbilt, I'm afraid Clyde passed away last night. You must have seen how frail he was."

I'm sure my expression betrayed me. "Did he leave anything for me?"

The moment the British fellow shook his head, I knew all was lost. I turned and left the hotel without a word.

Back at the Dorchester, the old ladies were making merry with eggnog and Christmas carols. Their holiday mood didn't infect me. I'd be stuck in a land of perpetual sun forever and would never find out where they'd buried Uncle Baron. Although I feigned cheeriness, I wished I could crawl into a hole and die.

"Merry Christmas, ladies."

Ho, ho, ho.

Chapter Ten
Los Angeles

December 22, 1931

The coffin lid creaked open. A creature in a tuxedo and black cape peered out from a world of black and pewter shadows. The demon's waxen face filled the screen. Suddenly, dissonant chords resonated throughout the theater. A lady shrieked and the audience broke out in nervous titters.

I'd improvised on themes from *The Rites of Spring* as three ghoulish beauties in flowing gowns, the vampire brides, prepared to feed on poor Mr. Renfield. The Mighty Wurlitzer mimicked the sound of a bat's wings as the bloodthirsty Count Dracula transformed himself. When the time came for my knock-'em-dead climax, I ramped up the dark chords as Van Helsing moved toward Dracula's coffin. The house lights flashed on and off, and then came the coup de grace: a stake driven through Dracula's black heart. The ceiling lights came on in a blinding flash.

The audience burst into enthusiastic applause and nearly blew the roof off the joint when I stood. Gaylord Carter may have been The King of the Wurlitzer, but that night the audience crowned me the Queen.

The regulars packed the theater, faithful and devoted fans who always showed up dressed in their

Sunday best. Maybe the two-for-a-quarter ticket price brought them in, or the rose-colored glassware handed out on Bingo Night. Perhaps they just wanted to forget the dark days of the present and remember better times in the past. They came all the same.

Although Christmas would be here in three days, *Dracula* remained the most requested of the movies on the Ritz's schedule. No one cared that we'd screened the silent print of the talkie. Whenever we showed our version, whether at a summer matinee, or on Halloween night, the line went around the block.

One old gal showed up at the Ritz at least twice a week. She tottered up, as giddy as a kid, then took my arm. "My darling Mitzi, you put on such a show tonight. It was so much better than those silly talkies with the stiff acting. Where did such a young girl learn to play so good?"

I always kept my curriculum vitae as short as possible. "I learned everything I know right here at the Ritz, ma'am."

The old lady touched my face. "No, darling, you're not from here. I can hear the New York in your voice."

Helen Keller could have heard the New York in my voice. "Such talent you have, Mitzi. A pretty little thing like you could take this town by storm."

Yeah, sure, I should have all of Hollywood at my feet. I'd heard it all before. Maybe the old dame had bats in her belfry, but I never argued with an admirer.

"Well, I'm happy you enjoyed the show, and I hope you come again."

She gazed at me, her eyes misting. "How can I come again? Aren't you closing the doors next week?"

Even she'd heard the bad news. "No, ma'am, we're

not closing down. Regal Pictures bought the Ritz, and they're wiring it for talkies."

A tear ran down the old gal's face. "How sad. I remember when you could go to the movies and see great acting and hear a splendid live orchestra. My daughter takes me to the talking pictures, a bunch of stiffs standing in one place, mouthing stupid stuff. If I want music, I have to listen to the radio or the Victrola. It's not the same."

"No, ma'am, it's not."

The old lady smiled. "It's the times, I guess." She took my hand once again. "Good luck, dear heart."

She ambled off without looking back. I'd been at the Ritz for an entire year now, and I sure would miss it. 1931 had proved to be even worse than 1930, but I had a job, at least until tomorrow.

Mr. Stein rarely visited the premises now, and for that everyone gave thanks. The guy never blew his stack, but he treated everyone—Edna, the twins, the projectionist, and the merchants who crossed the Ritz's threshold—with icy disdain. Everyone except me.

Unfortunately, his interest in me had deepened over the year I'd worked for him. With Mr. Stein around, I couldn't even have a chuckle with the fellows. The pill would give them the evil eye and then make a lousy comment like, "Hate to interrupt the party, but I believe there's work to do."

The nerve of the creep acting liked he owned me. I promised myself that one day, when I was in the chips, I'd tell him off, and not just for interfering with my social life. He'd continued his annoying habit of tossing his gold piece and leering at me like a Russian pimp. Once, he even pulled out a wad of cash and waved it under my nose.

"I'm a very generous fellow, Dollface. All you have to do is ask."

David Stein's money held no interest for me, and I'd never traipse down the primrose path with a married man. I thanked my lucky stars he only looked and never touched.

Leah had been under the weather with influenza, and I knew I shouldn't linger after the show. When I walked out to the lobby, Edna was entertaining her brothers by dancing a spirited Lindy Hop with the new vacuum sweeper. I joined Andy and Randy in applauding her antics.

She pushed the sweeper in my direction and whispered, "Mr. Stein is waiting for you, Toots. Let me know if you want the twins to hang around, just in case."

Drat. I shook my head. "No, Edna, tell them to go on. I can handle him."

I knocked, my heart palpitating like a bass drum. After a long moment, Mr. Stein opened the door. He fixed his eyes on me, his gaze so intense I wanted to head for the hills. Of course I'd already lost my job, so what else could he do to me? I breathed deeply and walked inside.

He pulled out a chair. "Sit down, doll."

Mr. Stein usually held court from behind his desk, but this time, instead, he perched on its front edge, his eyes never leaving my face. He looked imperious in his snazzy black suit and smelled as if he'd just left a barbershop. At twenty-three, the guy only had four years on me, but for some reason, I always quaked in his presence.

When I moved closer, I noticed he'd removed his wedding band. His philandering had become blatant. I felt like a sap for letting Edna and the twins leave, comforted in the fact that except for brushing up against me, he'd never made a move. After tomorrow, I'd never see him again.

"Mitzi, I wanted to tell you what a swell job you did tonight. I know the Ritz has been your home since you moved to Los Angeles, but all good things come to an end."

A compliment didn't mean much since I'd gotten the ax, but I smiled anyway. "Thanks for the kind words, Mr. Stein. If you don't mind my saying, it's a shame about the Ritz becoming a talking picture theater. There are still a lot of folks who prefer silent dramas."

His mouth tightened. "Are you trying to tell me how to run my business, Dollface?"

The bum hadn't paid me yet, so I couldn't afford to agitate him. "No, sir. Sorry."

His lips spread into a smile that didn't reach his eyes. When he slid closer, I could barely stop myself from squirming. "No need to be sorry, baby. Maybe the sound stinks, but it gets better by the day. Those fellows at Western Electric really know their stuff. Truth is I can't keep scrounging around for silent prints. They're not making many, just a few dribs and drabs. It's like I told you when you first came here—the days of silent dramas are over. We're getting rid of the Wurlitzer and going to recorded music."

Getting rid of the Wurlitzer? It really was curtains for the Ritz. They could spruce the old gal up, but without the mighty Wurlitzer, the Ritz had no heart.

"I'm sorry to hear that, Mr. Stein. I guess I should go now."

He barred my way when I stood. "Progress is the word of the day, little lady. Mankind must advance. Womankind too."

Mr. Stein had a laugh as chilly as his smile. He moved so close I felt his warm, peppermint-scented breath against my cheek. "Usherettes and popcorn schleppers are a dime a dozen, but you, you're a pip, baby. You've got talent, you're easy on the eyes, and with the right fellow in your corner you could go far. All you need is someone who knows the ropes."

He took a deep breath, then spoke in a rush. "Mitzi, I could be that someone. I'm doing big things with Regal Pictures. Maybe they're not much of an operation compared to Paramount or Metro, but everything will change when they own their own theaters. One call from me, and you'll be farting through silk panties. I just want to be your special friend. Is it too much to ask?"

Farting through silk panties? How could such an educated fellow say something so crude? I felt warm and knew the color had come to my face. "Being my special friend" meant I'd have to go to bed with the jerk. Mr. Stein laughed, probably because I'd turned as red as a tomato.

When I rose from the chair, Mr. Stein took me in his arms. We stared at each other for a long moment. From the look in his eyes, I knew he wanted to kiss me. I felt something stiff on the side of my thigh and noted the culprit poking the front of his pants. He wanted more than a smooch. When I tried to pull away, he held fast.

"Please, Mr. Stein, I'm not that kind of girl."

His voice sounded like satin. "Oh? What kind of girl is that?"

I hated having this crumb bait me. "Mr. Stein, let me go. Please. My sister is sick. She needs me."

"Then it would be my pleasure to drive you home, doll."

He released me and adjusted his trousers. I inched toward the door. "No, thank you, Mr. Stein, but you've given me an awful lot to think about."

Mr. Stein laughed in his frosty way. "Yeah, I guess I have."

When I turned to leave, he grabbed me by the arm, his fingers digging into my skin.

"Please, Mr. Stein, you're hurting me."

He released me, then blew on my neck. "I guess I don't know my own strength. Maybe it's because I have a thing for you. C'mon, baby."

Mr. Stein held me fast with one hand and turned my face to his with the other. The front of his trousers looked as if they'd pop open at any minute. He moved in for the kiss. "I made you mad, didn't I? How about a little smooch to make up?"

With the Ritz empty, no one would hear me scream. I struggled, but he was one strong fellow. "Please, Mr. Stein, let me go. What about Mrs. Stein?"

He released me immediately. I saw something vaguely resembling regret in his eyes. "She's…"

Before he could finish, I heard a most fortuitous knock at the door. The projectionist on the other side called out, "Hey, Mr. Stein, the wife and kids are waiting. It's time to lock up the joint."

Mr. Stein glared at the door, his schlong still rock

hard. "I'll be out in a minute!"

He flashed an icy smile as he adjusted his pants one more time. "Mitzi, you're a very special girl, and I'm a fellow you can lean on. Promise me you'll think about it."

"Yes, Mr. Stein."

He pulled me to him and whispered, "Call me David. Please."

I nodded, pushed his hands away, grabbed my pocketbook, and, though it took every bit of my nerve, strolled out instead of running for my life.

"Goodnight, Mr. Stein. I mean, David."

He called after me. "Make sure you look pretty tomorrow."

Boy, did I need that final paycheck. "Yes, David."

When I walked out the door, I felt his eyes burn a hole in my back.

Chapter Eleven
Farewell, Broadway Ritz

I left the Ritz at dusk. My arm throbbed from the goon's touch, and I felt like a sissy for not telling him off. Imagine him thinking I'd fallen for that baloney about Regal Pictures. They'd probably throw the bum off the Regal lot, smirk and all.

I thought I could take whatever that gorilla dished out, but no, I couldn't. Why hadn't I socked him in the jaw, or at least given him a piece of my mind? Because I needed my final paycheck, that's why. Still, despite his behavior, I knew a real human lurked behind the icy exterior. On a few occasions, I had seen a flicker of light in his eyes when he dropped his king-of-the-castle act. Sometimes he would stare at me as if he waited to share a secret, but he'd catch himself and walk away. What did it matter? The guy probably had a carload of dames stashed around town willing to do his bidding.

The scent of pine, chocolate, and cinnamon flooded Hill Street. An enterprising fellow stood in Bullock's open alleyway, selling Christmas trees, hot cocoa, and gingerbread. Some unfortunates kept the evening chill at bay by huddling around a steel drum filled with burning wood chips. I looked about the immaculate boulevards and thought about Manhattan. Snow covered the streets of New York, and some poor folks subsisted in Hooverville, a tent city in Central Park.

Still, no matter how brutal life in New York might be, I pined for her.

Christmas lights twinkled from every lamppost, and in shop windows fairy princesses danced with mechanical elves. A burst of light, a buzz, and the neon ribbons that decorated each movie house flashed on and bathed Broadway in garish colors.

The Palace Theater was screening Jill Carpenter's latest movie, *Platinum Madness*. The theater management had plastered her lovely mug all over the street, along with a rave by Walter Winchell: "This flicker has it all, sex, sex, and sex, personified by luscious Jill Carpenter. Everybody and his mother are wondering what hijinks she'll get up to next."

Jill Carpenter had money and fame, while I was a failure. What did I have? A heel who wanted to be my special friend, an uncle buried God knows where, and a sister with the flu. Reality hit me like a ton of bricks, and I bawled like crazy. I felt hopeless and knew I'd be out of a job. To top it off, I opened my pocketbook and only found one handkerchief. Life stank.

I sat down on the curb, wanting to die. Now I understood why folks bumped themselves off. At that moment, if we still lived in New York, I'd have jumped from the top of the Empire State Building.

Without warning, Paganini's Sixteenth Caprice, Pops' favorite, wafted through the air. I looked up at a Victrola sitting in an open window. It might be wacky, but it sounded as if the great Jascha Heifetz was making music in this lonely place just for me.

Then I noticed something glittering on the pavement: eight quarters, three dimes, a nickel, five pennies, plus four Red Car tokens. A treasure. I scooped up the coins, and plunked them into my pocketbook. Hopefully, whoever lost this fortune wouldn't miss it too much, but two dollars and forty cents meant I could take Leah out for a couple of decent meals as soon as she got well. I'd forget about Mr. Stein, Jill Carpenter, and that louse, Nussbaum, and celebrate.

I trudged up 3rd Street to the Dorchester, still marveling at my good luck. The chilly air had forced the ancients inside. When I unlocked the front door, I heard Omar's saxophone floating throughout the rooming house. Mrs. LaRue occupied herself by decorating a showy Christmas tree with ropes of popcorn, tinsel, and glass balls. She turned to me, a bright smile lighting her face. "How's tricks, kiddo?"

Tricks were lousy, but I couldn't dump my problems on her. "I'm fine, Mrs. LaRue, but I worried about Leah all day."

Mrs. LaRue tossed more tinsel on the tree. "Worrying causes wrinkles. Mr. Fournier gave her some wicked good medicine he swears could cure bubonic plague. Her fever must have broken by now."

More good news. When I opened the door to our flat, Leah lay asleep. The influenza had sapped every ounce of her strength, but sweat matted her hair and soaked her bedclothes. Omar's medicine had indeed broken her fever, but sleeping in a wet nightgown could worsen her flu.

"Leah, come on, wake up. We have to get you out of that damp nightie."

She rewarded me with a weak smile after I rubbed her down with alcohol and helped her into a fresh gown. "What a lucky lady I am to have a sister like you.

You take such good care of me. My little Mitzi, what a loving girl you are."

Leah fell back onto the mattress and passed out like a light. My stomach growled, and I searched the icebox for something to eat. Half a tuna sandwich and a cup of cottage cheese took the edge off my hunger. Time to hit the hay. I stripped off my dress and looked in the bathroom mirror. My arm throbbed, black-and-blue from Mr. Stein's fingers. I prayed the bruising would fade before Leah caught sight of it.

I climbed into my cot and thought of Zisel, prune Danish, and Central Park without a Hooverville. I remembered coasting down the hills of Washington Heights as a kid, my pals in bright winter togs, their laughter filling the air. We weren't likely to see snow in this land of perpetual sun. The occasional child played in front of the other Bunker Hill boarding houses, but Mrs. LaRue didn't allow kids in the Dorchester. Thanks to Nussbaum, I lived in little-old-lady land.

I rolled over, fell asleep, and dreamed of lying in the arms of a smiling Fuller Brush man.

****

Leah's cough roused me before the wake-the-dead din of the alarm clock. I pulled myself up from my cot, wrapped an old bed shawl around my shoulders, and shuffled over to her bed. Her eyes fluttered open, and she lifted herself up, barely able to whisper. "Hello, Mitzi, how's my bubala this fine day?"

She fell back onto her pillow. I let her slumber while I prepared for my last day of work. I walked down the hall to the bathroom we shared with the pensioners. From the bathroom window, I watched one of the carriages of the Angels Flight chug down to 3rd

Street while the other ascended.

Thank goodness for steam heat, because the unmentionables I'd washed the night before were dry enough to wear that day to my final performance at the Ritz. I planned to make it memorable. I dusted my cheeks, chin, and nose with face powder, mascaraed my lashes, then finished off with rose-red lipstick from Max Factor.

I donned the last pair of Mr. Roth's silk stockings, ones I'd hung on to for over a year, and in an attempt to disguise my chubby cheeks, I used a bit of rouge. It didn't work. I'd found a swell pair of Woolworth's earrings that didn't turn my ears green. Zisel had sent me a red velveteen dress courtesy of her beau, Seymour. The frock would set a festive tone. I knew Leah wouldn't mind if I borrowed one of her garter belts and her red pumps for this special occasion.

I gave my sister a mixture of aspirin powder mixed with seltzer water, and then I set off. She'd get well soon enough, but now other concerns loomed front and center. It might have been selfishness on my part, but I wished she hadn't insisted on paying back everybody who'd helped us leave New York. Leah had been too ill to work for a while, and we'd already hocked her fox fur and charm bracelet. She'd even hinted that Pops' violin might be next. Over my dead body.

Mrs. LaRue came in from the porch dressed in a silk kimono, a milk bottle in hand. She'd pin-curled her auburn locks and covered them with a hair net. She faced the morning sans eyebrows. Later, she'd paint, powder, and mascara herself into some semblance of glamour, but in the glare of the sun, she looked a fright.

"Good morning, Mrs. LaRue. You're up early."

She cackled and took a drag on her cigarette. "Can't be a sleepyhead. I ain't a debutante like Barbara Hutton. How's your sister doing?"

My mother had perished in the 1918 influenza epidemic. Every time Leah coughed, I feared she might be heading down the same path. "Well, uh…uh…"

Mrs. LaRue's psychic abilities were in full force that morning. "Listen, kiddo, there's nothing wrong with your sister, just a wicked bout of influenza. Leave her to me. With some hot soup and another dose of Mr. Fournier's medicine, she'll be fit as a fiddle in no time."

I'm sure folks could hear my sigh of relief all the way to the Broadway in New York.

"Thanks, Mrs. LaRue, you're a real pal. Say, there's a double bill at the Ritz this afternoon. I'll be playing some swell music, as good as Gaylord Carter. It would be wonderful if you could make the matinee."

Mrs. LaRue flicked the ash from her Chesterfield into a potted plant. "I don't think so. The ladies invited me to play bridge this afternoon, and I really should look in on your sister. Besides, if I showed up, it would only be to hear you play. You're famous, Mitzi of the Ritz. It's you who should be on the screen. I've told you a million times—I know folks who could help you."

Everybody in Los Angeles knew someone in the movies who could help me. What a bill of goods. If Mrs. LaRue really knew people, what was she doing running the Dorchester?

"Jeez, Mrs. LaRue, you'll give me a bigger head than I already have. I sure wish you'd come. In case you change your mind, I'll leave a couple of tickets for you at the booth."

Mrs. LaRue took another puff of her cigarette. "I mean what I say. Somebody with your looks and talent should be in the movies, not playing for them."

I laughed for the first time that morning, then dashed off. I rushed down 3rd Street toward Broadway, but stopped at the Grand Central Market and grabbed a couple of donuts and some orange juice along the way.

By the time I arrived at the Ritz, a crowd already formed at the box office. Everyone grumbled about the theater's closing, but as much as I hated admitting it, Mr. Stein hadn't lied. Silent movies were a thing of the past, but it didn't make reality any easier to swallow. The regulars weren't only grousing about the end of silent dramas. Talkies meant a hike in admission, too.

I stuck my head in the door of the ticket booth where Edna sat.

"Edna, my landlady, Mrs. LaRue, just might show up for the matinee. Could you save a couple of tickets for her?"

"Sure. By the way, it's our lucky day. Mr. Stein ain't around, and he left the pay in cash. He's the last of the big spenders, a regular Diamond Jim Brady. He dropped in an extra five bucks along with a letter of recommendation."

With that she handed me my pay envelope. I felt as though an invisible hand had lifted a millstone from my neck. David Stein would never torture me again. Hallelujah! I tore open my envelope and nearly fainted. In addition to my regular pay, I found two crisp ten-dollar bills. Two sawbucks! Twenty smackers! I could take care of the rent and get Leah's fox stole and charm bracelet out of hock. Christmas had come early for this

Jewish girl.

I started the first of three shows, thankful I'd breakfasted on juice and sinkers. This would be a long day.

The Southern Belle, Clarice Dumont's last film, told the story of a poor girl who went to Atlanta looking for a rich husband. She fell for a poor boy instead, then discovered he was really a millionaire. I must have seen *The Southern Belle* twenty times, but now that I knew about Clarice and Uncle Baron's romance, I'd watch it with new eyes.

Mr. Stein had managed to scrounge up a silent copy of the newest talkie from the team of Dallas and Sweet, *Where West is East*. It starred Rex Dallas, the bigoted rat, but showcased Buster Sweet's marvelous comic timing. The audience laughed at his every gesture, and he knocked 'em dead every time. Mr. Stein swore he knew Buster Sweet, but I figured his claim was a load of applesauce.

Regal had filmed *Where West is East* on the streets of Chinatown, so I pulled out all the stops, even worked in snatches of Puccini's *Turandot*. When I accompanied *The Southern Belle*, I threw in a bit of jazz and a few café society melodies.

By the second matinee, exhaustion overcame me. One of the twins, either Andy or Randy, brought me a grape Nehi and some fresh popcorn. Lunch consisted of five Saltine crackers and two slices of American cheese, but I still managed to pour my heart into the music.

Although I'm Jewish, you might say I'm an aficionada of Christmas carols. On my last evening at the old Broadway Ritz, I led a Christmas sing-a-long,

"O! Holy Night," "God Rest Ye Merry, Gentlemen," and "O Come, All Ye Faithful." For a magical moment, everyone got into the spirit of the season and managed to forget Old Man Depression.

By the third show, when the title card for *The Southern Belle* flashed on the screen again, I could barely concentrate. Edna brought my dinner—a package of melted bon-bons and four Sen-Sens, along with more Nehi. "Sorry, Mitzi, this is the best I could do."

I wolfed everything down and then, fueled by sugar, attacked the music as if I were a machine. Things were copacetic until the garden-party scene where Clarice meets Rex Dallas.

I'll never know why I looked up at the screen.

I saw him.

Uncle Baron sat on the bandstand, playing the piano. We'd shown *The Southern Belle* at least half a dozen times before, and twice that day, but I'd never noticed my uncle before. There were only a couple of shots of him, but when Clarice Dumont waltzed by, he winked into the camera.

The tragedy of Uncle Baron and the girl he loved dying together in a horrible fire hit me square in the gut. My eyes began tearing, and I feared I wouldn't get through the performance. Then, I remembered seeing Pops drag himself from his sickbed and go to work, to play his heart out. Now I had my turn. People paid for a show, and I gave them one.

At points, I syncopated the rhythms, borrowed a bit from Gershwin, then invited Mr. Chopin into the love theme. The final screen kiss elicited a cheer, and, when the house lights came up, the audience jumped to its feet. I had my pay, an extra twenty bucks, and Mrs. LaRue swore Leah would be on her feet soon. On top of everything, I'd just seen Uncle Baron in a movie. One day I'd find his grave. I knew I would.

I stacked my sheet music into a pile on top of the Wurlitzer. They were the past, and I wouldn't need them again. Edna and the twins had shoved off early, so the projectionist escorted me from the Ritz. We shook hands, and he uttered a polite, "See you around, kid."

I took one final look at the place I'd called home for a year, and then off I went.

Chapter Twelve
Ho Ho Ho

A Salvation Army Santa Claus stood outside ringing his bell, and I felt generous enough to part with a quarter. The closer it got to Christmas, the brighter the lights on Broadway and the more pungent the perfume of the evergreens wreathing every lamppost. Ladies wore wintry corsages and every passing gentleman tipped his hat. Carolers in costumes straight out of Charles Dickens warbled in front of Bullock's Department Store. A crowd surrounded them, maybe hoping the singers' tidings of comfort and joy meant better days ahead.

I thought about my Fuller Brush man selling his wares in wintry New York. A handsome fellow like him was probably occupied chasing skirts in a swanky night club. He had to have a girlie waiting in the wings somewhere. Oh, well.

When I passed 6th Street, a tingling sensation ran down my spine. I turned, but found nothing out of the ordinary except for a bustle of shoppers. Still, I had the inexplicable sense of being tracked. By the time I reached the corner of 5th and Broadway, I sensed something following my every move. I kept telling myself, "Mitzi, you're acting like a sap," but the feeling of someone stalking me like prey wouldn't go away.

My feeling of unease continued when I moved

north toward Bunker Hill. Without warning, an ivory Caddie crawled from one of the Second Street tunnels and made an abrupt stop in front of me. Mr. Stein slid across the seat and opened the passenger door. "Get in, doll."

I leaned forward to politely suggest he scram. "Thanks, Mr. Stein, but—"

Before I could finish, he'd grabbed me by the shoulders and pulled me into the automobile. My heart began almost to beat out of my chest.

"Mr. Stein, please, I have to get home."

He'd dressed to the nines, smelled of spicy aftershave and fresh mint, and had a nasty leer on his face. "I'll take you home, baby, but we have to have a little talk first."

I didn't want to think about what kind of "talk" he had in mind. "Please, my sister's sick and waiting for me."

He kept driving, turned into an alley, and finally parked the Caddie. The only illumination came from a shard of light traveling down from a second-floor window.

His eyes were feverish and his expression so intense it terrified me. One look at his face told me acting like a weak sister wouldn't get me anywhere. David Stein wasn't the kind of fellow who'd melt under a torrent of tears. He planted his lips on my cheek, his hot breath vibrating against my skin.

"Mitzi, can't you see I'm nuts about you? I can take care of you and your sister too. Why do you keep running away?"

The words came easy. "I'm no floozy. I can't step out with a married man."

He didn't respond, just took me by my shoulders, and pinned me down on the leather cushions. His lips parted, and I felt his perfumed breath on my face.

"I'm not married anymore. You don't know what I'm going through. C'mon, baby, I've been thinking about you all day. How about that kiss? Just a kiss. Please?"

I didn't know what he wanted for his twenty dollars, but I doubted he would stop at a kiss. "You gave me money because you think I'm a tart? Did you suppose I'd go to bed with you? I'm not a whore." I handed him my pocketbook. "Take your money back, Mr. Stein. I don't want it."

I made an attempt at the door, but he pulled my arm away from the latch. "To hell with the money. All I want is a kiss, just one measly kiss. Please, Mitzi. My wife is dead."

His eyes filled with tears, and he wrenched his body away from me. Fear stopped me from asking more questions. "I'm sorry about Mrs. Stein. Goodbye."

I flung the car door open and scurried away, pocketbook in hand. My legs must have carried me to the Dorchester faster than any runner in Olympic history.

Mrs. LaRue had left the front door unlocked. The dulcet tones of Louie Armstrong's magical trumpet greeted me. Laughter poured from the parlor. "Surprise!"

Food covered the dining room table: mock apple pie, deviled eggs, strawberry gelatin with fruit cocktail and whipped cream, a stuffed turkey, canned salmon molded into the shape of a fish, and potatoes au gratin. A big frosted cake sat between the two punchbowls, one filled to the brim with Kool-Aid and slices of lemon, the other with eggnog. The pensioners wore their glad rags, and it looked as if all had splurged on finger waves and manicures.

Mrs. LaRue smiled, showing off her new dentures. "We're having a little holiday cheer."

She looked me up and down, noting my bedraggled state. "Kiddo, if you don't mind me saying so, you look like something the cat dragged in."

What a sight I must have been, my dress disheveled, my hair all over the place, my makeup a mess. I uttered the first thing that came into my head. "I wanted to get home to Leah, and I ran all the way."

The old ladies tittered. Mrs. LaRue took my arm and barely spoke above a whisper. "You've had a hard time tonight, haven't you, kiddo? Go change into another of your pretty dresses."

I sped to our flat and looked at the mess in the mirror. Off came the red velveteen dress. I sponged my body with a damp rag, powdered myself with talcum, reapplied my makeup, then changed into another frock. Most importantly, I decided to put David Stein out of my mind, if only for a night.

When I walked back into the parlor, I found Leah and Omar giggling and whispering like a pair of kids. She still looked peaked, but she'd waved her hair, lined her eyes, and painted her lips crimson. Omar stroked her palm—No, how could it be? His hand must have accidentally brushed against hers.

Gold charms glittered from her wrist—her bracelet, the one we'd pawned after she got sick. I hadn't given her any money yet. How did she get it out of hock? Before I could ask, Omar jumped off the davenport and hurried over to the eggnog. He played the Egyptian to the hilt, and looked quite dashing in a tuxedo and a fez. One of the pensioners even asked him how the weather was in his country.

"Cairo's very sunny this time of the year, ma'am." He winked at the old dame, then handed me a cup of eggnog. "Don't tell your sister, but there's brandy in it."

Later that evening, Omar dragged out his saxophone to accompany Leah on the piano. Everyone joined in and handed out little presents. I'd bought handkerchiefs for all, and received a sachet, nail varnish, and perfume in return. Omar played Santa and surprised Leah with a bottle of her favorite perfume, Shalimar. It seemed awfully extravagant, but he had gifts for everyone, including a pair of chiffon stockings for me. I might not be an expert, but I'd been to a bunch of Christmas parties in my nineteen years. This had to be the best one ever.

The party ended at ten, and all the guests pitched in with the cleanup. Later that night I tossed and turned in my narrow cot, thinking about Mr. Stein. His wife might have died and left him in agony, but did her passing excuse his behaving like an orangutan in heat?

****

The morning after the Dorchester party, I dusted off Leah's red pumps and took a stroll down Broadway, hunting for another job. If my search didn't pan out, I'd join Edna and the twins when they made the rounds looking for extra work in moving pictures. Then, if working in the movies wasn't in the cards, I could always join Leah at the Dreamland Club. Leah hit the roof when I mentioned it and gave me the Look. "No sister of mine is working in that dump."

I ignored her. Perhaps I didn't have her dancing skill, but I knew how to waltz.

When I arrived back at the Dorchester after my job search, Mrs. LaRue called me into her overheated flat. She'd perfumed her apartment with incense to cover the stink of her cigarettes. Fringe, beaded curtains, peacock feathers, and ostrich plumes throughout the place recalled the tawdry opulence of the last decade. The stained glass lamps didn't provide much light, but Mrs. LaRue had the vanity of an aging actress and preferred the darkness. Her gaze remained on my face when she handed me an envelope. She pointed to a gorgeous bouquet of red roses.

"A handsome young gent brought these over. I told him you were out looking for work, and he seemed concerned."

I tore open the envelope and counted out ten crisp ten-dollar bills. "Jeepers!"

A piece of paper fell to the floor.

Mitzi,

I'm sure you and your sister can use this. I hope you like the flowers. I want to talk to you. Call the number on the note.

David

No apology for what he'd done or the way he'd acted. He'd typed his letter on stationery from a place called the Chateau Marmont. Mrs. LaRue smirked when I handed the missive to her.

"A lot of hanky-panky goes on at the Chateau Marmont because it's in West Hollywood, a wild and woolly place if ever there was one. By the way, this Stein fellow has already left a telephone message for you."

The nerve of that louse. "If he calls again, please tell him I'm out. I'll always be out to the bum."

She took a drag on her cigarette. "A lover's spat?"

The idea of pitching woo with that sex maniac made me nauseous. "No, he's the crumb I used to work for."

She chortled in a very suggestive manner. "He gave you a hundred smackers and beautiful flowers, yet he's a crumb?"

I should have shown her my bruises. "A hundred bucks is chicken feed to a guy like him. Leah will love the flowers, though."

Roses, especially red ones, were Leah's favorites, and they looked stunning in one of the vases I'd pinched from the Ritz. Despite rallying the night before, she still seemed a bit under the weather, so I placed them next to her bed in hopes of cheering her up. When Leah awoke, she gave a squeal of pleasure.

"Oh. how lovely, Mitzi! Are the roses from Omar?"

"No, Leah."

I walked away, wondering when Omar had begun buying her roses.

Chapter Thirteen

January 1932

The Monday after Christmas, Mrs. LaRue fired up the engine of her tin lizzie. The Model T turned over and off we went, four little lambs, with Mrs. LaRue as our shepherdess. I sat up front, while Edna and the twins took seats in the rear. We'd all dressed in our best, the boys in starched shirts and bow ties, Edna in a navy-blue sweater ensemble she'd bought with the five dollars from Mr. Stein. I wore my lucky outfit, the same black-and-red frock from my interview at the New York Ritz.

Mrs. LaRue cackled as she drove. "Kids, we won't bother with Central Casting. A little bird told me they need extras at Regal Pictures. Regal may be small potatoes, but they're always looking for young folks for their shorts. Best of all, I have pals there."

As the Model-T motored down Wilshire Boulevard, I marveled at how deftly Mrs. LaRue handled the gears and foot pedals yet still managed to carry on a conversation. Maybe one day I'd master the art of driving and speaking at the same time.

"Now listen, kiddies. I know the business, so let me do the talking. I've got friends all over Regal."

She turned the car onto Sunset Boulevard and headed toward West Hollywood, a small town on the border between Hollywood and Beverly Hills. She pointed to a faded sign that read Sherman. "In its lawless past, West Hollywood used to be called 'Sherman.' "

Edna turned her head from side to side, her eyes searching the quiet streets. "I hear West Hollywood is a den of iniquity loaded with nightclubs, speakeasies, and casinos."

It didn't look wicked to me—just another sunny California village with the usual mismatched architecture, citrus trees, and open spaces. The automobile sped onto Santa Monica Boulevard. Regal Pictures loomed ahead. I'd never shared Uncle Baron's story with Mrs. LaRue, but I felt my destiny had tapped me on the shoulder. My uncle lost his life on the Regal Pictures lot, and something told me I'd discover the truth about his death at Regal Pictures even if it took forever.

The studio gate might not have been as massive as Paramount's or MGM's, but it looked gigantic to me. Images of all their stars were everywhere, and garish posters and billboards affixed to the façade announced the studio's newest offerings. One displayed the odious Rex Dallas posing with Jill "Hateful" Carpenter while Buster Sweet watched in the background.

A ten-foot poster showed actor Bobby Fayette locked in a passionate embrace with Helga Nielson, the Regal star Walter Winchell had nicknamed "the dime-store Garbo."

A third figure stood over the romantic couple, ukulele in his hand, a handsome young fellow with wavy blond hair, bright blue eyes, and a million-dollar smile. It took me a minute to recognize the crooner, but

I'm sure my scream carried all the way to Sunset Boulevard.

"Mrs. LaRue, stop!"

She pressed the brake and the auto jolted to halt. "My goodness, I know the blond fellow in the poster. I met him in New York at Penn Station."

Edna tapped me on the shoulder. "You know Chick Hagan? Why didn't you say something? They play his music on the radio all the time."

For the past weeks, I'd been too busy to read a movie magazine or listen to the radio. No wonder I didn't know about Chick's fame. Suddenly, the sky turned into a field of verdant clover. We looked up at the giant arrow circling a massive globe of green and amber glass. The green sphere glittered from its perch like the world's biggest emerald.

Mrs. LaRue inched the Model-T to the front gate. Throngs of would-be extras, young men and women in their Sunday best, massed at the enormous wrought iron main gate. Every one of them hoped to be among the lucky few chosen to work for seven dollars a day, plus a box lunch. In the face of the massive crowd, it looked as if we were out of luck. Edna gave a sigh of disappointment. "Golly, I guess we were too late."

Then the guard, a tough-looking goon with a deep scar on the side of his face, caught sight of Mrs. LaRue. He smiled like a kid on Christmas morning.

"Gert, is it you? Where the hell have you been hiding?"

Not only did I learn Mrs. LaRue's first name was Gert, but I also discovered her skill at playing the coquette.

"I never left town, you big lug. You're still as

handsome as I remember."

When the big lug's face turned bright red, Mrs. LaRue turned up the charm. "These kids are looking for extra work. Since you know everyone on the lot, maybe you can help."

When the guy looked into the back seat, he gave Edna and the twins the once-over.

"Anything for you, Gert. One of the casting directors needs youngsters for a short with the Mischief Makers. He's a pal of mine, so leave the kids with me."

She took the guard's hand in hers. "And where do I find this Chick Hagan fellow?"

I jumped at the mention of his name. The guard pointed to a paved path that veered to the right of the front gate. "Just follow the old road and look for the hula girls." He grinned, revealing a mouth full of gold teeth. "Gosh, it was swell seeing you again, Gert."

Edna and the twins scrambled from the auto. When I opened the door to join them, Mrs. LaRue grabbed my arm. "Kiddo, you're not the extra type."

With that, she sped through the gate.

The Regal Pictures lot resembled a small town, the paved streets lined with pink stucco bungalows. Mrs. LaRue motored past the striped pole of the lot's barbershop, the music department, the doctor's office, an ice rink, a bowling alley, and two abandoned glass-roofed buildings.

"Those old stages were where we made silent dramas. The sun would bake you like a loaf of bread, and you'd go blind from the klieg lights, but I loved every minute of it."

We spotted a three-story brick warehouse sitting all by its lonesome near the rear gate. Some of those buildings must look menacing at night, but this place appeared dark and unsettling in the bright sunlight. Someone had bolted a "Keep Out" sign to the front door.

"What's that, Mrs. LaRue?"

Her face paled, and the auto sped away. "You don't want to go anywhere near there, kiddo. It was the Front Office a million years ago, but they started using it for storage in '25. The sign says Keep Out for a reason. They store old nitrate film stock in a vault in the basement. They planned to dump the old reels into the Pacific, but I hear they never did. If that stuff ever went up, it would be like Mrs. O'Leary's cow and the Chicago Fire all over again."

She didn't have to say another word. Everyone knew horror stories about nitrate fires. They'd fortified the projection booth at the Ritz like Fort Knox, with only the projectionist allowed inside. If anyone fried, it would be the poor schnook showing the movie, not the audience.

Mrs. LaRue slowed the Model-T to a crawl as we passed squads of men in overalls swarming toward a huge concrete building.

"That's Regal's first sound stage. When they switched to talkies, everybody prayed an earthquake would take the damn thing down. Making silent dramas was duck soup compared to talking pictures. Between the blazing lights and the lousy dialogue, I said to hell with the baloney."

The auto lurched forward. She continued gabbing away. "I read they're building another sound stage with nine-ton doors and concrete columns sunk into the ground. Metro has the biggest stage now, but Regal won't be outdone as long as Ben Roth is in charge."

She gestured at two garish caravans sitting outside the huge stage. "They wheel out those dressing rooms for the lead actors."

I remembered Uncle Baron died in one of those firetraps. Gorge crawled up my throat, but it vanished the moment we passed extras in cowboy regalia, dancing girls, knights along with their fair ladies. Most were kids around my age, and as screwy as it might sound, I felt the same sense of belonging as on my first day at the Ritz.

A bunch of girls in hula skirts, their bodies slathered in dark brown body makeup, rushed out of the sound stage, giggling and gossiping all the while. A young fellow strolled behind them, cool and collected. Purple eye shadow and black mascara defined his eyes and dark brown lipstick coated his lips. He flashed the same Fuller Brush man smile that had enchanted everyone in Penn Station a year before. I'd dreamed of him every night but never imagined our paths would cross again.

I jumped out of the auto screaming like a banshee. "Mr. Hagan, it's me, Mitzi, Mitzi Schector! Mitzi S-C-H-E-C-T-O-R."

He turned from the pack of hula dancers, broke into a brilliant grin, and sprinted toward me. "Wow! Mitzi? I can't believe it! I've been looking all over the city for you. There's a bunch of Schectors in the phone book, but no Mitzi."

I imagined his frantic search and couldn't stop myself from giggling. "I'm sorry, but we were in a bit of a jam when we arrived in Los Angeles and never got a phone. Golly, if I hadn't been searching for extra work, I wouldn't have seen your poster. You've made it into the movies."

My laughter must have been contagious because he chortled along with me. "Yeah, Dollface, old Chick is in the chips now, making movies and cutting phonograph records too. I'm going to be on the cover of *Photoplay*, can you believe it? Only problem is that they keep putting me with gals who can't sing. I need a partner."

"Your worries are over, Mr. Hagan. This gal is ready, willing, and able."

He laughed again. "It's Chick, not Mr. Hagan. I've got you now, and I'm keeping you."

A famous fellow like Chick Hagan wanted me to call him by his first name? Maybe he wasn't Jewish, but he had dashing looks, charm, and was a movie actor to boot. How lucky could a girl be?

Before I could say another word, a woman walked up to us with a determined stride. She appeared to be in her late thirties, a career gal with short marcelled hair. The woman wore a tailored suit with a narrow skirt, necktie, and oxford shoes. A dark-haired young lady followed her, camera and flashbulbs in hand. The older woman signaled to Chick.

"Chick, over here. We need some publicity shots with you and the girls."

He took my arm and marched me over to her. "Mitzi, here's a lady you gotta meet. May I introduce Miss Ida Cohen? Ida spotted me on the Broadway Limited when the boys and me were doing a number in one of the parlor cars."

Chick, grinning like the cat that'd swallowed the canary, pushed me toward her.

Miss Cohen extended her hand. "Hello, little lady."

Head of publicity? "Hello, Miss Cohen. I'm a friend of Chick's. Chick and I met on my way to Los Angeles a year ago."

Miss Cohen examined my face. "You've got a mug on you, kid. What's your name?"

"Mitzi, Mitzi Schector."

She raised an eyebrow. "Mitzi Schector? So you're the little girl with the great voice I've been hearing about."

Me? Who could have told her about me? I guessed Chick must have been singing my praises. "Yes, Miss Cohen, I sing a little, but I was afraid you might have heard about me from Mr. Roth. I got into some trouble with Rex Dallas a year ago on the Santa Fe Chief, and Mr. Roth helped me out."

Her face lit up as if she knew a secret no one else did. "Oh, so you're the girl. Yes, I heard the whole story. Unfortunately, Rex has a fondness for young ladies."

She placed an arm around my shoulder. "Well, Mitzi Schector, after what I've heard about you, I guess we'll just have to set up a meeting with you and the big man himself."

Zowie!

We may have left the Regal lot in the Model T, but the kids and I floated back on a cloud. Mrs. LaRue had come through for us like a real brick. Edna and the twins were going to be extras on a film with "those lovable jesters, the Mischief Makers," and I had a meeting with Mr. Ben Roth himself.

On the drive back, Mrs. LaRue, Edna, and the twins had a million questions.

"It's all set, Monday morning, nine sharp, in Mr. Roth's office. Miss Cohen said he has an old clunker of a piano there, the same one he played as a kid in his father's theater."

How Mrs. LaRue managed to pat my knee and maneuver the auto at the same time was beyond me, but she did. "I knew there was something special about you from the moment I saw you. You've got a mug on you, kid."

Funny thing, Miss Cohen said the same thing. "Say, Mrs. LaRue, why don't you come to Mr. Roth's office with Leah and me?"

She shook her head. "Aw, kiddo, you don't need me. Sure, I used to work at Regal Pictures, but it was mostly extra stuff, a few bit parts here and there. Let me tell you, if Mr. Roth offers you a contract, don't take a penny under fifty bucks a week."

Edna and the twins yelped in unison at the idea of making so much money. After all the trouble Leah and I'd endured because of Mr. Nussbaum, it looked like we were finally going to be in the chips. How I'd love to rub a certain Mr. Stein's nose in it.

Chapter Fourteen
Give 'Em Some Razzmatazz

I couldn't wait to share my good fortune with Zisel, but she beat me to the punch. The postman had delivered packages from New York the day after my reunion with Chick. I unwrapped the brown shop paper, then opened up a veritable treasure trove of goodies. In one box, Zisel had packed Elizabeth Arden cosmetics and a formal portrait of herself with her beau, Seymour. Although he dressed nattily, no one would call a gangly-looking fellow like Seymour handsome. Still, he'd been generous with us. What he lacked in looks he more than made up for in heart.

Zisel had sent twenty smackers, two beautiful frocks with hats, and a bias-cut evening gown of crimson Celanese satin with a matching jacket. With its jacket on, the garment would be très elegant, but remove it, and—Katy bar the door! The V-shaped bodice nearly exposed my bosoms, and the back dipped so low even Jill Carpenter might pause before wearing it. I wondered what my daring sister was thinking.

Zisel had also tucked a photo at the bottom of the box, the one she'd snapped just as Leah and I boarded the train. I hated the photograph on sight. I looked like a lunatic with a dopey smile plastered on my face despite the fact I wanted to die. I was sure Leah would add it to her "kvell collection" the moment she saw it. I found a letter addressed to me at the bottom of the box, opened it and discovered a sawbuck.

My Darling Mitzi,

Greetings and salutations! I hope times have gotten better for you, my sun-kissed darling. Here's your copy of that photo I snapped at the train station so long ago. I hope you like it. I've also enclosed two Hattie Carnegie dresses that will look smashing on you. Please don't show the bias-cut gown to Leah, she'll hit the roof. It's a pip from the French designer, Madeleine Vionnet. One day you might slip it on and trot off to some fabulous nightclub—stranger things have happened. I know you can use the cash. Buy yourself something swell.

Seymour is taking me to Florida next week. I'll be soaking up the sun but thinking of both of you with love. My darling, things are tough in Gotham, but I wish you were here instead of basking in the California sunshine. By the way, I haven't seen hide or hair of the detestable Nussbaum, and that's okay by me.

Are you still searching for Baron's grave? Somebody in Los Angeles must know something. Seymour says he will pay for a gravestone when you find it.

Zisel

****

On January 11, 1932, the sun deserted Los Angeles and it actually snowed. I ignored the chill and decked myself out in one of my new Hattie Carnegies, a navy sailor outfit with gold accents and a matching beret. Leah wore a chic frock of emerald green rayon. Our hose were of the sheerest cotton, and if you didn't look too close, you'd swear they were silk. Leah and I had finger-waved our hair, then powdered and rouged to the hilt.

We'd arrive at Regal in a limousine, riding in the lap of luxury, because when Omar wasn't working on the railroad, he chauffeured swells around town. Where he got the vehicle remained a mystery, but he insisted on driving us to my audition.

I had a million butterflies in my stomach, but despite not sleeping the night before and puking my guts up that morning, I'd never felt better. If Mr. Roth liked me, I wouldn't have to worry about crumbs like David Stein. I'd be able to take care of Leah and maybe even see New York again. But if he didn't like me— nah, I couldn't think about it.

Leah sat by my side as I vocalized the entire trip. Omar interrupted once to wish me luck. "Mitzi, I have a feeling this is your lucky day and mine too. I'm afraid we'll all be seeing a lot more of each other. You see, I'm quitting the railroad and going to work for Regal."

My sister squealed with delight. "Oh, Omar, that's wonderful, a dream come true!"

****

We arrived at Regal's front gate, and the scar-faced guard greeted us. Omar announced me, "Miss Mitzi Schector for Mr. Roth."

The guard glanced at Leah and me, then waved us in. "Oh, yeah, Mitzi Schector. You're expected."

Omar drove through the gate and down a winding path. He easily maneuvered the turns, then stopped the limo in front of a four-story stucco building. The perfect chauffeur, he jumped from the auto and opened the passenger door for us. Leah turned to him. "Omar, aren't you coming with us?"

He smiled that sad little smile of his. "No, Leah. There's no place for me in there. Mitzi, you knock 'em dead. Give 'em some razzmatazz."

Leah and Omar exchanged a long look before she took my arm. We walked through the massive doors of the front office, the pulse of Regal Pictures. My heart thumped like a bass drum as we skirted past the throngs of smartly dressed stenographers, hordes of lawyers, accountants, and errand boys.

Leah announced us to a bubbly receptionist. "Miss Mitzi Schector for Mr. Ben Roth."

The woman's face dropped; her jolly persona disappeared. She pointed to a waiting elevator, looked around, and whispered, "Ladies, just a warning, Mr. Roth is in a foul mood. He and his brother are tussling, and it doesn't help his personality. He always gets in a tizzy when he talks to the New York office. Good luck, dearie."

I squeezed Leah's hand as we went off to meet our future.

****

A skylight illuminated an office of inlaid mahogany, stainless steel, and tinted glass, the wooden floor a zigzag of chevrons. A massive fireplace filled one wall. The single incongruity among the otherwise elegant furnishings was a battered upright piano sitting alone and forlorn in a corner.

Mr. Roth sat behind an enormous desk so highly lacquered its reflection almost blinded me. The great man ignored us and finished off a plate of scrambled eggs and something that looked suspiciously like bacon. Between bites, he barked into one of three telephones on his desk.

"Look, tell that schmuck we have our own theaters now, and we don't need him. He only gets a Jill Carpenter movie if he takes a couple of westerns and a Mischief Makers short."

Miss Cohen was giving all her attention to Mr. Roth and had her back to us. Leah, mustering her courage, stepped forward. "Hello, Miss Cohen. We've never met, but I've heard wonderful things about you. I'm the sister of Mitzi Schector, musical genius."

Miss Cohen nodded but didn't utter a word. Mr. Roth's telephone conversation so engrossed him he never looked our way, just blustered on.

"Listen, Sam, he's just another schlemiel to me. You may think we need him, but we've got our theaters now, so we don't take crap from a jerk like him. Oh, yeah? The son-of-a-bitch can drop dead."

I'm sure Mr. Roth's language might have shocked a home girl, but Leah and I were modern babes, and his words rolled off our backs. Miss Cohen seemed amused and motioned us closer. "Ben is pretending to ignore you, but he knows you're here. He's talking to his brother in New York. If you ladies weren't present, I assure you his language would be a lot saltier."

All of a sudden, the doors opened and Chick strolled in. Without the heavy screen makeup, his skin glowed, his hair looked blonder and his eyes bluer. He'd dressed in an elegant wool suit and wore spats over his English oxfords. From the moment he entered, he didn't take those baby blues off me, and how they sparkled. He sauntered over and put his arm around my waist.

"Mitzi, you look swell. Let's get the show on the road so Mr. Roth can hear what you can do."

Our host's telephone conversation still engaged him. "So what if Metro has Garbo? We've got Helga Nielson. Nice kid, works cheap, speaks good English, and, unlike dear Greta, she can ice skate."

Chick ushered me over to the piano. "Mr. Roth is always on the phone, but he hears everything." He turned to Miss Cohen. "Gee, Ida, I wish she had some head shots. She's got such a pretty face."

Did Chick Hagan say I had a pretty face? I'm sure my skin turned a deeper shade of pink than my lipstick.

Miss Cohen patted my shoulder. "With a puss like hers, you don't need headshots. It's time to see if she's got the pipes. Ben isn't too keen about musicals right now, but don't worry, there's always a place for a song or two in our films—that is, if she can sing."

Her words cued Leah to tickle the keys of Mr. Roth's crummy old upright. The piano looked like a rickety mess, but it had a marvelous tone and, thank goodness, I was in voice. We got off to a rousing start with "I Got Rhythm."

Miss Cohen put down her cigarette holder and began snapping her fingers in time to the music. Mr. Roth ignored us. We slowed down the tempo with "Embraceable You" and then "But Not for Me." Chick applauded, Miss Cohen beamed, but Mr. Roth continued barking into the phone. "Joe Breen, the censor? He can kiss my ass!"

Could the gods be pouring ice water on our dreams? I murmured my fear to Miss Cohen. "I don't think Mr. Roth likes the way I sing."

She murmured back. "He likes you, all right, or you'd be out on your ear by now. Nothing gets past Benny. He hears and sees everything. Believe me, he can listen to music and talk on the phone at the same time. He used to juggle plates while selling candy during intermission in his father's Nickelodeon. Keep singing."

I belted out two songs I'd regularly performed at the Ritz, "Ten Cents a Dance" and "Sing, You Sinners." I threw in as much razzmatazz as I could, but Mr. Roth ignored me. He swiveled his chair away from the piano and continued his conversation.

Chick joined me in "Time on My Hands." Even without a rehearsal, our voices harmonized perfectly and couldn't have sounded any better with Paul Whiteman's orchestra behind us. Unfortunately, Mr. Roth blabbed away. "Are you bellyaching about those crumbs in the Hays office again? They're a bunch of penny-ante dictators. Aw, we can handle those bums."

I looked down at Leah. It seemed the time to give up the ghost. Perhaps the idea of work at Regal was just a pipe dream. Miss Cohen, however, had other ideas and asked the magic question. "Do you know any Yiddish songs?"

Leah nodded and began the opening vamp of "My Yiddishe Momme."

I took a deep breath, then threw in everything but the kitchen sink. I added trills and vocal acrobatics like the singers from the Yiddish theater. I remembered all the Jews who'd fled the shtetls of Poland and Russia only to end up in filthy, disease-ridden New York tenements. I thought of my family, of Pops and Uncle Baron, and wrung every ounce of emotion I possessed into the song.

A miracle happened. Mr. Roth finally looked up. He hung up the telephone, his attention on me, me alone, and his eyes like two aquamarine klieg lights. Silence. Then he burst into tears and bawled so hard no one could hear me above his caterwauling.

Leah spurred me on to the climax, and I finished, belting out as big a finish as I could. Talk about razzmatazz! Afterward, I doubted I could sing another note. I leaned against the piano, exhausted yet relieved my ordeal had ended. Except for Mr. Roth's sobbing, silence enveloped the room.

Mr. Roth looked so sorrowful that I thought I'd start crying too. "You're that kid from the train, aren't you?"

He picked up the phone and barked into the receiver. "Come to my office. Now."

He slammed the telephone down, rose to his feet, and walked over to Miss Cohen. "Well, Ida, I think we can do something with her. With that voice, we can use her for shorts, radio, and personal appearances. Sign her up at seventy a week."

Seventy dollars a week! I couldn't suppress a yelp. Mr. Roth glared at me.

"Okay, okay, seventy-five, but not a nickel more until we see how you look on the screen. I'm not worried about the acting. Anybody who can sing like her has to be able to act."

He moved a bit closer, gazed into my face, and turned back to Miss Cohen.

"Send her to Factor's, but don't let them tart her up too much. If we decide to team her with Chick, she can't look like a chippie."

Miss Cohen nodded. "Yes, Ben, she's a find, all right, but don't you think we should work on her accent?"

Mr. Roth looked at me and smiled for the first time that morning. The oversized room suddenly took on a toasty glow. "Nobody's worked with Stanwyck or Clara Bow, have they? The way she talks is okay by me."

There was a knock, and Mr. Roth marched to the door. "Mitzi, I want to introduce you to the man who'll be guiding your career. His office has been calling your number all week to set up a test. The guy's been talking about you for months and said he'd finally figured out how to get you onto the lot. Can you believe it? A year ago he told me about this kid he'd met in New York who sang like a canary and played the organ at the Ritz. He swore you were a natural, but musical movies were in the crapper, and I wasn't interested."

Miss Cohen put her arm around me. "The minute you told me your name I knew you were the gal he'd been talking about. It was in the bag from the first."

Right then I heard the voice I'd prayed never to hear again. "Hi, Mitzi, it's been a little while, hasn't it?"

I turned and looked into David Stein's smirking face.

Chapter Fifteen
Mr. Stein

Mr. Roth pushed me toward David Stein. "I bet you thought you'd escaped him, didn't you?"

Mr. Stein bounded over and wrapped his arms around me like a vise. I couldn't break free, and it took every bit of my self-control to keep from screaming in disgust. The bastard blabbed away to Mr. Roth while I stood imprisoned in his embrace.

"Yes, Ben, Mitzi and I go back a long way. We met in New York before she headed west. When she came out to Los Angeles, she played the Wurlitzer at the Ritz, before you and I made our deal, you pirate." He grinned like a Cheshire cat. "Ben, I told you she had what it takes. Gosh, Mitzi, I thought I'd have to hogtie you to get you here."

When he finally released me, he sauntered over to Leah, his hand extended, his smile so bright he managed to outshine Chick. In the year I worked at the Ritz, I rarely saw a glimmer of humanity. Now he put on the charm, acted like a regular Maurice Chevalier, and did everything but kiss Leah's hand.

"You must be Mitzi's sister. She always talked about you. It's such a pleasure to meet you, Leah." Then he did kiss her hand, and I wanted to puke. He turned back to me, an icy grin pasted on his mug. "I see the family resemblance."

When Leah tittered like a twelve-year-old, I knew the crumb had pulled the wool over her eyes. "Oh, thank you, Mr. Stein. You're so kind. I can't tell you how much Mitzi valued her time at the Ritz."

Chick brushed my cheek with his lips and, once again, I thought I'd plotz in front of everyone. "I have to be on my way, doll, but I'll be seeing you soon, real soon."

From the corner of my eye I saw Mr. Stein shoot Chick the same no-trespassing fish-eye he used to give the twins back at the Ritz. The nerve of the bum. Chick must have noticed, because he vamoosed before I could beg him to stay. Mr. Roth and Mr. Stein spent the next few minutes schmoozing with Leah. Mr. Roth mentioned our brush with destiny once again.

"Isn't it a small world? David's been raving about Mitzi for months, and now she's here."

Mr. Stein nodded in agreement, then glanced my way, the smirk gone. "As a very wise little girl once said, 'It was fate.' I kept telling Mitzi that I had connections, but I don't think she believed me. Of course, with all the phonies in Los Angeles, why should she? I had to talk her landlady into bringing her to the lot, and it worked, didn't it?"

Everyone laughed except me. He may have taken the rest of them in, but I knew the truth about David Stein—he was a fink and a sex-fiend. I now knew a rat, not a "little bird" had conned Mrs. LaRue into bringing me to Regal. I bit my tongue, smiled like a ninny, and didn't say a word.

Mr. Roth dismissed us with a flick of his hand and picked up the phone. On our way out, he shouted, "We'll sign up the sister too. Girlie, you can sure tickle the ivories! Now all of you, scram!"

Publicity photographs of Regal's stars covered the wall just outside Mr. Roth's office. One jumped out from the rest, an exquisite portrait of Clarice Dumont inscribed, "To Benny—my friend and savior, Your Clarice."

****

Leah and I would be in the money, but a big fat fly had just plopped into the ointment, namely Mr. David Stein. Although I couldn't let my feelings about him or the lousy way he'd acted that horrible night get in our way, I didn't have to like it.

Leah was over the moon, so cheerful I thought she'd leap into the air and click her heels together. "I feel much better knowing Mr. Stein, that is, David, will be taking care of you. You never mentioned how handsome he is."

I rolled my eyes at her words. Maybe the guy had leading-man looks, but a skunk lay underneath. "Gee, Leah, I never noticed him. He spent most of his time in New York, and besides, he was a married man."

She shook her head and began to tear up. "But not anymore, Mitzi. Miss Cohen told me that his poor wife died."

How could I forget? "Yes, I knew she'd passed away."

Leah dabbed her eyes with her handkerchief. "She died two months ago, Mr. Roth's niece, very young and quite sickly. Oh, the pain that poor guy must be feeling."

I kept my lips buttoned, but I was willing to bet poor Mrs. Stein got wind of her husband's Romeo ways and he bumped her off. Maybe he laced her chicken soup with arsenic.

Omar insisted we celebrate my triumph and invited us to dinner that evening. When he stopped by our flat, Leah, the mistress of kvelling, pulled out our childhood photos, the ones she kept next to her bed. I stifled a scream and prayed, "Don't let her drag out my baby pictures!" She did, but thankfully not the naked ones.

"This was Mitzi at three, already reading and playing the piano. Such a beautiful baby. Did I ever tell you she sang before she spoke?"

I'd have been mortified if it had been anyone but Omar. He'd become so much a member of the family I didn't really mind.

That evening, the three of us celebrated my triumph with a dinner at Clifton's Pacific Seas Cafeteria of the Tropics, a fancy automat. Clifton's served colored people, one of the few downtown eateries that did. Omar insisted on paying for dinner.

We sat under a neon palm tree scented with coconut perfume and tropical flowers. The three of us dined on Clifton's signature meat loaf and toasted my good fortune with limeade as we enjoyed the waterfall and a Hawaiian band replete with ukuleles. A musician plucked out "When I Take My Sugar to Tea," then burst into song. My heart sang along with him. The ukuleles reminded me of Chick, and I'd soon be working with the real thing.

Leah's attention never strayed from Omar. "Dearest, tell Mitzi your story, please."

He looked at me, a shy grin on his face. He looked around our table, then spoke in a whisper. "There's not much to tell. I'm from New Orleans. Daddy raised me to be a hard worker. I did a little of everything, including bootlegging with my uncle and playing the saxophone in a jazz band. A cousin got me the job on the train. I met Mr. Stein, and he introduced me to Mr. Roth. I drive for Mr. Roth sometimes, bring him 'medicinal wine' when he entertains, and do odd jobs."

Leah and Omar held hands and cooed like turtledoves throughout dinner. How could I have been so blind? I tried to ignore them but couldn't. Some celebration of my success this turned out to be.

When we returned to the Dorchester, Omar walked us to the door. Leah took his face in her hands, and they shared a long, passionate kiss.

"Omar, my dear, sweet Omar."

Her charm bracelet jingled from her wrist. So that's how she got it out of hock. Not that I minded at all. The Schectors were Bolsheviks who treated everyone the same. I knew Pops would have approved of anyone who made Leah happy.

I guessed our lives would now include Omar Fournier.

****

Two days after our celebratory dinner, Leah and I stood at the entrance of the renowned Max Factor & Company. Mr. Factor had located his beauty factory inside a concrete bunker near Hollywood Boulevard. Inside this bustling temple of feminine pulchritude, Mr. Factor and his minions would pluck, shear, and paint me, transforming Mitzi Schector from schnook to ravishing beauty.

Before we crossed the threshold, however, I exacted a promise from Leah.

"Whatever they do to me, even if you think I look like a hussy, don't make a peep. I need this job—we need this job. Not only will we now have three square meals a day, but I can find out more about Uncle Baron. Swear to me you won't say anything."

Before she gave me the Look, I gave her one of my own. She nodded with a pout. "All right already, I swear."

Factor's exterior wasn't much, but inside the place rivaled the grandeur of a movie palace. We entered a salon as grand as the court of Louis XIV. Gilded mirrors reflected the light from coffered ceilings, blazing crystal chandeliers illuminated trompe l'oeil columns, niches, and recessed walls. A small perfumery adjoined the grand salon and filled the air with vanilla, rose, lavender, and a hundred other scents. A beveled-glass showcase displayed everything from toupees to powder puffs.

"Hello, Mitzi. Hello, Leah."

Miss Cohen stood in wait in front of our destination, the consultation room, a broad smile on her face. A few of Mr. Factor's patrons left the place, all made-up like kewpie dolls. The Factor team had bleached a young lady's marcelled head to match Jill Carpenter's platinum tones, dyed another girl's hair banana yellow, and turned another's tresses cherry red. All had used the newest Factor product—lip-gloss— and their mouths looked shellacked. Mr. Factor's patrons all sported pencil-thin eyebrows. Oh, the horror of it—I might end up looking like Mrs. LaRue.

Miss Cohen took the arm of the doe-eyed young lady I'd seen with Chick. The girl carried a camera and a bag of flash bulbs. "Good day, Mitzi, and glad to see you again, Leah. Let me introduce you to my niece, Miss Rose Amelia Dupree."

Rose extended her hand. "How you doing?"

The moment Rose opened her mouth, her Brooklyn roots spilled out. Leah and I exchanged a look, and Miss Cohen chortled.

"I know what you girls are thinking. Her name is really Rose Cohen, and yeah, the name Rose Amelia Dupree was one of my brainstorms. When you're in the glamour business, you better have a glamorous name. If Ruth Goldstein can call herself Ruth Harriet Louise, my Rose can be Rose Amelia Dupree."

A diminutive, bespectacled gentleman strolled into the room, kissing the hand of every lady he passed. He spied Ida and called out to her, "Hello, Ida. It is good to see you."

Miss Cohen rushed over to him, hand extended. "Max, my old friend!"

Could this nebbish be Max Factor, the master of Hollywood glamour? With his heavy accent, he sounded like some greenhorn just off the boat. In fact, Mr. Factor was the spit and image of the tailor who had made Pops' shirts. Mr. Factor kissed Miss Cohen's hand, then scrutinized me through thick glasses. He mused out loud as Rose's camera flashed.

"Interesting face, a child turning into a woman, and the hair, marvelous, so thick, so glossy. Too bad it's not blonde. Her eyes are dramatic, but we must thin the brows."

I suddenly had a vision of Mrs. LaRue's shaved forehead. Luckily, Miss Cohen interceded.

"Max, no. David Stein nixed waxing off her eyebrows. He hates the penciled-in look."

Mr. Factor seemed exasperated. "Factor does mystery, glamour, and eyebrows, but we will try to make Mr. Stein happy."

For my pre-glamour photograph, Rose positioned me between Leah and Mr. Factor. Flash, pop. Then Mr. Factor, followed by his underlings, led me into the Consultation Room. After the opulence of the grand salon, its white-walled sterility reminded me of a hospital surgery. Instead of perfume, the place smelled of astringent, ammonia, and cold cream. Beauticians in white smocks spoke in the hushed tones of operating room nurses.

I disrobed and donned a special gown. A beautician trimmed my hair before washing it with Mr. Factor's special shampoo. He arranged it into a shoulder-length bob and gave me the same tousled look, minus the red dye, that Clara Bow currently sported. Rose flashed her camera while I stared into a mirror and focused on my image. Not bad. Good, in fact. I thought my coiffure quite becoming.

The pop of flash bulbs accompanied each step in my transformation. Another cosmetologist shaped my eyebrows but left enough so I wouldn't have to pencil them back on. Why girls plucked away their brows only to draw them back on again had always eluded me. I pondered that question as a member of the white-smocked squad examined every inch of my face under a magnifying glass. Mr. Factor had one mantra: "Clean skin is the foundation on which beauty is built."

His lackeys took those words literally. After one technician squeezed my imperfections into non-existence, another fellow drenched my face with astringent, and then tested every shade of Society Make-Up on my skin. He sponged the winning color on my face, then began working on my eyes. The Factor folks tried shades of eye shadow from lilac to emerald green. I thought the shadow gave me a dramatic look, but Leah shook her head, finally, breaking her oath. "You look like one of those chippies from Dreamland."

I hissed at her. "It's for my art, Leah. Remember? Seventy-five dollars a week."

Despite her objections, the Factor mob agreed on a shade of brown shadow they said brought out the flecks of gold in my eyes. It didn't make much sense since I'd be photographed in black-and-white, but I wasn't about to quibble. Mr. Factor vetoed false eyelashes. "She does not need them. The child has the lashes of Garbo."

One of Mr. Factor's minions coated my lashes with globs of mascara instead. Another flunkey applied rouge to the apples of my cheeks. I looked like someone had slugged me. A fellow brushed lip rouge on my mouth, then covered them with so much lip gloss they looked varnished.

I hoped I'd escaped the worst. Unfortunately, I was wrong. The staff whispered among themselves and I heard murmurs of "furry" and "hirsute." A six-foot-tall Valkyrie entered the room, examined my armpits and legs, then grinned like a demented fiend. "Poor girl, like an organ grinder's monkey. I will remove all hair from body the Egyptian way and make her beautiful."

She proceeded to put me through an ordeal as tortuous as anything devised by the Spanish Inquisition.

Some of my Barnard sisters shaved their legs, or used smelly depilatories. Others eschewed plucking and shaving, and thinned their brows and waxed their legs with Zip Wax and No-Tweeze. I didn't know some ladies used wax on their underarms or that special place. Memories of Jill Carpenter's bald privates floated into my psyche. "Please, I beg of you. Don't touch me down there."

My tormentor stared at me, shocked and repelled. "I am not degenerate. I do not touch that place."

The torture of hair removal with a concoction of heated lemon, honey, and sugar began. It didn't feel so bad when she applied it, but I screamed bloody murder when she snatched it off, ripping out hair and removing layers of skin. The lady torturer seemed to take pleasure in my agonized yelps. She grinned like a sadist when she showed me pieces of cloth covered with the clumps of leg hair torn from the roots.

"My poor hairy child, you must be waxed at least once a month just to look human."

After four hours, this Cinderella emerged: plucked, powdered, and perfect. Everyone oohed and aahed at my grand transformation, an assistant handed me a mirror, and Rose's camera flashed as I gazed at myself.

I'd once attended the funeral of a gentile classmate and made the mistake of looking into the casket. The embalmer had applied the makeup with such a heavy hand the deceased resembled a wax statue. I looked like that embalmed corpse.

Chapter Sixteen
Clarice

Ida ushered us from Factor's. "Girls, I have a feeling we'll be fast friends, so from now on, please call me Ida. How about lunch? The eats are on me, and I know just the place, right up the street. Everyone in the business dines there, and their lamb is this side of heaven."

The restaurant's host greeted us warmly and led us to a mahogany booth where a gang of waiters in bright red jackets swarmed around us. I looked up at ceiling beams carved from French oak, pointed at the murals depicting a bucolic France, then smiled for the camera. Rose had tagged along, her camera snapping my every move.

A slender, nattily dressed man spied Ida and strolled over to our booth. Two young fellows in sailor suits followed him. Ida nudged me in the ribs.

"It's Bobby Fayette with his pals. Don't say a word. I'll do the talking."

Her admonition was unnecessary. Bobby Fayette, Zisel's favorite actor, had been the face of American youth from my childhood. Just the idea of meeting him left Leah and me speechless.

Mr. Fayette sauntered over, a million-dollar smile spread across his handsome puss. "Ida, my darling girl, please introduce me to these two lovelies."

Before Ida made the introductions, she signaled to Rose to shoot Mr. Fayette with his arm around Leah's shoulder. Mr. Fayette, his blue eyes twinkling, bowed to Leah, then took my hand in his. The fine lines creeping around his eyes and his mouth belied his youthful features, but he grinned like a mischievous schoolboy, and as the flashbulbs popped, kissed my hand. Boy, it seemed as if every fellow I met was a hand kisser.

"Ida, my dear, tell me, who is this ravishing creature?"

"Bobby, we're keeping this little beauty a secret for now, so mum's the word."

Ida looked around the restaurant, then spoke in a whisper. "Bobby, I trust you to keep it under wraps. She's David Stein's newest discovery, a musical sensation named Mitzi, uh, Mitzi Charles."

"Uh, Ida, my—"

Before I could correct her, Mr. Fayette said, "Mitzi Charles? Charming, absolutely charming, the perfect name for an ingénue, especially one so lovely. Oh, to be a boy of nineteen again."

Although his once-dazzling teeth were nicotine stained, he smiled even brighter. I felt the warmth of a blush edging up my face, but thankfully, the makeup probably hid it. Snap, pop, snap, pop. Mr. Fayette bowed. "Mitzi Charles, I am your slave."

He winked once again before strolling off.

Ida patted my hand. "That Bobby's a delightful rascal, isn't he?"

She continued smiling at his retreating figure. "With Fayette around, you always know when the fleet is in."

I had no idea what the heck she meant, but I had another question. "Ida, Leah and I appreciate every effort you've made for us, but our last name is Schector, not Charles."

Ida leaned closer and spoke in conspiratorial tones. "The change in the moniker was David's idea. I thought he'd told you. Schector is a fine name, but it's too Jewish sounding. We can't have that, especially since our Mitzi looks like a gentile."

But I was Jewish. Before I could argue the point, a waiter escorted an elegant young couple to the booth across from ours. My head throbbed when I realized the young man was Mr. Stein, arm in arm with an exquisite blonde. He acted like a block of permafrost as usual, but his companion appeared to be quite animated and chatted away. He saw us, waved, seated the beauty, then whispered something into her ear. Whatever he said must have amused her because she threw back her head and brayed like a donkey. Mr. Stein strolled over to our table, a greasy grin plastered on his pompous mug, his eyes flashing in my direction.

"Hello, Ida, I hope I'm not intruding."

Leah simpered like a little girl when he kissed her hand. "Leah, I'm one fortunate fellow to get to see you again." Then he turned to me. "You look beautiful, Mitzi."

I felt myself flushing red, but managed to keep my aplomb. His lady friend wore full war paint: eye shadow, false eyelashes, plucked, rouged, and powdered. Mr. Stein obviously had an attraction for girls who looked like pickled cadavers.

He stared at me for another moment, then glanced back at his table. "You'll have to excuse me. I shouldn't keep my luncheon companion waiting."

After Mr. Stein had returned to his guest, Ida turned back to us. "In case you don't know the details, David and Ben have a grand business scheme. David owned the movie theaters, and Ben had the studio. He feared David might strike a deal with RKO or MGM, but lucky for him, they'd already filled their quota of boy wonders. David's a brilliant kid, but he can be a cold fish at times."

I had to admit, Mr. Stein had brains enough to run the family business with his father at twenty. Edna had told me that when she started working at the Ritz, Mr. Stein wasn't even old enough to sign the payroll checks. Now that he and Ben Roth were partners, Regal would take its place as one of the premier studios. Mr. David Stein would finally become a big man, a real Hollywood macher.

Leah piped up before I could agree with her. "You're wrong about him, Ida. David Stein is a lovely fellow."

Ida lit a cigarette and placed it in her holder. "Oh, he's all right. I've known him since he was in diapers. Believe me, he's a ray of sunshine compared to his mother. She hovered over that kid, indulged his every whim, but there's a sad story behind the way she treated him. You see, once there were three Stein boys. The oldest died when David was six. The other passed away in 1918 during the influenza epidemic."

Leah and I exchanged looks before Leah piped up with, "Our mother died of the flu in 1918 too."

Miss Cohen put a comforting hand on hers. "Sorry to hear that, Leah. David was the baby of the family, and his mother made keeping him happy the most important thing in her life. Problem is, she never denied him anything."

If Mr. Stein weren't such a stinker, I would have felt sorry for him. Before I could comment, Mr. Stein's luncheon date brayed like a donkey again and spoiled the mood. Leah glared at the young lady, her lips curled in displeasure. "Ida, who's the girl?"

Ida glanced toward their table, a nasty smirk on her mug. "Her name is Beth Cushing, a little Vassar girl David plucked from the New York stage. He insisted Ben sign her. I'm afraid Beth and David are more than friends, but you didn't hear it from me."

The bum's wife wasn't even cold in her grave, yet he already had a high-hat squeeze and had made a play for me too. I wanted to scream at the louse, but I didn't say a word. I wondered if he'd told his girlfriend she'd be farting through silk panties.

Leah couldn't hide her disappointment. She'd already picked David Stein out for me, but Mr. Stein and his lady friend weren't my concern.

"Ida, where did the surname 'Charles' come from?"

She put down her fork. "Oh, that. Well, as Bobby pointed out, Charles is a perfect name for an ingénue, and it's ritzy too." Ida placed a cigarette into the holder and lit it. "You know, a few years ago we were going give the name Bernard Charles to a handsome boy and put him on the screen. His name was Schector too, Baron Schector. Sort of a coincidence, isn't it? Unfortunately, he died, but I always liked the name Charles."

Leah gasped so loud that every eye in the restaurant turned to our table. The mention of Uncle

Baron knocked the wind out of me. I couldn't speak, but Leah could. "Ida, Baron Schector was our uncle. We came to Los Angeles to find out where they buried him. Mr. Roth knew about us when he gave Mitzi her contract."

The color drained from Ida's face. "I had no idea. Ben never said a word. Schector is a pretty common name, but now that I look closer, I see the resemblance. Perhaps I shouldn't mention it, but at the time of his death, Baron and Clarice Dumont were madly in love."

I'd never told Leah about my sleuthing at the Hotel Hollywood. She gasped at the news, and I feigned shock.

Ida tapped a fresh cigarette on her gold-toned case. "It's been nine years, but I wonder if anyone will ever forget their end."

Leah twisted her napkin. "Please, Ida, can you tell us where Baron is buried?"

Ida took a drag on her cigarette. "I don't know where he is, and neither does Ben. Clarice's mother had her hand in everything to do with the investigation. Maybe she paid off the sheriff to dispose of poor Baron. One of the benefits of Baron dying in Sherman, as they called West Hollywood in those days, rather than Los Angeles, was the studio not having to deal with the police."

I took her hand. "Ida, are you sure the sheriff disposed of Uncle Baron?"

She lowered her voice. "Ben wanted to let sleeping dogs lie, but I didn't. The world believes a lit candle in Clarice's dressing room started the fire, but those in the know at Regal knew the culprit was Clarice's mother."

Ida called Rose over, leaving Leah and me to mull

over her words. "Rosie, you can go home now."

We waved goodbye to Mr. Stein and his shiksa lady friend, and Ida loaded us into her roadster. "Before I drive you home, I'm taking you gals to the cemetery where Clarice Dumont is buried."

****

A few minutes later, we entered a city of the dead, secluded behind a huge wrought-iron gate. Granite gravestones nestled among groves of palm trees swaying in the afternoon breeze. Ida drove her roadster past rows of marble tombs and headed to the rear of the graveyard. A limousine going the other direction passed us. I glimpsed a woman in the back seat, her face obscured by the veil on her cloche hat.

Ida suddenly cried out and brought the auto to a halt near a poplar grove. She sat at the wheel shaking. "No, it can't be."

Her hands trembled as she grabbed a flask from the glove compartment before taking a generous slug. "Ben would murder me if he knew I took a drink in public, but I needed it. Clarice's killer was in that car."

The source of all our pain had just driven past us. We left the roadster and followed Ida to a beautiful pink marble sarcophagus guarded by a smiling cherub. The inscription read:

Heart of our Hearts, Clarice Dumont, 1904—1923

Clarice had been nineteen when she died, the same age as Uncle Baron. A fresh spray of white roses lay atop the tomb. Ida stared at them as if absorbed in a daydream. I hated disturbing her reverie, but I had to know about Uncle Baron.

"Tell us, please, Ida. Did Clarice's mother start the fire?"

She looked up, her eyes rimmed in red. "Yes, but we couldn't prove it."

She pulled a handkerchief from her vest pocket and dabbed at her eyes.

"Her mother was a drunken parasite who'd dragged Clarice from pillar to post from the time she was a child. After Clarice met Baron, she developed a backbone and threw the witch out on her ear. Somehow, she got back onto the lot. You've seen those old portable dressing rooms? They're firetraps on four wheels."

Ida stopped speaking long enough to take another swig of booze. "Clarice was changing costumes when her mother got together with some bum with a grudge and started the fire. Ben's father heard Clarice's cries, but the fire spread so quickly he couldn't get to her and had a heart attack. Baron broke into the dressing room, but, well, he and Clarice died together."

I looked from Ida to Leah. " 'Some bum with a grudge' helped that woman murder my uncle?"

Ida gave a nod. "Yes, a schmuck who worked for the old man. He's long dead, but the mother walked away scot-free and made off with all of Clarice's money. There's no justice in the world."

"What's her name?"

Ida, lost in thought, pulled a card from the bouquet of roses and handed it to me. "Carlotta, Carlotta Dumont."

Written in a feminine cursive were the words, "I am sorry, C." I pocketed the card.

My uncle's murderess walked the streets of Los Angeles as free as a bird. At that moment I hated Carlotta Dumont even more than Joseph Nussbaum.

Chapter Seventeen
There's No Business Like Show Business

My screen test turned out to be as much of an ordeal as the visit to Factor's. A makeup man slathered my skin cadaver white with a greasepaint called Silver Stone No. 1, a favorite of the great actress Norma Shearer. They caked my eyes with purple eye shadow, then painted my lips mud-brown. When they finished, I looked as if I'd joined the ranks of Dracula's wives. One look in a mirror and I howled like a mad woman.

Luckily, Bobby Fayette, the biggest actor on the lot, tested with me. Although he played the romantic foil, they'd covered him with ghoul makeup—so much for Hollywood glamour. Bobby and the director worked like Trojans, giving me rushed lessons on acting in front of a camera. Mr. Stein flipped his gold coin and watched every take while I broiled alive under the lights.

Gossip about Bobby Fayette buzzed throughout the studio grapevine. Everyone swore his star had waned, but for the life of me, I couldn't figure out why. He spoke beautifully, everyone found him amusing, and most importantly, his films made money for Regal. Still, something seemed amiss, but I couldn't put my finger on it.

I soon learned.

Edna, the twins, and I lunched in the studio

commissary, a cozy place that always buzzed with rumors and smelled of chicken soup made from Mr. Roth's mother's personal recipe. When I mentioned Bobby, the three of them snickered. Extras always knew the real dirt, so Edna figured she'd wise me up in her favorite lingo, pig Latin.

"Obbybay Ayettefay isway away ansypay. Bobby Fayette is a pansy. He's a three-dollar bill, a fluff, a queer."

It couldn't be true. I turned to the twins. "But Bobby's a he-man—isn't he?"

Both boys shook their heads in the negative and one of the twins, I think Randy, said, "Take it from me, Bobby's a fruit. Women all over the world are nuts for the guy, but he's a big powder puff. I still can't figure out why a pip like Jill Carpenter married him. We heard Mr. Roth won't renew his contract, and no other studio wants him."

It all fell into place, except for being wed to Jill Carpenter—the fawning male extras, chorus boys, and sailors flocking around him. Ida's remark about Bobby and the fleet being in suddenly made sense. None of it changed the way I felt about him—the guy was still aces in my book. Edna said folks in the know swore Mr. Roth had hired Chick Hagan to be the "new Bobby"—younger, better looking, and most of all, a real man. Poor Bobby.

****

I managed to run into that smirking, sex-happy jerk David Stein every day. He cornered me in the commissary a few days after my screen test. "Dollface, I want to see you in my office tomorrow at nine."

I answered politely, "Yes, Mr. Stein, I'll be there."

I showed up all right, but to be on the safe side, I brought Leah along.

We met in an office almost identical to the one Mr. Stein had at the Ritz but much grander, with an adjoining suite of rooms. The place reeked of masculinity, the walls painted bottle green, with leather and metallic accents. Spit-polished and orderly, Mr. Stein kept his office in the same meticulous order as the one at the Ritz.

Mr. Stein posed in front of his desk waiting for us, his arms crossed like an omnipotent deity. He'd positioned the photograph of a waifish young woman with a sad smile in the corner of his desk. The poor girl must have been his late wife. He greeted Leah with open arms, smiling brightly. "Leah, it's wonderful to see you again, especially since I'm the bearer of good news. Mitzi's screen test was terrific, and we're going to start working her right away."

He turned to me, his teeth gleaming white and feral like a wolf's. "Doll, we'll need publicity shots. Ida will meet you in Wardrobe, so you better be on your way." Leah grinned like an escapee from a loony bin when he moved in closer and took my hand in his. "Little lady, I'm afraid we'll be seeing a lot more of each other in the next few weeks."

The thought of having to work with this heel almost ruined the good news about the test. Still, I managed a smile and a quick, "Thanks, Mr. Stein."

Leah went on her way, and I hotfooted it over to Wardrobe Department. Mr. Roth made his way across the lot as he did every morning, a human hurricane speeding through the narrow studio paths. He'd march around the studio in a cloud of Carnival in Venice cologne, moving at the speed of light, walking the length of his kingdom, poking his nose into every production, large and small. His subjects greeted him like a king, and he either ignored his serfs or acknowledged them with a curt nod.

As usual, Mr. Roth had dressed to the nines in an elegant suit with a white carnation boutonniere. We were heading in the same direction, past the Scribes' Palace, a Spanish-style bungalow where the screenwriters cranked out the spine of a movie, the scenario. In his rush, Mr. Roth almost knocked me on my tush. He stopped in his tracks, but not because of me. He stood in front of the building, his face scarlet, eyes blazing. Normally, the place pulsed with the tapping of Underwood typewriters, but that day, the building had the energy of a mausoleum. He yelled out in the silence, "You lazy bums, I don't pay you good money to loaf. I should fire the lot of you."

Without warning, the clicking of a hundred typewriters exploded the silence. Mr. Roth screamed to the heavens, "Liars! I'm surrounded by liars!"

He muttered a few choice words in Yiddish, then caught sight of me. "Why the hell aren't you working, girlie?"

"Mr. Roth, I'm meeting Miss Cohen in Wardrobe. I'm supposed to be measured today."

His eyes lit up. "So the great Alexandre of Paris is waiting for you, huh? You better hope he's had his oatmeal, because he eats little girls like you for breakfast."

Before he said another word, a battered Conrad Brothers Piano Tuners truck chugged past us. Ben Roth demanded a perfectly manicured lot. Trash, bubble gum, and banged-up autos were persona non grata. Mr. Roth took one look at the heap, and nearly went into an apoplectic fit. "What the hell is wrong with you guys? Make sure to hide that piece of junk before you clowns set foot in my office."

He gave a loud cackle in my direction, then walked off to inspect the rest of his fiefdom while I continued to Wardrobe.

The world of international style bowed to the feisty little Frenchman Alexandre of Paris. My stomach knotted at the thought of meeting him, but thankfully, Ida hung around to protect me. Mr. Roth hadn't exaggerated Alexandre's reputation as a heartless martinet who devoured actresses alive if they gained an ounce. I shuddered to think what he'd make of me.

Five minutes later, I walked into the Wardrobe Department, an older brick building housing a tailor shop, sewing room, and assorted fitting rooms. I heard the drone of sewing machines and stuck my head into the sewing room. Fabric dust blanketed the air, and the place smelled of coffee, cigarettes, and sweat. Bolts of cloth, of every hue and texture, fell against each other in cupboards. Harried seamstresses rolled fabric out onto massive cutting tables or draped it over dressmaker manikins.

Sketches and photos of evening gowns, modern frocks, and period costumes plastered the walls. Only one image held any interest for me: a faded shot of Clarice Dumont. Clarice had struck an aristocratic pose in a ruffled eighteenth-century gown, a powdered wig covering her blond curls. An older, fleshier version of the young actress imprisoned Clarice in her bejeweled arms.

"Ida, who's the lady in the picture with Clarice Dumont?"

Ida turned her head toward the photograph. "That's Clarice with her bitch of a mother. Take the damn thing down."

A hapless worker plucked the photograph off the wall and handed it to her. Ida promptly ripped it in two. Tailors and dressmakers who'd been slaving at a fevered pitch stopped and stared at her. She didn't say a word.

A little fellow dressed in a vest and checkered trousers stormed into the room and glared at the paralyzed crew. "Get on with your work, you goldbricks."

In an instant, the din began anew. The diminutive man ignored the bedlam and continued perusing each frock, poring over every seam and hemline. Ida called to him, "Hey, Al, here's the new girl."

He marched up to Ida, bussed her on the cheek with a cursory peck, and gave me the once-over. If he'd worn a skirt, he could have been Ida's double. "So she's the girlie David's been blubbering about. Well, at least she's got a pretty face and a trim figure."

Ida threw a protective arm around me and pushed me over to the tiny tyrant. "Her name is Mitzi Charles. Mitzi, allow me to introduce my brother, Al Cohen, known to the world as Alexandre of Paris."

My jaw must have dropped to the floor. Regal had imported the famed Alexandre of Paris straight from Hester Street. I extended my hand, and he gave it a limp squeeze. "Yeah, yeah, pleased to meet you, too. Don't call me Alexandre—the name's Al. Alexandre is some baloney Ida dreamed up, like the great Adrian at Metro.

He's Adolph Greenberg, from Naugatuck, but what the hell does it matter? She renamed my little girl too. Rose Amelia Dupree, what a pile of horseshit."

He looked me over again and pulled out his measuring tape. "Kid, be prepared to work nonstop until you learn the ropes or get canned. They'll put you in a few shorts, a couple of programmers, a gangster film, and you'll probably work with the Mischief Makers."

Ida's mouth tightened. "David would be crazy to put her with those little shmendriks."

Al snorted. "Aw, he knows what he's doing. Let's get her measured. Follow me, girlie."

We left the bedlam of the sewing room for the tranquility of the dressing rooms. Paul Whiteman played on the phonograph to set the mood, mirrors reflected the light from walls painted in soft azure tones. Al fixed his eyes on two contract players being fitted by his assistants. "Look at the hips on this one! Sister, believe me, you won't have any problems with childbirth. As for the other one, put her in the rust-colored gown. We've got to hide her giant tuches."

The girl with the giant rear end broke into tears, but the vile little fellow ignored her. He raked back the hair from his forehead and looked around the shop for someone else to torment.

Al pulled a tape measure from around his neck and began barking out the numbers to a harried assistant. "Hmmm, bust thirty-six. She may look like a kid from the neck up, but she's got a set of knockers on her."

Ida stepped in. "Al, the kid's shy."

He shook his head. "She's shy? So what the hell is she doing in movies?"

I ignored his glare and thought about seventy-five dollars a week instead. I stepped out of my dress and stood in the middle of the room in my camisole and panties. Heat came to my face, I must have turned ten different shades of red, but no one looked at me. Maybe I wasn't a glamour puss, but I'd hoped Al would dress me in something special. He did—a black skirt slit up to my panties, along with a satin blouse cut low enough to expose my bosoms. Fishnet stockings and a pair of stiletto pumps, the kind trollops slithered around in when they pounded the pavement, finished the ensemble.

"Put these on."

I had a hard time hiding my disappointment. The greatest designer in motion pictures had costumed me like a chippie. When I changed into the outfit, he sketched me from different angles and then ordered me to stand as still as a dressmaker's dummy.

Al clasped his hands together, and Ida applauded.

"Can I pick an outfit, or what? Exactly what David wants, a baby-faced vamp with a woman's body, a tootsie who'll bring every horny shmendrick in America to the movies."

I glimpsed myself in the mirror and almost burst into tears. All I needed was a pimp and a lamppost.

Chapter Eighteen
Hurrah for Hollywood

Dear Zisel,

Life is fine in Los Angeles and Leah is doing well with her young man. Can you believe it, my screen test was a success! Unfortunately, if you ever see me on the screen, the credit will read Mitzi Charles. Mr. Stein decreed that "Schector" is too Jewish and changed it. My dear sister, keep your fingers crossed that I make good and earn enough money for Leah and me to get back to New York. If I do, I'll look up Mr. Nussbaum and spit in the bum's eye, and then we'll paint the town red, maybe even go to Harlem and meet Duke Ellington.

Your loving sister,

Mitzi, once Schector, now Charles

****

A gangster flick called *Havana at Midnight* marked my first appearance in motion pictures. Regal shot *Havana at Midnight* on a miniscule budget in nine days. I played a tousle-haired floozy who sang a peppy little rumba in a Cuban nightclub. Max put me in a bias-cut skirt covered with embroidery and sequins and a lovely ruffled blouse that showed off my shoulders. The ensemble achieved the desired effect—I looked like a hussy. Judging from the reactions of the fellows on set, I must have been hot stuff. In fact, Ida called me to her office a week later. "Mitzi, David wants to use you for the *Havana at Midnight* foyer posters."

Rose started working on the photo image right away. I posed in the elaborate outfit against a sultry backdrop, a pair of maracas in my hands.

"Mitzi, you look like a million bucks. The fellows in the art department will turn this into a color poster, and your gorgeous mug will be everywhere. Now, sit up, toss your head back, and give me a big smile."

I did as requested, pushed out my bosoms, smiled, and waited for the camera's flash. It didn't come. Seconds ticked away. Nothing happened. I wondered if Rose had dashed off to the powder room, but she hadn't. She'd gotten into a discussion with a man whose voice I knew only too well.

"But David, Aunt Ida said to go for a winsome look."

I heard his annoyed sigh. "Rose, I'm the one who signs your paycheck, not your Aunt Ida. I've told you a million times, I hate winsome. Fellows pay to look at a real tomato, not a winsome one. Get her to pout and show off those lips. She's got terrific gams and great shoulders, so let the world see them. Get rid of those crummy maracas while you're at it."

I could feel the color working its way from my toes to my face. Mr. Stein caught my eye, winked like some dime-store Casanova, and then walked off tossing his coin. A costume assistant slit the skirt up to my thighs, then lowered the ruffled bodice enough to expose my shoulders and most of my bosoms.

"Mitzi, you heard the man. Look over your left shoulder and pout."

I pouted all right, like a big, fat floozy.

After an afternoon of photos and costume changes, exhausted and sore, I dragged my weary bones from Rose's studio, silently cursing David Stein. Why I took a different path to the gate, I'll never know.

I almost missed it, an alcove covered by white bougainvillea. The flowers concealed a rose-filled garden with stone benches flanking a small fountain. No one had ever mentioned it, but I knew how special it was the minute I saw it. I pushed my way through, looking for anything that would tell me about the place.

A bronze plaque glinted through the floral wall:

Samuel Roth, Senior
Clarice Dumont
Bernard Charles
Forever in Our Hearts
April 25, 1923

Thank goodness I wasn't wearing mascara. I'd have had a million black streaks trailing down my cheeks.

Chapter Nineteen
The Mischief Makers

March 2, 1932
Dear Zisel,
Isn't it awful about the Lindbergh baby? That sweet little thing kidnapped from the safety of his bed. It's all anyone talks about nowadays, and everyone is keeping watch over those darling tots the Mischief Makers.

I made three more musical shorts, sang on the radio, and made a live appearance at the Orpheum Theatre. Regal has cast me with those adorable tykes the Mischief Makers, and I can't wait.

You wrote about Uncle Baron. Sorry, no news on that front.

With love and great affection,
Your Mitzi

****

On that March morning I showed up for the first movie in which I had real dialogue, a comedy short starring the Mischief Makers, Regal Pictures' premier troupe of child actors. The sound stage bustled with workers positioning giant electric fans around the stage. Janitors mopped the floors with bleach. An assistant director stopped me before I walked inside.

"Sorry, honey, there's no filming today. Some of the little bastards had a pissing contest and peed on the lights. The whole place reeks to high heaven. We'll start work tomorrow."

So went my introduction to the Mischief Makers. They may have looked like adorable moppets, but demons lurked behind those angelic faces. The children spent sunup to sundown in high-paid drudgery, shooting, while their greedy parents stood by, their palms open. The little monsters let off steam by tormenting each other with spitballs, flicking nose pickings, having flatulence contests, and worse. Then puberty reared its head and rendered them obsolete. With the exception of Buster Sweet and snotty Jill Carpenter, most faded into obscurity or ended up working as bit players.

I arrived on set the next morning just as Mr. Stein escorted his girlfriend, the braying shiksa from Vassar, off the set. He'd cast her as a plucky orphan, but with her false eyelashes, finger-waved hair, and manicured claws, orphan material she was not. From the gossip on the lot, everyone found her phony, hoity-toity accent off-putting. The director didn't think much of her either. I took her place after one of the Mischief Makers screamed, "Hey, this broad is stinking up the joint."

Mr. Stein placed a protective arm around his sweetie's shoulders. I overheard him whispering to her as he spirited her away, "Don't worry about this piece of fluff, Beth. I'm working on a little drama with a perfect part for you."

Miss Vassar flashed a triumphant smile that faded when the cast and crew applauded her departure. We had five days to complete this masterpiece, so shooting started immediately.

Edna had warned me about the Mischief Makers.

"Mitzi, take it from me, you'll never survive unarmed. Get yourself a knife and a gun."

They were just children. How bad could they be?

I soon learned, and it wasn't pretty. Most of the kids behaved more like simians than humans, except monkeys had nicer manners and smelled better.

The smaller children acted as if possessed by demons, and no female was safe from the pranks of the older boys. When I arrived on the stage that first day, three boys got down on all fours and crawled about the floor, sniffing up my skirt. They barked like dogs, and then one snapped at my ankles.

When the director rushed to my defense, the tiny monsters gave the poor fellow the ol' fingeroo. After he stormed off the set, the tykes regaled the crew with new tricks they'd perfected, belching and farting in unison.

One of the worst of the pack, a pint-sized Lothario, already smoked. He couldn't have been older than ten, but he sidled up, cigarette in his hand, and declared his animal attraction for me. "Listen sister, I've got a yen for you."

"Beat it, you little pipsqueak."

He took a drag on his ciggie and slunk away.

I spent every moment bucking myself up to work with those chimpanzees. I vowed to keep my job, work with Chick Hagan, and maybe one day, with God's help, find Uncle Baron's grave.

For some reason, only Mr. Stein could handle the little terrors. He actually seemed concerned about their welfare but made no effort to hide his disdain for parents who pushed their children in front of the camera. I overheard him talking to one mother who always dolled herself up like a society matron yet dressed her little girl in the rattiest dresses.

At first, Mr. Stein spoke politely, but his voice took on an icy edge. "I have a special place in my heart for mothers, but not mothers like you. Lady, you should be ashamed of yourself, dressing that sweet kid in dime-store rags while you wear the finest fashions. By the way, I know about that fancy man you're keeping on your daughter's dime. I hope you enjoyed your ride on the gravy train, sister, because you're getting off right now."

The lady stammered, "But Mr. Stein, uh, I depend on my little girl."

I could hear Mr. Stein's barely controlled rage. "Yes, I know you do. I've taken a personal interest in her welfare and arranged to have her next check spent on decent clothes and toys. I'll be watching you, lady. If you keep throwing away her money like a drunken sailor, when her contract is up I'll have you both barred from every studio in Hollywood."

He lowered his voice. "Once the poor kid can't get work, I guess you'll have to get off your fat rump and find a job like everybody else."

With that, he strolled away, leaving the lady in tears. Her little girl ran over to Mr. Stein, who picked her up and tossed her in the air. That sight would normally have warmed the cockles of my heart. It didn't. His act didn't take me in. I knew the real David Stein, a sex maniac and a cold fish without feelings. Everyone on the lot knew it too and called him the Icebox behind his back.

He walked past, tossing his gold coin high in the air, savoring his power with a wiseacre grin on his arrogant mug. I wanted to give him a swift kick in the pants.

Still, except for one mishap with a whoopee cushion, I survived the Mischief Makers and lived to tell the tale. For that, I gave thanks.

****

March 20, 1932

Dear Leah and Mitzi,

Seymour and I took in a double bill at the Strand, Havana at Midnight *and* Shanghai Express. *When we entered the lobby, we saw a gigantic lobby poster of a beautiful raven-haired gal with a lovely smile. The lovely creature resembled my beloved sister, but who is Mitzi Charles? Oh, yes, now I remember. Our Mitzi had to sacrifice her Jewish roots on the altar of Christian artifice!*

Zisel

****

I didn't want to seem ungrateful. I had a job when folks were starving, but working with the Mischief Makers had made me question what the heck I was doing in the movie business. I'd never dreamed of seeing my mug plastered all over the silver screen; I wanted to be a schoolteacher. Sure, I had cute looks and could sing, but girls like me were a dime a dozen. Most child actors were unemployed after the first pimple, and Regal was easing Bobby Fayette out of his stardom.

I became lost in thought during my morning walk. Instead of the music department, I found myself in front of the old building that warehoused the nitrate stock. Mrs. LaRue's admirer from the front gate stood guard. I turned to hightail it before he saw me, but unfortunately I wasn't fast enough. From the grim look on his kisser, I was in for it.

"What are you doing here, sis?"

"Nothing, sir."

"Well, then, beat it."

The nitrate stock in the cracker box could ignite at any time, so he didn't have to ask twice. I noticed an open window on the second floor and abandoned scaffolding leading up to the roof. Breaking into the place would be duck soup. When I turned to point it out to the guard, his grim expression made me hold my tongue.

I circled around and headed to the music department. Someone whistled at me as I neared the steps. I turned and nearly jumped out of my shoes. The wolf was Chick Hagan, the handsomest fellow in Hollywood. My head pounded, my heart leapt to my throat, and I felt the heat of a blush rising to my face. Chick walked over, spun me around, and planted a kiss on my cheek.

"Is that you, Mitzi, my little Mitzi? Wow. You look like a million bucks."

Chick smelled of Eau d'Orange Verte, the same fragrance Bobby Fayette wore. He took my hand and held it for the longest time. "Dollface, you've grown up so fast."

My giggling started, and I couldn't stop. "Golly, Chick, when you shoot with the Mischief Makers you'd better grow up fast." I stepped closer. "When are we going to work together?"

Chick grinned, his teeth glinting white in the California sun. My heart soared—I could have floated across the lot like a dirigible. "It can't be soon enough for me, baby. Have you seen that swell poster of you they put it up at the gate?"

Poster? What did a poster matter to me with Chick here? We gazed at each other, smiling and laughing nervously while we thought of small talk. I didn't have the guts to say, "I adore you, Chick, and think about you every waking moment," so I simply gazed into his eyes.

A voice woke me from my reverie.

"Chick, darling, who's your little pal?"

Jill Carpenter strolled toward us, looking as glorious as a Botticelli nymph. Miss Carpenter sparkled in white linen, and I wondered how a girl could be so beautiful. She sized me up as she slithered over to Chick, entwining herself in his embrace.

He flashed an even bigger smile at her than the one he'd given me. "Say, Mitzi, have you and Jill met?"

I extended my hand as I had before, but she never took her paws off Chick. "C'mon, Chick, the gal from *Photoplay* is waiting."

They walked away with Jill's maid following them like a trained dog. The girl flashed a conspiratorial smile. "Hello, Miss Schector."

Jill Carpenter had hired Betty, the ladies lounge attendant from the Santa Fe. Betty rolled her eyes at Miss Carpenter, put her forefinger to her lips, then sashayed after them. I'd have to wait to get the lowdown.

Chapter Twenty
The Golden Falcon

That evening Mrs. LaRue waited for me at the Dorchester's threshold as usual. "So, Little Star, what happened at work today?"

Mrs. LaRue loved hearing the latest studio gossip. Normally, I enjoyed chronicling my adventures, but I still hadn't stopped reeling from my encounter with Chick and Jill Carpenter. Omar, Leah, and I dined on Mrs. LaRue's stewed chicken and dumplings. I begged off a game of charades and went to our flat.

Leah came to me a couple of hours later. "Mitzi, what's wrong? You were so quiet at dinner."

My lip quivered, tears flooded my eyes, and try as I might, I couldn't stop myself from bawling. "Everything is horrible, Leah. I'm a failure, and I don't know what to do."

Leah stroked my hand. "How can you call yourself a failure? You're doing so well in the movies, and you're the most wonderful sister a gal could have. We'll find Baron, just you wait and see."

Perhaps I shouldn't have brought up Chick, but I had to tell someone. "No, it's not that. Leah, I'm in love with Chick Hagan, and he doesn't love me back."

She placed an arm around my shoulders. "Of course you're in love with him. He's so handsome and charming. A lot of girls are in love with him, but Mitzi, he's not the boy for you."

Why couldn't she understand the depth of my feelings for Chick? "How can you say that, Leah? He's the man of my dreams, only he doesn't know it."

She stroked my cheek. "I've met my share of guys like Chick Hagan. Believe me, a pip like you can do better. You need someone who's educated and not chasing after everything in a skirt. From what I've heard, Chick Hagan runs with a very fast crowd. He's a drinker, he gambles, and gets into a lot of hanky panky with the extra girls. Now, David Stein is a different matter, cultured, and so ambitious. He's the right sort, Jewish, and only four years older than you."

Why would she mention him? I couldn't tell her David Stein was also a sex fiend. If Leah knew the truth, she'd make such a big stink we'd be out on our ear.

"Leah, Mr. Stein is attached to a young lady, and that's the end of it."

She pulled away with a shrug. "A girl can dream, can't she? I found a decent guy. I want you to have the same."

She'd never understand the ways of my heart. "I think it's time for me to go to sleep, Leah."

Leah kissed my forehead and turned off the lights. I fell asleep to Omar's saxophone.

****

I took a gander at my poster the next day. An artist had added vibrant colors to the image of a smiling girl affixed to the Santa Monica Boulevard gate. It might be immodest to say, but my poster was the most beautiful one plastered across the studio wall. Could the girl with the pouting lips and flirty eyes really be Mitzi

Schector? Chick thought so, and that was enough for me. Although I hated admitting it, Mr. Stein had been right—the maracas had no place in that poster.

Ida summoned me to the publicity department where she commanded an army of workers laboring in the Regal Star Factory. The studio spared no expense to become the most up-to-the-minute in Hollywood, and publicity utilized the newest technology: wire photo transmission and dictation machines. I passed rows of secretaries typing away and studio drones answering fan mail and autographing stacks of glossy eight-by-ten photos.

Ida had filled her "lair" with no-frills, black lacquered furniture, and covered the gray walls with images of actors from years past and a gallery of family photos. She pointed to a little boy of color dressed in short pants. "Wasn't Buster the cutest little schwartze you've ever seen?"

The Schectors never called people of color schwartzes, but I didn't correct her.

Ida wiped the image with her handkerchief. "His mother took him on the road when he was just a pisher, barely out of diapers. We signed him up for the Mischief Makers. Most of those kids outgrew the movies, but Buster just got better. Those were the days. We worked out of that brick box where they store the old film stock, and we shot in the glass stages. We made movies day and night, but what fun we had."

Ida pointed to another photograph. "Here's Ben twenty years ago with his father and his older brother, Sam, breaking ground for the Regal lot. Here's Al with Rose when she was a baby."

She moved to another photo, David Stein

embracing a sweet-faced girl in white. "And that's David with his late wife on their wedding day."

The late Mrs. Stein looked delicate enough to have blown away in a strong breeze, but she glowed when she looked up at Mr. Stein. They seemed happy, but now the poor girl was dead. Maybe he hadn't bumped her off after all.

"Golly, Ida, I didn't know she was so young. Life isn't fair, is it?"

Her eyes misted. She turned away, wiped a tear from her face, then her sunny demeanor returned.

"No, it isn't. Let's talk about other things. Mitzi, my girl, have you seen your poster? Believe me, it's caused quite a stir. Can you believe there've been four auto accidents since we put it up? Fellows are rubbernecking to get a look, and David is over the moon. I've arranged a short interview and pictorial with *Modern Screen Magazine*. Of course, we've already written the entire piece. The magazine just needs some photos. I'm having Rose shoot some new publicity stills, some provocative ones, so expect to be busy for the next few days."

Ida slid a portfolio, musty with age and bearing a faded Regal Pictures watermark, onto the desk. "I have something else for you, and I'd appreciate if you didn't mention it to anyone."

Considering the ratty condition of the package, I expected an eight-legged beastie to crawl out. Instead, I found several stunning photographs of my dashing uncle. He'd tipped his Panama hat at a rakish angle like John Gilbert, the great matinee idol.

I vowed to discover his grave no matter what. "Ida, if you find anything else, please give it to me."

She appeared hesitant. "Ben ordered everything destroyed after the fire, but I managed to hang onto a few clippings. They're probably around somewhere. I'll find them."

The photos of Uncle Baron reminded me of my raison d'être, as the French say, my real reason for working at Regal Pictures. It meant more than a regular paycheck and Chick Hagan. It meant God put me in the perfect place to search for the truth about Uncle Baron's death.

A freckle-faced boy stuck his head into the room and announced, "Excuse me, Miss Cohen. The *Modern Screen* photographer is here."

****

Ida had already written the interview, all the lies.

Modern Screen: It's my pleasure to introduce to the legions of readers Regal Pictures' newest ingénue, Miss Mitzi Charles. Mitzi, I understand Regal plucked you from the debutante circuit to become one of their new personalities.

Mitzi Charles: Yes, they did. You see, I come from a long line of New Yorkers. Members of the Charles family fought in the Revolutionary War. I was studying at Barnard College when a scout for Regal Pictures saw me performing in a school musical. Everything since has been a whirlwind of excitement. Regal Pictures brought my sister and me to Los Angeles. I've been working ever since.

Modern Screen: We've noticed that Regal has dubbed you the "smiling vamp." A very saucy moniker for a debutante, isn't it?

Mitzi Charles: Golly, it's 1932, after all. I'm just a girl of the times.

Modern Screen: Which of Regal's personalities have you worked with, and whom did you like the best?

Mitzi Charles: Everyone has been so swell, it's hard to choose who's the nicest. I met Rex Dallas and Jill Carpenter and they both were wonderful and so encouraging to a neophyte. Chick Hagan has been fabulous, and the Mischief Makers are such darling children. They kept me laughing throughout every scene I had with them. Bobby Fayette is a real gentleman too.

Modern Screen: What's next for you, Mitzi Charles?

Mitzi Charles: Well, I'll be in the latest Dallas and Sweet mystery, *The Golden Falcon*. Working in motion pictures with such marvelous people has always been my dream, and I pinch myself every single day. I'm such a lucky girl.

****

By the time I walked onto the set, *The Golden Falcon* had been shooting for two weeks. The moment I caught sight of Rex Dallas, I became a mass of jangled nerves. Thankfully, Leah came with me to buck me up. I'd taken special pains with my hair and makeup and donned a pert frock of crimson bouclé because I wanted to make a favorable impression on the director, the famed Willy Taylor.

Everyone in Hollywood knew Willy Taylor, a wiry fellow with bushy red hair, by his nickname, "One-Take Willy." He'd worked with all the greats and had once been the most skilled director of silent dramas. The advent of talking pictures caused him to go loose in the upper story, and he hadn't shot a film since '28. Edna gave me the lowdown.

"Willy Taylor abandoned Regal for better pickings at Paramount, only it didn't pan out. Everybody knew silent dramas were passé, and the soundmen ran roughshod over everybody, especially directors. They'd yell, 'Bad for sound,' and order a reshoot even if the director liked what he had."

She spoke in a gleeful whisper. "Mr. Taylor attacked a sound guy with a claw hammer and then ran around the Paramount lot in his skivvies. They committed him to the bughouse, and he hasn't worked since. He came crawling back to Regal with his tail between his legs and begged for a job. Poor fellow has to learn to direct all over again."

The moment we arrived on the sound stage, I felt heat, but it didn't emanate from the blazing arch lights. The set reproduced the lethal squalor of a Chinatown alley. Mr. Taylor and the crew watched in silence as Dallas and Sweet, their faces slathered in heavy movie makeup, squared off. Who, I wondered, would strike the first blow?

Before I could introduce myself, an assistant director tiptoed over and whispered, "Sorry, ladies, you came at a bad time. The guys are at it again, and it ain't pretty."

Rex Dallas's mouth twisted into a vicious grin. "My dusky friend, you were still rooting around in the watermelon patch when I visited your sister. Best poontang I've ever had!"

Buster Sweet looked about thirty, muscular, with velvety dark brown skin, flashing black eyes, his lips spread in a faux smile. "I didn't have time to joke with her about that pea shooter of yours. Wanna know why? I spent the night servicing your mother. For a dame who's up in age, she's one hot-ass gal. This poor ol' darky gave it to her good."

Mr. Dallas gritted his teeth. "Back home we have ways to deal with bucks like you!"

By this time, Mr. Sweet and Mr. Dallas were nose to nose. "I know about the pointy white hood you keep in your dressing room, but guess what, Cracker? We ain't 'back home!' ''

I thought they'd come to blows, but a miracle occurred. Mr. Taylor called, "Roll camera!" In an instant, they transformed into Paige and Sweet.

Detective Paige looked at his comrade, "Buster, are you thinking what I'm thinking?"

Buster Sweet bugged his eyes out, looked from right to left, then rolled his eyes some more. "Yes, suh, boss! Them Chinese devils done took Miss Peggy and, jumpin' catfish, we gots to save that poor little gal!"

Detective Paige nodded. "Time's a'wasting, Buster, time's a'wasting!"

They walked out of frame, and Mr. Taylor yelled, "Cut! Print it!"

In an instant, the two men were back at each other's throats again.

Dallas's mouth twisted in a grimace. "You black son-a-bitch, you stepped on my line!"

"Stepped on your line? My hair turned gray waiting for you to spit it out, you drunken bastard."

Dallas stormed up to Mr. Taylor. "You're in cahoots with the chocolate drop, aren't you? He has more lines than I do."

Mr. Taylor appeared ready to throttle Dallas. "He has more lines than you because he's not soused all the time and can spit them out."

Then the once-esteemed director suddenly burst out in tears. The crew turned away in embarrassment when he looked up to the heavens.

"To think I once directed Fairbanks and Valentino. Now look at what I'm stuck with. I should've stayed in the nuthouse. Anything's better than working with you lugs."

Mr. Taylor glared at the soundmen, then looked up at a microphone dangling overhead. "As for that thing, if one of you baboons starts that double talk about how the wa-wa is connected to the woo-woo, I'll kill you!"

The crew remained silent, praying this ordeal would end soon. Unfortunately, it didn't. Rex Dallas's moans and groans grew progressively louder.

"This coon is making as much money as I am. How can that happen in the United States of America? The South may have lost the War of Northern Aggression, but this is something only a Bolshevist Jew would have thought up."

I didn't think things could get any worse, but they did. Dallas walked over to me, a salacious grin on his face.

Dallas bowed with a flourish. "Goodness, I didn't know I'd have such a lovely leading lady."

I nearly retched. "I'm pleased to meet you too, Mr. Dallas."

I'd prepared myself for a fiery encounter, but I needn't have worried. Perhaps the liquor he'd consumed in the past year washed my image away, or my new glamour-puss look made me unrecognizable. Maybe I just wasn't memorable. An assistant director introduced us, and the freshness of the predatory glint in Dallas's eyes reassured me he didn't remember me from the train.

Mr. Dallas took Leah's hand and placed it to his lips. "You've got a real peach of a sister, and may I say, you're as lovely as she is."

Although she probably wanted to rear back and punch him in the nose, Leah remained the soul of decorum. "Yes, Mr. Dallas, I'm so proud of Mitzi."

I turned to Buster Sweet and extended my hand. "How do you do, Mr. Sweet? I'm pleased to meet you, too. Leah and I are your biggest fans, aren't we, Leah?"

The place suddenly went silent, everyone holding their breath. It seemed I'd committed a faux pas, but for the life of me I couldn't figure out what.

Mr. Sweet turned to me with the broadest smile imaginable, and proclaimed to everyone within earshot, "I'm pleased to meet you too, Miss, but it's not Mister Sweet. Just call me Buster, plain ol' Buster."

I heard a collective sigh of relief from the crew. Mr. Taylor strutted over and pumped my hand. "The name's Willy, Willy Taylor. Sorry about that little dust-up, but you'll get used to it. Those two are at each other's throats all the time. I've heard good things about you, little lady."

"Gee, thank you, Mr. Taylor. I promise I won't cause any trouble."

Everyone had broad smiles on their faces. In fact, everything was copacetic until a roar came from the rear of the sound stage. "What the hell is happening? I heard those two almost came to blows."

Mr. Roth strode over to the two actors, his blue eyes blazing. He acknowledged Leah, "Hi ya, Leah, glad to see you," then pecked me on the cheek. "Hey, Mitzi, did you see your poster? Another accident this morning, two cars slammed head on. Nobody died, though. Swell, ain't it?"

He turned to Buster and Dallas with a scowl. "Listen, you mugs, since the last supervisor quit, no one else will work with you crumbs. I'm bringing in the big guns. David, come in."

Mr. Stein sauntered onto the set, acknowledging everyone with a chilly smile. A grip whispered, "We're doomed. It's the Icebox."

Mr. Stein's reputation had preceded him.

Chapter Twenty-One
An Education

That evening after the debacle on the set of *The Golden Falcon*, I sat alone in the Dorchester's dining room framing Uncle Baron's beautiful photographs. Leah walked in and tossed down the Society Page of the *Los Angeles Times*. "Mitzi, read this."

A photo showed Miss Vassar smiling radiantly as she clung to Mr. Stein's arm. He looked glum as usual. The caption read, "Regal Pictures Vice President David Stein enjoys a night on the town with actress Beth Cushing."

Leah appeared upset. "The thought of a grand guy like David with that dizzy dame breaks my heart. I've seen the way he stares at you, Mitzi. That could have been you stepping out with him."

Leah would have loved to mate me with that sex-crazed baboon, but thankfully, he had Beth, the Vassar slut. Unfortunately, my sister wasn't the only one who loved sticking her nose into my personal life. Edna felt it her duty to wise me up about sex. I found out that she knew plenty in the most unpleasant way.

I'd finished work for the day and went searching for Edna on a deserted sound stage. I heard moans that sounded like some severely constipated fellow trying to relieve himself. Then a woman's voice that sounded like Edna's whispered, "Come on, big papa, show mama how much you like it."

When I looked out from the darkness, I could barely believe my eyes. One of the producers, a perpetually horny young man, had dropped his trousers down to his ankles. Edna stood behind him, stroking his penis. I wanted to look away, but I'd never seen a schlong before and watched their hijinks out of curiosity. His member looked big, flushed pink and hard as a rock. One thrust of her hand, and he ejaculated with a grunt, sperm all over the place.

I called out, "Edna, oh, Edna!" The fellow pulled up his pants and rushed away.

Later I confronted her on the ride home.

"Edna, I saw you with your hand on his, uh, thing—you, a nice Christian girl!"

She giggled. "Where did it mention that in the Bible?"

After I witnessed her exploits, Edna decided to tutor me in all things of a sexual nature. Our talks usually occurred in the studio commissary. We sat near the extra girls, many of whom were no older than we were. All of them had painted their faces, lacquered their fingernails, and tinted their hair in hues that had nothing to do with nature. I'd watch them make goo-goo eyes at the producers and listened as they regaled each other with stories of their naughty adventures.

Edna filled me in on what fellow was "on the make" and which "hussy" had given in to him. She couldn't stop talking about everyone's carnal hijinks.

"Some of the gals sit on their fellows' laps and call them 'daddy.' If they're really fast, they let them touch their boobies too."

Edna pointed to a group of girls she swore were all

hot-ass mamas. "That one over there, the one with the platinum hair, is definitely loose. I hear she signals she'll do it by hanging her douche bag on the shower where the fellows can see it."

"What's a douche bag?"

Edna wised me up about douche bags in her own unique style. "It's a rubber thing you use to squirt warm water mixed with Lysol up your honey-pot. It kills sperm so you won't get knocked up."

How fascinating these Christian girls were. "It's a vagina, Edna."

My friend made a face. "Yeah, yeah, a vagina."

Now I knew what a douche bag was, but the meaning of "do it" eluded me.

"She'll do it? Do what?"

Edna seemed clearly exasperated. "You went to college and you don't know anything. 'Do it' means they put out, and don't ask me what they put out. It's the ultimate, you ninny, screwing, how married folks make babies." She scooted closer and whispered into my ear. "But there are other things a girl can do with a fellow so she can still be a virgin and not get in the family way."

Then she elaborated on the nature of those "other things." I'd taken hygiene in college, and I knew how men and women made babies, but I'd never heard such lurid descriptions in my life. Edna sprinkled her conversation with expressions I'd never heard at Barnard: "honey-pot," "knocked-up," "dong," and a host of others. For nineteen years, I'd thought "dick" was short for Richard, and a "pussy" was a kitty cat. Edna let me know just how ignorant I'd been.

Edna pointed to a bosomy girl with henna-red hair

sitting at a table across from us.

"See that girl over there? She has hot pants for this guy from Europe, and they do all kinds of fancy stuff. Wanna know what they do?"

"No, I don't."

Edna ignored me and went on to detail the grossest, most sickening and repulsive things I'd ever heard, in addition to being the most shocking and nauseating, with fingers, hands, mouths and tongues, licking, stroking, and sucking in the strangest places. She swore she'd never done any of these acts, so I assumed her prurient interest must have been the result of her deprived childhood.

"You know something, Edna? I could have gone to my grave and died a happy old lady without hearing such trash. You're full of baloney, and I don't believe human beings do such things."

We stared at each other for a moment, but my curiosity got the better of me. "What happens to the sperm when she's uh, finished?"

"She either spits them out or swallows them."

I ended our revolting conversation. "Well, I hope they both gargled with Listerine afterwards and wore gloves. I don't know why you listen to such filthy stories anyway. Some of us want romance, not just hanky-panky."

Edna tossed her head in the nonchalant manner she'd learned from the more worldly extras. "Oh, I get it. You're still waiting for Chick Hagan to give you a tumble. Well, it ain't gonna happen, dearie. Besides, you-know-who sticks to him like glue."

She would remind me that I hardly ever ran into Chick anymore, and on those rare occasions I did, Jill

Carpenter attached herself to him like an extra appendage.

Edna ended our conversation by confirming my worst fears about Chick. "You don't have a snowball's chance in Hell, and I'll tell you why. Chick Hagan likes hot-ass mamas, so that leaves you out, toots."

When I arrived home later that evening, I recited my conversation with Edna to my older sister. I didn't leave out any of the sordid details. "People don't really do all that vile stuff, do they?"

Leah gazed into my face long and hard. "Yeah, Mitzi, everybody does it, at least in Los Angeles and New York."

Thank you, Leah.

****

Regal's saucy silent dramas had brought the studio notoriety, but with David Stein at the reins, raunchiness rose to new heights. Whether a society drama, gangster flick or comedy, Mr. Stein managed to fit in half-naked girls, booze, and jazz music. He peppered the scripts with dialogue that made censors tear their hair out, but all of it ensured his theaters did boffo business.

The Golden Falcon highlighted all the elements of Mr. Stein's signature touch in addition to opium dens, pansies, and risqué banter. I'd be playing my role, half-caste innocent sold into white slavery, in my underwear and chained to a brass bed, something David Stein, the pervert, had added to the script.

What would the Barnard sisterhood think? The dean would probably blow a gasket, convinced the degenerate influence of Hollywood had destroyed the virtue of one of her flock. I doubted any of my school chums would care. The girls always snickered behind the old bluestocking's back.

The costuming choice didn't please Leah. She could never get used to the fact everyone in the movies paraded around in their skivvies.

"How could they ask you to lie there in front of a camera with no clothes on?"

"They're paying me one hundred smackers a week. That's how they could ask. Besides, I'll have on a camisole."

At times I wondered if looking at David Stein's smirking face every day made the money worth it. He supervised other productions, but somehow he and his gold coin managed to show up every time I had to shoot a scene. Thankfully, he kept his distance, yet he treated the crew with his usual icy contempt. A gaffer might greet him with a simple, "Hello, Mr. Stein," and he'd walk past as if the fellow were invisible. A soundman declared, "That guy must piss ice water." I agreed.

I hadn't counted on Mr. Stein's taking a personal interest in every inch of celluloid they shot of me. He insisted on key lighting, soft-focus lenses, and more close-ups. When Willy complained about the additional expense, Mr. Stein responded with a frosty, "Willy, I didn't ask your opinion. I told you to do it."

Perhaps I should have been flattered. After all, close-ups were time-consuming and costly, but every time he showed up, I wanted to scream, "Go away, you two-timing pill. I hate you. Leave me alone." I never uttered a word.

One day, Mr. Stein strolled onto the set just as the cameraman worked on framing my bondage scene. I sat chained to the bed in my camisole and panties, covered in makeup, a key light frying my scalp. No one had the courage to defend me against the Icebox, so I found myself on my own. He strolled up to the bed, looked down at me, and licked his lips. "For a girl who's been chained to that bed for three days, she looks rather dewy, doesn't she?"

Then the crumb yanked down the sheets and ripped my camisole before pulling the right strap so low my bosom nearly popped out. Willy, the gaffers, and the lighting men shuffled around, but no one said a word. Mr. Stein treated me like a cheap floozy, and the makeup fellow didn't have to use glycerin drops to make tears. The nerve of the big lug!

Willy took me aside after we'd finished for the day. "I've seen the way Stein looks at you, the old Hollywood song and dance—a randy son of a bitch with power bullies a girl into submitting to him. We're almost finished, so I can't re-shoot your scenes. I need this job, and I don't have the guts to fight the bastard, but I'm telling you, it'll get worse unless you go to Ben."

I knew Willy spoke the truth, but I didn't want to ruffle any feathers. For the next two days, I lay in that brass bed with my bosoms half-exposed, all because of that louse. He slunk around the set like a gangster, flipping his gold coin, and on more than one occasion I'm sure I heard him pant. David Stein might be the boss, but I wasn't planning to take it lying down—except for right now.

On the final day, Willy yelled, "Cut. Print it. It's a wrap." The crew broke out in applause. He placed his arm around my shoulder. "Great work, kid! You really turned on the tears."

Mr. Stein stood next to the camera, grinning like

the cat that swallowed the canary. I appreciated the kudos, but I still wanted to knock his block off. Instead, I decided to take Willy's advice and talk to Mr. Roth.

I pulled up the errant strap, slipped a kimono over my underwear, and walked off.

Mr. Stein had arranged for my own portable dressing room, a brightly painted caravan with running water and a toilet. The thought of having my name affixed to the door overjoyed me, but I remembered Clarice and Uncle Baron burned to death in one of those wooden boxes, a fact that took the thrill away.

Boy, would I give Mr. Roth an earful and the lowdown on what kind of a man David Stein really was. I'd be earnest, maybe shed a few tears. It would serve the bum right if Mr. Roth threw him out, right on his fat head.

Mr. Roth expected his contract players to look spiffy, so I refreshed my makeup and chose my loveliest frock. The one hundred simoleons Mr. Stein had left at the Dorchester sat on my makeup table. After I spoke to Mr. Roth, I'd make a dramatic entrance into his office and throw the money in his leering face. I couldn't wait to see the worm's reaction.

Without warning, the door swung open. Mr. Stein stood at the door without saying a word, staring at me. I stood in my brassiere and panties, my heart pounding out of my chest. Instead of panicking, I acted like a cool tomato, and wrapped myself in my kimono.

"Uh, Mr. Stein, I'm afraid I'm not dressed for company. Will you please excuse me?"

If Casanova made a move in my direction, I'd scream bloody murder. To my great relief, he stayed where he was.

"I just wanted to make sure it met with your approval."

"Well, uh, thanks very much, Mr. Stein. It's lovely and a swell surprise, like the beautiful poster on the studio wall. Thank you for that too."

He didn't smirk, just focused his cold eyes on me. "So I finally did some things that pleased you. Maybe you'll do something to please me. It would make me happy if you'd call me David, and if you'd think about our last conversation at the Ritz. I'm not such a bad fellow. You could do a lot worse."

With that, he closed the door. My hands shook so violently I had a hard time buttoning my dress. Boy, would I wise up Mr. Ben Roth about a certain David Stein—no, I wouldn't. I'd confront the crumb myself.

On my way to the front office, I passed the floral alcove and thought of Uncle Baron. If Mr. Stein fired me, would I ever find his grave? I'd have to take the chance. I couldn't let this goon run roughshod over me anymore. I sat in wait for him. He strolled in two hours later, cool and dapper in a blue serge suit. He didn't seem at all surprised to see me. In fact, he grinned like a toad.

"Mitzi, this is a pleasure. Do come in."

If the crumb thought he'd bullied me into submission, he had another think coming. He opened his office door and gestured for me to enter. My heart began to race when he closed it, but I refused to let him see how frightened I was.

He pointed to a chair, but I didn't move. "Mr. Stein, Mr. Stein…"

From the way he smirked, I knew the bum enjoyed tormenting me. "Didn't we agree that you'd call me

David? So what have you come to say?"

I decided to let this crumb have it and have it good. To avoid losing my nerve, I looked down at my feet. "You bum, you worm, you sex fiend! I'm not afraid of you anymore, David Stein!"

I threw his money on his desk then dropped my eyes once again. "Here's your lousy hundred bucks. Count it—it's all there. I never spent a penny of it. I'm not some Polish whore you can toss a few shekels and use anytime you want."

Suddenly, I felt emboldened enough to recite the litany of his sins, but I still didn't look at him.

"After nearly breaking my arm in your office, you said if I stuck with you, I'd be 'farting through silk panties.' How disgusting. You grabbed me off the street like a common thug, you big gorilla. You touched my bosoms and humiliated me in front of everyone. How dare you open the door to my dressing room without knocking? You did it just to show me you were the boss, but all it did was make me hate you even more. I hate you. I hate your guts! I'll make your movies and prance around half-naked because I need a job, but I'm not a whore. If you try any fresh stuff again, I'll buy a gun and shoot you full of holes like a piece of Swiss cheese, and laugh all the way to the electric chair!"

My tirade left me exhausted. I wanted to sit but didn't dare chance it. The room went silent. Maybe he'd walked out during my harangue.

I looked up. Mr. Stein stood in front of his desk, staring straight at me. My stomach lurched, and I almost tossed my cookies right on the spot. Then I noticed his eyes had welled up.

"Mitzi, you hate me? You really hate me?"

For a smart guy, he was one dumb cluck. "What did you expect, my enduring gratitude? Yes, you lox, I hate you. I hate you a whole lot!"

A tear rolled down his cheek and took me by surprise. Suddenly, my anger subsided. "Well, maybe 'hated you' is more like it. Maybe I don't hate you as much as I used to, but I still hate you a little bit."

He took a step in my direction, but I backed away. "Make a move and I'll scream."

I'd promised myself I wouldn't cry but, weak sister that I am, my own tears started. Then, I remembered how awful mascara looks when it runs. Maybe my lower lip quivered a bit, but I refused to sob.

"You scared me to death, Mr. Stein."

He walked back to his desk. "I'm sorry." For once, David Stein looked almost human.

"What were you going to do to me that night?"

Mr. Stein slumped onto his desk. "I wanted a kiss."

How stupid did he think I was? "Aw, come on. You wanted to do more than just smooch."

He bowed his head, and I really felt sorry for him. "No, no, no, I swear, I just wanted a kiss. My wife had died, and I went nuts. I needed you to make me feel better, but when you asked about her, I couldn't go through with it. I sent the money as an apology."

"You could have told me you were sorry, and it wouldn't have cost you a dime."

Mr. Stein looked at me with such a soulful expression, a wave of pity swept over me. I walked over to his desk and picked up his wife's photograph. "You have my condolences, Mr. Stein."

He took the photo from my hands, and I saw another flash of humanity—or perhaps regret.

"I married a sweet girl, but it wasn't a love match. She was Ben's niece, and our families wanted the marriage. Believe me, I cared for her, but I wasn't in love with her. She had the misfortune of loving me."

Maybe he was a louse, but at least he was an honest louse. "I'm sorry, Mr. Stein. I sure wish you had told me all this before that night."

He looked up, and his eyes bore into me, but I didn't get the creeps as I usually did. I finally saw vulnerability in his handsome face. Neither of us spoke, and I found the silence unbearable. I'd gotten everything off my chest. Time to shove off.

"I guess I should be on my way. Goodbye, Mr. Stein."

He called out to me when I turned toward the door. "Mitzi, are you still afraid of me?"

"No."

"Do you still hate me?"

"No, sir." I turned and faced him one final time. "May I ask, what was Mrs. Stein's name?"

"Dara. Her name was Dara."

"I'm sorry for your loss, Mr. Stein."

His sobs began the moment I closed the door.

Chapter Twenty-Two
Aftermath

Leah chattered away the entire drive home. "Omar, darling, you should hear the praise for my Mitzi. They worked on one scene for two whole days. David insisted on close-ups, special lighting, everything they do for stars. Today, I heard that Mitzi cried on cue. I had reservations about this movie, since she'd be working with that louse Rex Dallas, but wiser heads prevailed. She made her sister proud."

I ignored Leah's blabbing and thought of Mr. Stein's dead wife, Bobby Fayette getting kicked out on his ear, and Buster Sweet stuck working with that bigoted toad Rex Dallas. The folks at Regal didn't need writers to make up stories; they could have filmed their own lives. I needed to sort it all out in silence, but Leah never stopped talking. It was "David" this and "Ida" that. I bet she would have shut up quick enough if I told her how Mr. Stein kept fiddling around with my bosoms.

"David and I were talking earlier today. He wants us to leave the Dorchester for a place closer to the studio. They have lovely accommodations for the contract players, and two flats have just become vacant. It looks like we'll be moving up in the world."

Swell.

I'd had some peace since Leah had started stepping

out with Omar. Strange, wasn't it? She loved a colored man, the ultimate forbidden fruit, but since no one really knew exactly what Omar was, nobody said a word. I guess that's what they call irony. That night I cried myself to sleep and dreamed of Chick running to me, his arms open, smiling. I woke up and cried even more.

Leah and I spent the next few days packing for our move to West Hollywood. I didn't make a peep when Leah informed me Omar would be joining us. She hadn't been so happy since before Pops became ill, and I didn't want to be a wet blanket. The Dorchester may not have been the swankiest place in town, but it had been our home for over a year. We were abandoning our old life, and although it didn't seem to matter to Leah, it did to me.

Before we left, I said my goodbyes to Mrs. LaRue, the pensioners, and all the familiar places, including the new Broadway Ritz. They'd gussied up the old gal and fashioned her into a medieval castle, minus the moat. I peeked through glass doors into the refurbished lobby. The ushers wore hunter green uniforms with gold epaulets. A massive mural of the English countryside decorated the lobby, and grand chandeliers hung from beams of solid oak.

The ticket seller looked at me with a haughty air. "Hey, miss, do you want to buy a ticket?"

I shook my head and walked off. Without the Mighty Wurlitzer, the Ritz had lost her soul.

****

Regal Pictures built the Casa de Monte in 1924 to house its contract players and designed it in the Spanish Mission style with a red tile roof and stucco walls resembling ivory meringue. Twelve spacious apartments surrounded a terra cotta courtyard, quite a change from the respectable squalor of the Dorchester and Bunker Hill.

Fiery bougainvillea crawled up the walls of the rear terrace. Trees of every kind—orange, lemon, peach, and fig—surrounded the place, including one bearing a marvelous fruit called avocados. The entryway to our flat led to a pale yellow living room with parquet floors polished to a high sheen and a vaulted ceiling embellished with carved moldings. Once Omar positioned our furniture to Leah's satisfaction, anyone visiting our new apartment would have sworn we'd lived in the Casa forever.

Omar took a smaller flat near ours, and Leah spent much of her time there. Minus his Pullman porter's uniform, our neighbors referred to the swarthy young fellow as "that Turkish gent who works for Mr. Roth." Although I loved the Dorchester, I knew life here would be better. For one thing, Leah and I wouldn't have to schlep across town for work. The builders had located the Casa only four short blocks from Santa Monica Boulevard and the Regal Pictures lot.

I tried to concentrate on finding Uncle Baron's grave, but night and day, my thoughts were on the elusive Chick Hagan. I even sought out Betty to give me the lowdown on Jill Carpenter and the man I loved. She shook her head and sniggered. "You can forget about Chick Hagan. Miss Carpenter is one determined lady and has sunk her claws into him. No other dame gets near him if she's around."

Still, nothing could dissuade me. When I slept, I dreamed that he swept me into his arms, swore he adored me, and planted a big one on my lips. It had better happen soon or, I swore, I'd curl up into a ball and die.

At twilight, I walked into the courtyard where a whimsical fish statue covered in Mexican tiles spouted into a fountain. The fragrance of jasmine, gardenias, and sage enveloped the courtyard. A breeze set the wind chimes in motion. The metallic tinkling, the music of gushing water, and the scent of the perfumed air swept me away. Everything would be perfect if only Chick would appear and take me in his arms. I made a wish: Please bring me my one true love, and make it snappy.

"A penny for your thoughts, Dollface."

A man's shadow moved toward me—Chick coming to make my dreams come true. No, just my luck, David Stein strolled over carrying a huge bouquet of red roses.

"Hello, Mr. Stein."

He moved close enough for me to see his smile. "Gee, Mitzi, I didn't think you'd turn back flips to see me, but why the downcast face?" He chuckled, yet his laughter seemed hollow. "Were you expecting someone? A beau, perhaps?"

What a first-class dip. "No, I wasn't expecting anyone, and you know very well I don't have a beau."

When he chortled at my words, I wanted to kick him right in the keister. "Well, I was in the neighborhood. I thought I'd drop by and see how you and your sister are settling in."

Before I could tell him to beat it, Leah stepped out of our flat. "Mitzi…" She paused and her eyes brightened. "Oh, my goodness, it's David. Please, come in. Come in."

The worm grinned at me as he sauntered into the living room. He handed Leah the bouquet with a grand flourish. "These are for you, Leah, just a little housewarming gift."

When Leah squealed like a twelve-year-old, I knew all was lost. "Oh, David, they are lovely." She rushed off to the kitchen.

Mr. Stein gave our apartment a quick once-over and called to her, "Leah, you've made this such a charming place. It proves home is where the heart is."

Brother, did he lay it on thick, and Leah swallowed his bushwah, hook, line, and sinker. She waltzed back into the dining room with the flowers arranged in the vase I'd pinched from the Ritz.

"You must stay for dinner. Now that we have a real kitchen, I'm cooking up a storm."

He placed his hat on the end table and grinned. "Gee, thanks." Drat, he'd marked his territory as surely as if he'd peed on it.

Leah plunked the vase in the middle of the dining room table. "Mitzi darling, set another place."

He flashed another triumphant smile. What else could I do? Lacing his food with rat poison would be inhospitable. Then it happened, the most embarrassing, humiliating thing in the whole wide world, my dear sister uttered those fateful words. "David, let me show you some photos of my family."

I raced into the kitchen to avoid witnessing something as inevitable as the sun rising in the east and setting in the west, her showing off our family and my childhood pictures.

"This is my dear mother. She died in the influenza

epidemic, as did your poor brother, or so I heard. This is Pops, such a handsome fellow, me in the Jewish Girl Scouts, and Mitzi at four, already in grade school, reading and writing. Our little genius at six, her first recital. But these are my favorites."

While I set the table, I suffered the ultimate humiliation. She pulled out my baby pictures, the naked ones. The kvelling began with renewed vigor and reached a fever pitch.

"David, have you ever seen a more beautiful baby? Look at that adorable tush. My mother would kiss her little rump every morning after she bathed her."

I heard a masculine chuckle. "I would have kissed it too."

Nothing is more mortifying than a conversation about tush kissing, but I refused to let that crumb enjoy my discomfort, so I stayed in the kitchen.

I listened to the oohing and aahing as Leah dragged out all the other family photographs and plopped them in front of Mr. Stein. At one point, he asked, "Is this Mitzi?"

Leah answered with a giggle. "Not our Mitzi, but her namesake, our great-aunt Mitzi. You're not the first person to notice the resemblance."

I knew they were looking at a print of the enameled image affixed to her tombstone. The first Mitzi had concealed her black locks beneath a sheitel, one of those ugly wigs Orthodox matrons wore, but her heart-shaped face and doe eyes were testaments to her beauty.

Something must have amused him because Mr. Stein laughed. I popped my head into the living room to see what had caused the laugh. He held the photo Zisel had taken of me the day we left New York, the one I hated like the plague.

"This is the way Mitzi looked when I first met her. I wonder if you could bear to part with it for a few days. I'd like to make a copy of it for, uh, publicity."

Leah handed it to him with a laugh. "Take it, take it. Mitzi never liked it anyway."

He pocketed the photo and continued perusing other images of Schectors, all the while mumbling polite comments. When I finally emerged, I found Mr. Stein at the bookcase examining Pops' collections— Dickens and Shakespeare, his bound folios of violin music, and the Yiddish stories he loved.

He moved on to the photos of our long-dead Viennese relations, sepia-toned ghosts from an era of bustles and lace fans. One of Uncle Baron's portraits sat on the mantel next to great-grandmother's menorah. Leah had placed a photograph of my matinee-idol uncle next to one of my father posed dramatically in his tuxedo.

"My, what a good-looking family, Leah." He picked up Uncle Baron's portrait. "Who is this dashing fellow?"

"Baron, my late uncle. I'd hoped that Ida had mentioned him to you. You see, Uncle Baron died with Clarice Dumont in that horrible fire."

He whistled. "Gosh, Leah, I didn't know. Does Ben have any idea you were related?'

Leah took the photo from him and placed it back on its perch. "Yes, he does, but, well, he won't talk about Uncle Baron. Could you, would you, ask him?"

Mr. Stein shook his head. "No, no, no. Sorry, I'd love to help, but the surest way to get Ben's dander up is to mention that fire. You see, it's personal with him.

His father had a bad ticker and died trying to put out the blaze. Take it from me, nobody talks about that fire to Ben, nobody."

Perhaps I should have kept my mouth shut, but couldn't stop myself. "Uncle Baron was Clarice Dumont's lover."

Mr. Stein's mouth jaw dropped, and the front door opened at the same moment. Omar strolled in. He dined with us every night, and I knew he didn't expect to see the Icebox talking to Leah. The two fellows stared at each other for what seemed an eternity. Then Mr. Stein smiled and marched up to him, hand extended.

"Hello, Omar, it's good to see you. So we're all having dinner together? That's grand."

Well, at least he wasn't a bigot.

Leah served her special brisket of beef garnished with potatoes and carrots, and Mr. Stein kept up the palaver the whole time. Omar and Leah seemed enchanted by our guest, and he regaled them with stories of his life. I, on the other hand, remained silent because I knew he was a fink and a degenerate.

"Ben offered me a job after high school, but my parents wouldn't hear of it. Pop said, 'Benny, my boy is a scholar, and he's going to a big university so he can learn to handle the goyim.' "

Leah tittered, Omar guffawed, and Mr. Stein glanced at me sideways as if he wanted me to join in the festivities. I didn't.

"Pop had his heart set on Harvard, but they had an even tighter quota than Yale. All those Boston gentiles were sore about Jews winning academic honors, but, well, Pop knew some people and pulled a few strings."

He smiled, but his green eyes were smoldering. I'd

heard all the horror stories about Jewish boys at Harvard and the other Ivy League schools, so I understood. "They barred us from the fraternity houses and all the societies, but I couldn't let a bunch of spoiled brats stop me, could I? I'd been called Jew Boy before."

He looked at Leah's shocked face and flushed with embarrassment. "Sorry about being a killjoy. Anyway, that's all behind me. I'm Ben's partner, and here I am."

Leah patted him on the knee. "And it's our gain, David."

Goodness, Leah laid it on almost as thick as Mr. Stein did, and I wanted to puke. I took a deep breath and stifled my yawns while he told Omar and my sister his plans for Regal's future. "People may chide us over the content of our films, but the box office proves folks want more from movies than just a bunch of pretty people waltzing across the screen in nice clothes."

Yeah, now they wanted pretty people waltzing across the screen in the buff.

By the end of the evening, Mr. Stein had eaten so much brisket I figured it would probably take a crane to get him out of the chair. Omar kept refilling his glass with some of the "medicinal" wine he sold on the side. Mr. Stein sipped a bit and settled back in his chair. Maybe he'd move in with us. Leah had had one glass too many and giggled like a fourteen-year-old.

"Now that we have a Frigidaire, we can enjoy some of the finer things in life, like ice cream."

Her words were my cue to leave the room. "I'll take care of it, Leah."

I raced into the kitchen and spooned ice cream into Bubbe's Austrian china dessert bowls. Finally, we got to use our good dishes. David Stein walked into the room and toward me. I glared, and when he realized he'd moved too close, he took a step back.

"I have to leave after dessert, but here's some good news for you. You're going to start work on another picture, and, Dollface, you're the leading lady."

Every girl on the lot hoped to hear those words, especially a contract player like me. Of course, it didn't mean I was the star of the film, but I'd never played a big role before. I finally did have something to blush about. "Really? Me? A leading lady? That's swell, David."

He was silent for moment and stared into my face. "You called me David."

I guess I had. "That's your name, isn't it?"

From the way he looked at me, you'd have thought I'd handed him the moon on a silver platter. Then a sly smile danced across his lips, and I knew something was up.

"Since I'm truly the bearer of good news, guess who your leading man is? Chick Hagan."

I had to grab the counter so I wouldn't swoon like some damsel in a Victorian melodrama. I'd finally be working with the man I loved. The sheer bliss must have shown on my face. David started laughing, but as usual, it sounded empty.

"You're sweet on that guy, aren't you?"

"I'm just happy to be working. Does it really matter how I feel about Chick? A lot of girls are mad about him." I looked him dead in the eye. "Why do you care anyway? Aren't you stepping out with that high-hat shiksa, Miss Vassar?"

David laughed, a real laugh, not one of his fakes.

The nerve of the guy. "Doll, I didn't peg you for the jealous type. I'm flattered. By the way, her name is Beth."

I refused to take the bait. "I simply stated a fact, and by the way, I don't care who you see."

He took my face in his hands, and I didn't pull away. "Maybe one day you will care."

We stood gazing at each other for a long moment. David looked as if he was angling for a kiss, but once again remembered himself and stepped back with a nervous laugh.

"The title is *Kids on the Lam*. It's no epic, but it will be a heck of a lot better than what you've done so far. We have a decent budget, the script is aces, and Willy is chomping at the bit to prove he's got the hang of talking pictures. In two weeks, we start filming in a little dump called Carlisle, a farming town in the Central Valley, about two hundred miles from here. Funny thing about Carlisle, it's where Clarice shot *The Southern Belle*."

My stomach nearly dropped to the floor. Uncle Baron and Clarice had been in Carlisle together.

David searched my face. "Is something wrong? I thought you'd be pleased."

I prayed my smile would convince him that life is just a bowl of cherries. "Oh, nothing's wrong. Everything's hunky-dory."

Chapter Twenty-Three
Carlisle

Hollywood Invades Carlisle
The Carlisle Republican, *June 11th, 1932*
Our quiet hamlet will be the location for more than growing grapes this summer! The citizens of our fair city have become stargazers since the Southern Pacific Railroad chugged into town with the cast and crew of Regal Pictures. The illustrious director Willy "One-Take" Taylor is at the helm of the modern drama Kids on the Lam. *Popular Negro comedian Buster Sweet and crooner extraordinaire Chick Hagan are the principal players along with lovely newcomer Mitzi Charles, whose rise to stardom has been spectacular.*

Regal Pictures has not been a presence in Carlisle since 1923 when they filmed The Southern Belle *here. The silent drama starred Clarice Dumont in her final role before her tragic death.*

The studio has built a vast set near Bradford Creek. All of Carlisle is grateful for their return after a too-long absence. Now Carlisle's glorious fields will soon heed the clarion call of the movies: "Ready! Action! Camera!" and "That's good—Cut!"

****

A hellish stench enveloped the hobo jungle snaking around the railroad tracks, the stink of rotting produce and fumes from the portable toilets nicknamed "honey wagons." To make matters worse, the June sun blazed hotter than usual, the trains produced a maddening din, and coal dust coated everything and everyone.

Welcome to glorious Carlisle, the location of *Kids on the Lam*, a tale of poverty, deprivation, and squalor ripped from the headlines, a "riches to rags" opus. The camera followed me past glum mothers in faded aprons and sullen men in threadbare overalls. It shadowed me when I passed a toddler trailing a filthy blanket, and a morose little girl clinging to a tattered doll. I stopped to watch a group of urchins playing a game of tag.

"Okay for sound. Cut, print, that's a wrap."

Whenever Willy ended the day's filming, the denizens of Carlisle, America's raisin capital, costumed in their shabbiest clothing, would abandon this hellhole and scurry away to their farms and homes. The cast and crew were outsiders and stayed at the local hostelry, a massive Beaux Arts building, the only hotel in town. A former actress, Mrs. Dagmar Carlisle, owned the place, which had gone into a decline since the Depression. Folks whispered the biggest cash crops were raisins and marijuana.

When David arrived to supervise the production, he got right into the spirit of the place. He still tossed his twenty-dollar gold piece, but he'd abandoned his usual sartorial elegance, and dressed in jodhpurs and riding boots. Since I'd swear he'd worn a necktie to his bris, seeing David in open-collared shirts shocked me.

He insisted on a type of naturalism I hadn't seen in most Regal productions. He barred the purple eye shadow and brown lips. The actors looked as if we'd rolled in dirt instead of makeup. We wore Depression glad rags, but Chick still managed to look Adonis-like despite his ratty dungarees.

Though Chick still dominated my dreams, Uncle Baron managed to steal into every waking thought. I imagined him strolling down the palm-lined streets with Clarice on his arm. Acres of orange trees, grape vines, and forests of eucalyptus, magnolias, and cypress spread beyond the railroad tracks and our hobo camp. I'd wander through the groves thinking about Uncle Baron and Clarice. Perhaps my uncle had romanced his ladylove in a wooded area perfumed with the deadly sweetness of oleander.

At sunset, Carlisle rolled up its streets, leaving cast and crew at loose ends with no place to play. Ida traveled from Los Angeles weekly and encouraged us to make the best of the situation.

"It could be worse. You could be filming in Death Valley."

Ida's publicity machine worked nonstop, arranging interviews for Chick and a front-page placement of my photo in the *Carlisle Republican*. The cast and crew ate together, sweated, and labored together into the night. The time spent shooting in steaming boxcars made me wonder if working in movies was worth the perspiration, tears, and long hours. Then I'd remember my uncle and Chick and realize the ordeal was worth every minute.

Chick was a keen fellow, but he had one teensy problem—he never read anything more challenging than the funny papers. *The Katzenjammer Kids* was his favorite. He'd stand in the chow line, quoting from the strip out loud, then convulse into gales of laughter. He loved repeating the characters' corny German dialect. "Und I vent to Coney Island und I took Schatz mit me!"

I admit it was goofy, but when he smiled his Fuller Brush smile, I fell in love with him all over again.

One day when some in the crew groused about the demands of the shoot, I changed the subject by bringing up the newest book by Pearl S. Buck. "Has anyone read *The Good Earth*?" Chick looked up from the funny papers.

"Sorry, baby, I don't spend my time with books. I leave it to brainy gals like you. Don't read too much. You'll get lines on your forehead like some dried-out librarian."

He went back to the comics and started chortling. "Wow, The Katzenjammer kids are a hoot today."

David happened to be nearby going over the shot-list. He exaggerated clearing his throat, and made sure I heard him. He even had the nerve to smirk at me when I glared at him. I knew he considered Chick a dolt, but someone needed to remind Mr. Smarty-Pants Stein that not everybody went to Harvard.

****

In *Kids on the Lam*, the boy and girl meet after she hops onto the boxcar where he's sleeping. Willy rigged up a trolley track alongside the path he'd laid out for action, mounted the sound camera onto the trolley, and ran it parallel to the actors. People around Hollywood said Willy had lost his visual flair when the microphone became king, but he had the last laugh. He'd figured out how to add wings to the bulky sound cameras and bring motion back to talking pictures. This simple setup showed me why folks had nicknamed Willy Taylor "One-Take Willy."

The writer added motion to his scenario, and Willy even wanted to capture my character jumping onto a boxcar. At first, he expected me to hop onto the moving car, but David nixed the idea. He hired a diminutive stuntman who doubled for actresses and children to do the shot, but I thought David made a big megillah over nothing. Jumping aboard the train would be a piece of cake, and besides, the boxcar wasn't moving at any real speed. My double, however, claimed the stunt was too dangerous for a non-pro to try, but business as usual for him.

"Girlie, I've hopped on the backs of stallions in full gallop. I know what I'm doing."

The little fellow reeked of whiskey, didn't have a tooth in his head, and sported a face covered in a mass of battle scars. Just how skilled was the guy?

Chick and crew roasted alive inside the boxcar while Willy cracked the whip. Willy had already shot my close-up and planned to photograph the stuntman from behind as he jumped aboard. "It'll be duck soup. One take, and once we get it in the can—"

Willy didn't finish his sentence. The train from Los Angeles arrived, its engine blanketed in steam. A porter dropped the trap to the ground, and Ida jumped down, a wicked grin on her face.

"Hi-ho, Mitzi, hi-ho! Look who I brought all the way from Los Angeles."

Jill Carpenter stepped from the car, a vision in pink, carrying a large picnic basket. Some of the crew called out to her, and she responded with her glorious movie-star twinkle. As soon as she saw me, her upper lip curled, but she recovered quickly, and smiled even more radiantly.

Edna whispered. "Ooklay! Idaway oughtbray atthay eachedblay ondblay ussyhay ithway erhay."

Translation: "Look! Ida brought that bleached-blonde hussy with her."

Ida called out again. "Guess who else came for a visit?"

Another blonde stepped from the train and posed on the trap. She hee-hawed like a donkey, and everyone knew Miss Vassar was on the premises.

Edna nudged me in the ribs. "Owway! It'sway Avidday Einstay's orewhay inway ethay eshflay."

"Wow! It's David Stein's whore in the flesh."

Miss Vassar must have gotten a whiff of the honey wagons, because she wrinkled her pretty little nose the moment she stepped off the train. Ida had recruited Rose to photograph every detail, and the young shutterbug busied herself with her tripod. Jill glared daggers, Miss Vassar guffawed, and Ida seemed amused.

"Mitzi, darling, I know you've met Jill Carpenter, but I'd like to introduce you to David's discovery, Beth Cushing."

I attempted a smile, but my heart wasn't in it. "Hello, Beth."

I decided not to bring up the infamous Mischief Makers short or mention Beth Cushing was a snotty no-talent trollop who everyone knew slept with David Stein just to get into movies. She probably stank at screwing, too, but being polite and well brought up, I kept my thoughts to myself.

Beth responded like a hoity-toity quiff. "Mitzi and I met on the lot, when she still looked like a girl."

She brayed in her donkey laugh, and I wanted to plant a right hook on her kisser. Ida put her arms around both actresses. "Girls, since you're Regal's three rising starlets, I thought it would be fabulous to have Rose photograph you together. All of you move over to the front of the train."

Just my luck to have Rose shoot me dressed like a ragamuffin between two beautiful prima donnas garbed in the height of elegance. The idea probably came from David Stein. I'd give the skunk a piece of my mind when I next saw him. We posed, the camera flashed, and Jill tried her hand at wit. "Gosh, two beauties and one beast."

Beth brayed again, even louder.

Flash! Pop! Rose aimed the camera for another picture when a shriek stopped her cold. Willy yelled loud enough to wake the dead. "Cut, damn it! Cut!"

I took my leave of Ida and company and ran back to the tracks. The toothless stuntman lay on the ground moaning in agony, his leg twisted at an unnatural angle. Willy looked down at the injured man with utter disgust.

"We almost had the shot, too. Somebody get a doctor for this worthless turd. Damn the drunken bastard to Hades. Now the whole day is ruined. Where the hell am I going to find a runt stuntman in this Godforsaken rat hole?"

I grabbed his sleeve and pulled him aside. "Willy, I can do that jump. I swear I can."

He looked at me as if I'd gone buggy. "The Icebox would have my head if something happened to you. I know it ain't worth much, and it sure ain't pretty, but I like it sitting on my shoulders, all the same."

I decided to press my case. "But Willy, you told me yourself that in the old days actresses did their own stunts. I know I can do it."

Willy kept shaking his head. "Thanks for the offer, but I can't let you."

Before he could walk away, I took his arm once again. "You're the one who called the shot duck soup, and it is. We've all been hopping on and off the boxcars when no one is around. I tell you I can do this."

He looked around. "Suppose Stein catches us?"

I looked around the tracks. "I don't see him, do you? Let's shoot it before he finds out."

For the first time that day, Willy smiled. "You're all right, kid, all right!"

Willy ordered the boxcar rolled back into position and the cameras reloaded. No one knew exactly what he planned, but no one with any sense argued with Willy Taylor. Steam nearly obscured the camera mark. A grip tensed up when he saw me move into place. "Hey, Mitzi, whatcha doing?"

An assistant director yelled out, "Quiet on the set."

Willy bellowed, "Roll 'em!" and I started running for the freight train. Without warning, the train lurched forward and picked up speed. I chased that boxcar, running so fast I thought my lungs would burst. My legs burned as I sped through the coal-filled air, the steam from the locomotive obscuring my vision. Finally, I grabbed the handlebar and Chick pulled me inside the car. Perspiration and dust covered every inch of me, but I did it.

Applause and yelps of admiration followed Willy's shout of, "Cut! Print!" He muttered, "I'll kill that bastard," and stormed over to the engineer. "Why the hell did you speed up like that? I ought to knock your block off, you son of a bitch!"

Ida abandoned the two actresses and directed Rose

to photograph Chick and me together. We were both black with grime, but Chick lifted me down from the freight car. In the blinding flash of Rose's camera, he planted a big one on my cheek.

"That was swell, Mitzi! I've never met a gal like you before."

Let me die now, a happy girl. Unfortunately, it was not to be. Leah rushed up and dragged me from Chick's arms. "Mitzi, you could have been killed!"

I didn't tell her I would have jumped onto a locomotive speeding at two hundred miles an hour if the reward was a second in Chick Hagan's embrace.

"You're as reckless as Uncle Baron. Promise me you'll never do something like that again."

She'd never compared me to Uncle Baron before, but then I'd always been her obedient kid sister. How could I explain those days were over?

"Yes, Leah, I promise."

I hadn't counted on David Stein's getting in on the act. David arrived just as I made my leap. There he was, arms crossed, giving me his version of the Look. He smiled ever so sweetly at Leah, and then grabbed me by my wrist.

"Leah, may I have a moment with Mitzi?"

Since David didn't show anger like other people, few would know he was furious. He still had a big smile on his mug when he dragged me out of earshot and pulled me over to his automobile. By the time he turned to face me, he'd dropped the cheerful act. "I should wring your neck."

The crumb didn't scare me one bit. I wasn't in the mood for a lecture and pulled my arm away. "Yeah? You and whose army?"

He had a nasty glint in his eye. "If you ever pull anything like that again, I'll…"

I felt pretty nasty myself. "You'll do what, David Stein? I saved your bacon, and this is the thanks I get?"

Of course, being a Jew, he didn't have any bacon to save, but I'd made my point. We were nose to nose, and for the first time, he blew his lid. "Don't you mouth off to me, little girl! I don't take lip from a smart-ass, wet-behind-the-ears pisher!"

The nerve of the guy! "Well, how about you planting a kiss on my smart ass and telling me it smells like a rose?"

He laughed and gave me the leer of the century. "Is that an invitation, Dollface? I wouldn't mind if it was."

I stood there like a lox, trying to think up a witty retort when Miss Vassar interrupted.

"Woo-hoo, Davie darling, we're waiting for you. Don't you want lunch?"

I couldn't resist imitating her tight-jawed, snotty, Locust Valley accent. "Davie darling, I wouldn't dream of keeping you from dining with your chums."

If I hadn't stormed away in a huff, I would've kicked him in the keister.

For the next two days, everyone treated me like a conquering hero—that is, everyone but Leah and David Stein. Leah kept shooting me the Look but it had lost its power. Then she tried the silent treatment but couldn't keep it up. I found David a different story. Whenever I caught him glaring at me, I saw admiration and lust mingled with rage. Honestly, a psychiatrist wouldn't know what to do with the guy.

Chapter Twenty-Four
When I Take My Sugar to Tea

Four days later, an ill-humored Mr. Roth jumped from the Los Angeles train, a dog-eared copy of the script in his hand. Mr. Roth looked spiffy in his striped suit, gleaming white shirt, silk tie, and spectator brogues. His Carnival in Venice cologne battled against the stench of the honey wagons. He looked around the hobo jungle and bellowed, "Who picked this dump anyway?"

No one dared say a word, but everybody knew he'd insisted on shooting in Carlisle because he knew Mrs. Carlisle was movie crazy and would make shooting here cheap. Omar arrived with him and took me aside. "He's in a foul mood, Mitzi. Stay away."

Some poor chump of a grip made the mistake of saying, "Hello, Mr. Roth."

Mr. Roth glared at the fellow, screamed, "Drop dead!" and stormed over to David, who was going over the shot list with one of the assistants. His upper lip curled when he eyeballed David's attire.

"You look like a bum."

David appeared unperturbed. "Sorry, I'm having my tux pressed."

Mr. Roth waved everyone away with a curt, "Scram! Mr. Stein and I have things to talk over."

The crew scrambled like mice from a hungry cat.

David and Mr. Roth walked to an orange grove that adjoined the railroad tracks. I followed at a short distance, since Mr. Roth had a voice that could cut through solid granite.

Mr. Roth stopped in his tracks and the bellowing began. "Are you trying to ruin my company?"

David barely spoke above a whisper, and I strained to catch his reply. "It's our company, Ben. We're making money, aren't we? Before our deal, you were one step above a Poverty Row outfit, but now the bucks are pouring in. The money from every ticket, every bag of popcorn, every bon-bon goes into our pockets, not to some other putz."

Mr. Roth caught himself and softened. "All right already, we're making money. I had a meeting with Joe Breen about this piece of trash, *Kids on the Lam*, and he ain't happy."

David took a breath at the mention of Breen, the notorious screenplay censor. "Don't tell me you called on Breen in that get-up? No wonder he was sore."

Mr. Roth snapped back. "What's wrong with the way I dress? I spent a lot of dough on these duds."

He looked Mr. Roth up and down. "Nothing's wrong, if you're a pimp. Breen already told me the script was a piece of trash, and you know what I told him? The screenwriter won a Pulitzer Prize. He's the toast of Broadway, the one that matters, the one in New York. Maybe Breen doesn't know about that Broadway since he was just a scribe for some Catholic rag in Philly. What makes him qualified to tell us how to run our business? You should have suggested he try selling rosary beads instead of sticking his nose into movie making."

"Yeah, I'm sure he would have loved that. Think you're smart, Harvard Boy, don't you? Well, maybe you are, but I'm the one who has to deal with him. He told me no fairies, no cute lesbian scenes, no whites and coloreds together, no drugs, no naked broads, and no profanity."

I heard the quiet fury in David's voice. "What's the matter with you, Ben? We're businessmen, aren't we? What about free speech? What about art and creativity? What about Bobby Fayette's acting? This is his greatest performance."

"To hell with that pansy!"

When David finally piped up, his voice matched Mr. Roth's in pitch. "Bobby has been in movies since the silent days, and he's never given a performance like this. Ben, this is his last film for Regal. We should let him go out in glory. You owe it to him."

Mr. Roth exploded. "What a load of horseshit! I made the fluff a star, and how did he thank me? By picking up every piece of queer ass from here to Honolulu. Forget about that powder puff."

David sounded as if he was pleading with Mr. Roth. "Ben, I know you're angry, but you've seen the early rushes. We've got something."

"Yeah, and we need to talk about that 'something.' All these close-up and soft focus shots of Mitzi, that's your doing, not Willy's. What's going on between the two of you?"

I guess his words blindsided David. He didn't answer, but I could have told Mr. Roth what was going on with me and David Stein—a big fat pile of nothing.

"David, you've gone sappy over that little girl, haven't you? You can have any broad on the lot and you pick her? Yeah, I know she's a cute kid, but screwing a Jewish girl is like sleeping with your sister. Oh, well, you're young and full of fire. Just keep it in your pants, at least until after we finish this movie. Oh, and that scene by the lake? I've thought it over, and maybe all is not lost. Have some pretty girls take a midnight swim. Fellows like that. We'll keep the raunchy patter and can probably get away with showing some body parts, as long as they're not Mitzi's. Make sure you cut that kiss between Mitzi and Chick, while you're at it. The guy's laid everything except the Atlantic Cable."

Atlantic Cable? What did the Atlantic Cable have to do with anything? When I first read the script, I'd done a back flip because I'd finally get to kiss Chick. Maybe it would be in front of a crew and our lips wouldn't really meet, but beggars can't be choosers. Now my kiss had gone down the drain, and I could barely keep from bawling. Mr. Roth might as well have hacked out my heart.

When I returned to the hotel that evening, I asked Leah what Mr. Roth meant about Chick laying everything except the Atlantic Cable.

Gosh, I wish I'd kept my big mouth shut.

****

After working like pack mules all day, the gang usually ended up in Chick's suite to blow off steam. In addition to disliking Chick, Leah disapproved of me mingling with the crew after hours and hated the idea of me attending his soirees.

"Those parties last all night. I hear they drink bootlegged liquor, smoke reefer, and the fellows try to make as many girls as they can. I worked at Roseland

and had my share of guys like that. I don't want my little sister rubbing elbows with those mugs and their loose girlies."

"Leah, everyone goes to Chick's parties. I'm having such a bum time." Finally, after a great deal of cajoling and pleading, she gave in and decided to join Edna and me.

It thrilled me to have a chance to don my prettiest summer frock. Leah wore a snazzy floral print, and Edna looked cheery in a Hawaiian-style dress. The elevator doors opened as we reached Chick's floor. Someone had strung up brightly colored paper lanterns in the hallway, and hot jazz music spilled out of the rooms. A girl in a disheveled dress darted from the suite with a grip running after her. Both their lips were smeared with her lipstick. She simpered as she ran from him. "Roscoe, you're a devil." The guy caught her, and they shared a passionate kiss before he threw her over his shoulder and took off. Leah rolled her eyes but didn't say a word.

The place roared like a house on fire. Cab Calloway blared from the Victrola as Buster demonstrated a few new dance steps to some of the crew.

"You want to see what they're doing in Harlem? It's called the jitterbug. Watch Uncle Buster and learn."

One of the boys grabbed Leah, and they began dancing up a storm. Edna jumped into it with an assistant cameraman. I looked around for the host and managed to make my way past a group of kids passing around bottles of homemade wine. "Say, can somebody tell me where Chick is?"

An extra gal tittered and pointed to a closed door. I

moved past lovebirds spooning in a dark corner, took a deep breath, and opened it. Two young couples sat on the floor, passing a strange-looking, strange-smelling cigarette back and forth. A kid inhaled deeply, then handed it to the girl sitting next to him. Sharing a cigarette seemed awfully unhygienic to me, but no one cared. Another fellow hand-rolled another cigarette using what looked like dried herbs instead of tobacco.

Chick reclined across his bed like the Grand Pasha of Istanbul, but jumped up the moment he saw me. "Hey, Mitzi."

He looked at the kids on the floor and grinned sheepishly. "They're smoking Turkish cigarettes."

For some reason Chick's guests started laughing. "Yeah, Turkish cigarettes."

He hushed them right away. "Show some respect, you mugs. This is my leading lady."

The smokers waved in greeting, and went back to the cig. Chick sauntered over to me. "Sugar, you know what? You look good enough to eat."

His remark brought on a round of lewd snickering, and he glared at his friends again. "Can it!"

He moved closer, and I thought I would faint. "Don't mind them, baby."

"Baby!" Chick called me "baby" as if I were his girlfriend!

Someone put "When I Take My Sugar to Tea" on the Victrola. He pulled me close, and I forgot about the Turkish cigarettes and his smirking friends. I'd practiced with Leah, and the thought of dancing with Chick was the most thrilling thing I'd ever imagined.

He put his cheek next to mine and sang into my ear. "When I take my sugar to tea, all the boys are jealous of me."

I felt the warmth of his breath, smelled his cologne and the smoke from that funny cigarette, but I didn't care. This must be the way you feel when you're in love.

"'Cause I never take her where the gang goes, when I take my sugar to tea."

He pulled me even closer and whispered, "Baby, you know what?"

"What, Chick?"

"I think about you all the time. How about I throw these bums out and you and I have a real conversation?"

My heart pumped a million miles an hour. A real conversation? That would be fabulous. "Yes, Chick, just us."

He moved his mouth closer to mine, and I knew he wanted to kiss me. I shut my eyes expecting the most important experience of a girl's life—her first kiss.

I'd waited an eternity for this moment. Seconds passed and nothing happened. I felt Chick move away and opened my eyes. I found myself looking right into David Stein's smiling face.

"Sorry, Cinderella. The clock just struck midnight. The ball is over, time to go."

I wished him to the frozen wilds of the Yukon. The clock said half past eight. I was dancing with the man I loved. Romance perfumed the air, along with Turkish cigarette smoke.

"I'm not going anywhere. Chick and I are about to have a private conversation, and that means you're not welcome."

David's jaw tightened, his eyes flashing a vitriolic

shade of green. He looked as if he wanted to slug Chick. Instead, he grinned in a very disturbing way.

"Private conversation, huh? Gosh, I'm afraid that won't be happening anytime soon, Dollface. Chick, how about you and I having our own private conversation later tonight?"

The kids started their snide giggling again. "Chick, better watch your step, the boss man's sore!"

Although both men continued smiling, they looked like they were about to come to blows. "Okay, Stein, you win, this time."

How could he give up so easily? "But, Chick, I don't want to go. Please tell him we were going to talk. Please."

Chick stroked my face. "There'll be plenty of time to talk later, baby." He kissed my forehead and threw himself back onto the bed.

David grabbed my arm and dragged me out of the room. Leah stood in the hallway, a silent witness to my mortification.

"Leah, you're a Benedict Arnold!" I swiveled toward David. "David Stein, you're a big drip. Please let me stay. I don't want to go."

He pushed me ahead of him. "I'm taking you to your room."

How I hated the guy. "You've ruined everything. Now Chick and I won't have that talk, and it's your fault."

This pill didn't have an ounce of romance in him. "Yeah, well, I can guess what kind of talk Chick had planned. Did he get you to smoke any of that marijuana?"

What a silly man. "You don't know anything.

Those were Turkish cigarettes. And no, I didn't smoke one. Smoking is bad for the voice, and besides, those cigarettes smelled horrible. The way they were passing them around looked unsanitary."

The jerk had the nerve to laugh, and it angered me. "Mr. David Stein, for a smart guy, you are one dumb cluck. Do you know what everyone calls you around the studio? The Icebox."

He grabbed at my arm once again, but I pulled away and stood my ground. "You're just a big Gloomy Gus who never gives anyone the time of day. It's really quite simple. When some poor sap says, 'Hello, Mr. Stein,' all you have to do is say 'Hello' back to them."

I stood before him, humiliated, lovesick, and strangely famished. "Say, David, would you happen to have a cookie or maybe a Hershey bar on you? Don't know why, but I'm awfully hungry."

The nudnik started laughing again. "Baby, when you hang around hop-heads smoking marijuana, you get an appetite."

He took me by the shoulders and looked me in the eye. I expected a tongue-lashing, but he didn't say a word. Instead, he stroked my cheek. I guess he wasn't really angry. "Mitzi, if you only knew."

From the way he gazed into my face, I knew what he wanted. I tossed my shoulders back. "David, I don't have the energy to fight you off. If you're going to kiss me, go ahead."

He tilted his head as if he were going in for a smooch. I closed my eyes, and stood still. I waited, but nothing happened, not even a peck on the cheek.

"No, Mitzi. Not like this."

He took my wrist and marched me down the

corridor. I didn't know what had angered him, but there wouldn't be any kissing that night. We arrived at my room, and he handed me over to Leah, who had already arrived and was waiting for us.

"Leah, your sister needs to rest now. She's had too much excitement this evening. I'll go find Edna."

The bum had the nerve to wink at me. He went off to search for my lost friend, and I searched for some chow.

"What kind of sister are you, Leah? You betrayed me. I'll never forgive you. David Stein is a dreadful man and a terrible killjoy. I hate him very much."

She didn't say a word when I dug through our larder and devoured two peanut-butter-and-jelly sandwiches, a banana, and a nectarine. Later David returned with Edna. I really wanted to give him a piece of my mind, but I'd caught sight of the most fabulous chocolate cake.

Poor Edna staggered in looking a bit worse for wear, followed by a smirking David Stein. "I'm afraid Edna drank a bit too much of the local wine, but she'll be fine tomorrow. Get the girls to bed. It's an early call."

David turned, a smile dancing on his lips. I would have made a biting comment, but I couldn't stop eating that divine cake. Maybe it was because of those Turkish cigarettes, but by a quarter past nine I was out like a light and slept through the night. The next morning I bounced out of bed ready for work, but poor Edna woke up with a horrible headache.

"I want to die. Please, someone, shoot me!"

She was right as rain after she drank two cups of black coffee and tossed her cookies.

Chapter Twenty-Five
La Rosita

Five days later, our time in Carlisle ended. Ida marched into our room, bristling with nervous energy. She cut quite a striking figure in her double-breasted ice cream suit. For once, she had opened her silk blouse at the collar.

"Time to go, girls. Can't keep Mrs. Carlisle waiting. We've been invited to lunch, and I expect you to make a good impression."

Leah had left for the Carlisle mansion an hour before, and Ida acted as our chaperone. We dressed lightly while the merciless summer heat beat down on us. Edna donned pale green cotton, and I wore white. Ida turned me around, scrutinizing my dress from every angle.

"Very nice. White goes well with your complexion and dark hair. Rose should get some lovely photos. Now girls, listen well. Dagmar Carlisle is a lovely lady, but she's a bit, shall we say, eccentric. In the old days, she made a few stabs at a movie career, but returned to Carlisle a sadder but wiser girl. It didn't hurt, since she married the heir to the Carlisle raisin fortune. Her mansion, La Rosita, is as famous as her rose gardens. Regal filmed *The Southern Belle* on her estate, and the good citizens of Carlisle talk about Clarice Dumont to this day. By the way, Mrs. Carlisle fancies herself a singer and will probably serenade us, so no smart comments."

Edna tittered, Ida shot her a dirty look, and she stopped snickering. "Who, me? I'll be good, I promise, Miss Cohen."

Ida continued lecturing us on proper etiquette as we walked to the limousine. "Be polite and ladylike and, Edna, no wine. Mrs. Carlisle is keen about movie folks and even invited Buster to her little fiesta. Her driver is waiting, so let's shove off."

****

How do I describe La Rosita? I'd seen grand estates in the Hamptons. Los Angeles was chockablock with sprawling manor houses on great tracts of land. La Rosita, however, was unique. Before we set eyes on the great house, an overpowering fragrance hinted at the wonders awaiting us. Acres of roses bloomed in every imaginable hue. La Rosita loomed high on the horizon, a massive Queen Anne mansion. With eight oversized gables and two mammoth towers painted in shades of green and fuchsia, La Rosita dwarfed the adjoining guest cottages and hunting lodge.

Our driver stopped and opened the doors of the motorcar. A metallic soprano voice singing "Ah, Sweet Mystery of Life" assaulted our ears. I looked at Edna and bit my tongue.

We walked into La Rosita through an intricately carved portal. Everything about the place screamed gargantuan, from the piazza to a mahogany hat rack that dwarfed the ones in a haberdashery. I stopped in front of two enormous portraits, obviously the works of a master. One was of a demure young blonde, the other a mature gentleman with a steely gaze.

Ida whispered, "John Singer Sargent painted them when Dagmar and her husband honeymooned in London."

Did she say "honeymoon"?

"Gee, Ida, she looks awfully young to be a bride, especially to a geezer like him."

Ida chortled at my remark. "Mr. Carlisle always got what he wanted. Dagmar was sixteen; he was a forty-year-old robber baron. To quote Dagmar, 'He came, he saw, he conquered.' All things considered, she did well for herself."

Yes, I'd say she did well for herself. The vestibule was probably larger than our whole apartment. The architect had utilized the rose motif throughout and even had the chandelier globes blown into the shape of Mrs. Carlisle's beloved flower. Stained glass windows bathed the rooms in a delicate, rosy glow.

Our hostess wore her wealth with great elegance. Mrs. Carlisle dressed in billowy organza, her finger-waved hair lightened into a tasteful lemon parfait coiffure, her makeup understated. Her diamonds, though large, weren't the least bit vulgar.

Mrs. Carlisle's voice, however, was brassy enough to make a lullaby sound tawdry. Mr. Roth had instructed everyone to reward the lady of the manor's efforts with lavish applause. After her final song, we all stood for an obedient ovation. She threw her head back, gave a hearty laugh, then blew us all a kiss.

"Thank you, thank you so much, my friends. Trapped here in the hinterlands as I am, it's a pleasure to host true aficionados of my art. You shall be rewarded."

She nodded to her accompanists, a harpist and

pianist, and began another song. We stood in silence, smiles frozen in place. I avoided looking at Edna for fear we'd both collapse into giggles. Leah's shoulders already shook in amusement. We endured another ten minutes until, mercifully, Mrs. Carlisle concluded her concert. Rose's camera snapped away as we lined up to greet our hostess.

I couldn't wait to ask Mrs. Carlisle about Uncle Baron, but just as she turned to me, a woman's voice called out, "Dagmar!"

All eyes turned to the vestibule where Jill Carpenter posed. Rose snapped her, and she entered, followed by Betty, dressed in a white maid's uniform, and a harried local fellow carrying her luggage. Betty glanced at me and rolled her eyes to the heavens. Working with Jill Carpenter must have been sheer torture. Still, despite the heat, I had to admit Jill was a vision in her cream-colored linen suit.

"Dagmar, it's me, your little Jilly!"

Jill Carpenter became the center of the universe and everyone, including Mrs. Carlisle, rushed to her. Well, almost everyone. Leah and Omar walked me onto a veranda as large as the First Class Promenade of the Titanic. My pulse quickened when Chick came in and took his place near the entrance, a cigarette dangling from his lips. My heart nearly jumped out of my chest when he looked at me, but Jill waltzed over and flung her arms around him before he could say hello. He dropped his cigarette and threw her into the air.

"How's my girl?"

So she was his girl, and I meant nothing to him. Leah's lip curled in a sneer whenever she saw him, and I'm sure his choice overjoyed her. I figured it was time to vamoose. David and Mr. Roth were deep in conversation off in a corner. I made myself inconspicuous, because I didn't want to acknowledge the pill, also known as David Stein. Unfortunately, the moment my blabby sister caught sight of the two, she called out to them, "Yoo-hoo, Mr. Roth. Hello, David."

Mr. Roth gave her a polite wave before returning to his conversation. David bowed to Leah and leered at me, obviously remembering our last encounter. I hadn't spoken to the crumb since that night in Chick's room. How could I have ever thought of letting him kiss me? I needed my head examined. Telling him off that night did have a silver lining, though. People said the Icebox was a changed man. All of a sudden, he acted like a swell guy, greeting everyone by name from the lead cameraman to the lowliest gaffer. On occasion, he even smiled. The word soon got out—the Icebox had thawed.

I still wanted to chew him out for messing things up with Chick, but decided on the silent treatment instead. His discussion with Mr. Roth finished, David sauntered over and greeted Leah with a kiss on the check, a mischievous grin on his face.

"Hello, Leah, it's grand to see you. Hello, Mitzi."

When I turned up my nose, the bum had the nerve to laugh. I refused to let the worm annoy me. A bell announced they were serving lunch. I grabbed Leah and flounced off while Omar strolled behind us.

To say Mrs. Carlisle served the fatted calf would be an understatement—it was three fatted calves roasted on spits alongside suckling pigs and chickens. An army of Mexican servants garbed in authentic dress saw to our every need. We dined al fresco on the incredible fare.

Chick walked arm in arm with Jill and flashed a weak smile in my direction. Leah was in a spirited conversation with Mrs. Carlisle's accompanists, while Omar joked with Buster. Edna abandoned me for dessert, leaving me alone. David's attention remained on me, but I ignored the louse. Thankfully, Mrs. Carlisle took me aside, coming to my rescue.

"Dear girl, I've been told you are a budding star. Oh, how I envy you. I dreamed of a career in motion pictures, but I was young and naive. I made a couple of silent dramas for a studio in San Diego. Perhaps you've seen *Man and Maid*? *Beauty is Gold*?"

I hoped my smile looked genuine. "I'm sorry I haven't had the pleasure."

Dagmar laughed theatrically. "No? Oh, well. They were before your time. How I hated the eighteen-hour days and the rigors of movie making. I'm afraid I was too accustomed to a life of luxury. I finally packed my bags and came home. I marveled at how dear Clarice could bounce back after working those long hours."

My pulse surged at her mention of Clarice, but I forced myself to speak in a casual tone. "When they were shooting *The Southern Belle* at La Rosita, did you ever meet a young man named Baron?"

Her jaw dropped. "Baron? You mean Bernard Charles? Yes, of course I knew him, even his real name. Such a dashing young man, so handsome, so talented. He'd play our piano for hours. The dear boy adored my voice. He often said that Broadway was the place for me, but my late husband would not hear of it. It devastated me when the poor darling died alongside Clarice. They were an item, you know. Why do you ask?"

"Well, you see, he was my uncle. My sister and I are trying to find out where he's buried."

She moved closer. "Oh, my dear, dear girl, I'm so sorry, but I can't help you. I can tell you something no one else knows. Bernard is still here at La Rosita. Don't think me mad, but at times, especially while the roses are blooming, I feel his spirit."

I was pondering her words when David strolled over to us. Mrs. Carlisle simpered like a schoolgirl when he kissed her.

"David, I was speaking to Mitzi about poor Bernard, her Baron. It's strange you asked me about him too."

His color changed into a deep blush. "Uh, well, I knew Mitzi had questions, and I—"

Before he could say another word, Mrs. Carlisle caught sight of Buster. "Oh, you must excuse me. I do so adore Negroes."

She floated away, and David took my arm. "Are you still angry about Chick?"

That night, after I had consoled myself with milk and chocolate cake, my anger took a powder, but he didn't have to know. I swerved away from him in a mock hissy fit. "Yes, I am. I'll never forgive you."

He turned me around to face him, his green eyes dancing with mirth. "Yeah, I can see devastation etched on your face. I'll beg for absolution on bended knee, but first I need to show you something. Come on."

David led me to the great rose garden behind the house. For a second I feared a repeat of our earlier encounters, but I thought better of it. An arrogant fellow like David Stein wouldn't be so foolish, especially with Mr. Roth within screaming distance.

****

My jaw dropped at my first sighting of the La Rosita garden. The biggest wisteria tree on earth made the giant gazebo look as if it sat in a purple mist. Wisteria painted the afternoon sky violet as if nature had dropped an amethyst-colored awning over La Rosita.

I pointed to the bandstand. "My uncle played the piano there in *The Southern Belle*. I know you think it's crazy, but Mrs. Carlisle said she feels Uncle Baron's spirit here. Maybe she's right. I once read the soul is energy and never dies."

David and I locked hands as we raced up the steps. He knelt at one of the pillars that buttressed the delicate roof. He took my forefinger, tracing it over an inscription carved into the wood and covered with a dark patina. "It says 'Baron loves Clarice and Clarice loves Baron, forever.'"

"How did you find it, David?"

His attention remained on the carving. "I don't know. I wasn't looking for anything, just took a walk, and landed here."

The gazebo with its copper dome, carved spires, and elaborate finials looked like something from a Victorian fairytale. I spread my arms and spun around the bandstand.

"Oh, David, just think, this might be the place where they fell in love. Uncle Baron and Clarice died together. It's so romantic, except for the part about being burned alive."

I knew I shouldn't pry, but for some reason my curiosity got the best of me. "David, have you ever been in love?"

He looked away. "Maybe."

For some reason, I felt a bit disappointed. "Oh, so you're in love with Beth Cushing. Forgive me for saying so, but I don't think you have very good taste in ladies."

I found his snickering extremely annoying. "Excuse me, Mr. Stein, but I thought we were having a serious discussion."

David stopped laughing and all of a sudden became sincere. He turned his head, and I looked into his face. What a handsome guy.

"No, I'm not in love with Beth, and there's nothing wrong with my taste in ladies. Beth and I have a complicated history."

I wanted to hear about that history. "David, I'm not a kid. You can tell me anything."

David hemmed and hawed; it seemed to take ages to find the words. "I'm not proud about what happened with Beth. At Harvard, I ran into a guy from an old New England family. The fellow hated Jews, me in particular. I didn't care if some crummy fraternity wouldn't let in Jews, or about the general dislike of everything Jewish. The thing is, this fellow and his pals went out of their way to make it clear I stood under a special Hebrew light only goys could see. I vowed to get even with him and did just that. He was nuts about Beth, wanted to marry her, and I took her away from him."

It seemed to me that David ended up with the booby prize, but who was I to judge? "Of course, your revenge was sweet."

From the smug grin on his face, I figured he savored the memories of his depraved encounters with

Miss Vassar. Then he stopped smiling.

"At first, absolutely sugary. I knew it was wrong, but my wife had problems. She was delicate and, well, we couldn't have relations, you know, relations between a husband and wife. I'm afraid I used Beth to scratch an itch."

"I guess you don't mean eczema."

His face colored. "Doll, excuse me. I really shouldn't be talking about this with you."

I felt my back stiffening. "Well, I don't appreciate you treating me like a baby. You think I'm just a kid? Well, I'll be twenty in October. The last time I checked, that makes me a woman. You have to talk to someone, don't you? Why not me? So Beth wrecked your home."

I didn't pull away when he took my hands in his. "Don't blame her. Forget all that bullshit about Vassar. She never finished her freshman year. Her father blew his brains out after the Crash. A friend of the family gave her a role in a play so she and her mother wouldn't starve. I met her after the swells cut her out of the social register. Pop had died, Dara wasn't doing well, and I was going wacky. I know I sound like a cad, but it wasn't supposed to be anything serious."

He sighed in resignation. "Dara had a bad ticker. The doctors said not to chance having relations, in case she got in the family way. Mitzi, you have to believe me when I tell you I was quite fond of her. I'd hoped for a real marriage, a family, and kids, but it wasn't in the cards for us." He dropped my hand and plopped down on the bandstand steps. I plopped with him.

"Unfortunately, the Harvard guy was a vindictive son-of-a-gun. When he heard about Beth and me, he spilled the beans to Dara. I think it killed her. When I found out what he'd done, I beat the bastard to a bloody pulp, only it was too late. I should never have married Dara. And I wish to hell I'd left Beth alone."

Perhaps David wasn't really the playboy I'd thought. He remained silent for a long while; then his mood lightened. "Enough of my sordid past. What's going on with you and Chick?"

Why did he have to bring up Chick? "Bubkes. I keep hoping, but I don't think anything will ever happen."

"Maybe it will, doll."

I gave a shake of my head. "No, not with Jill Carpenter in the picture."

He gave me one of his intense looks and moved closer. Maybe he wanted to tell me something else. David hesitated as if searching for the right words. "Uh, Mitzi, uh, I, well, would you—"

He never finished his sentence. A sudden breeze stirred the branches of the great wisteria and a million purple blossoms rained down on us.

"I think we better get back, Dollface."

I don't know what he'd planned to say, but I guess it wasn't important.

****

A worried Buster waited for us on the veranda. "Mitzi, your sister is in the salon. She needs you."

Leah in trouble? We followed Buster into an opulent room with silk wall covering and a ceiling festooned with plaster-of-Paris roses. Leah sat on a gold damask divan, tears rolling down her face. Omar had an arm around her shoulder, but she refused to be consoled.

I bent over and whispered, "Leah, what's wrong?

Tell me."

She didn't speak, just pointed to a framed photograph affixed to a wall. Buster led me to it. "We took this picture nine years ago, on the last day of filming *The Southern Belle*."

Someone had shot the beautiful image on the bandstand. Dagmar had locked arms with the elder Mr. Roth, who looked dapper and proud as punch. Bobby Fayette posed next to a smiling Buster costumed in a white waiter's jacket. Willy looked very much the silent screen director in his jodhpurs and riding boots. Little Jill Carpenter stood in the front row, an impish smile lighting up her face. Uncle Baron beamed at Clarice, who was ensnared in her mother's arms. Dozens of extras, the men in tuxedos, and the ladies in gossamer gowns, surrounded them.

Leah, unable to speak, kept her index finger pointed at the photo. I looked again and finally saw what so upset her. At the very edge of the photo, I could make out a man partly hidden behind a pillar. I reached for David to keep from sliding to the floor. The corners of his mouth turned up, in a furious smile. I saw a ghost from the past—no, a dybbuk, a demon no one had exorcised.

The man in the photo was Joseph Nussbaum.

Chapter Twenty-Six
The Plot Thickens

I lost my footing. I would have crumpled onto the floor if David hadn't caught me. "Are you all right, Mitzi?"

Seeing Nussbaum's face had taken the air out me. "Thank you, I'm okay, just shocked. The fellow in the corner was the reason we left New York. Leah and I thought we'd never see his ugly puss again."

Buster and David both hovered over me, while Ida stared at the photograph in silence. Mr. Roth spoke in a hoarse whisper. "Your sister told us he went by the name Joseph Nussbaum. We knew him as Jacob Neuberger. Later, we found out the cops wanted him for arson, larceny, battery, and murder, under the name Joshua Noll."

The monster didn't even have to change the monogram on his handkerchiefs.

Ida stood in front of the photo, transfixed. "Leah told us Nussbaum, or whatever his name is, killed his wife. His copper friends in the New York police force must have helped him get away with it. The bastard came to Los Angeles, changed his name, then worked as a bodyguard for Ben's father. After the fire, we searched for that son of a bitch everywhere—Mexico, Cuba, New York. We heard he'd died. I guess he was too smart for us."

Mr. Roth slumped on the settee. "That son-of-a-bitch robbed my father blind, so I threw him out on the streets like the dog he was. When he picked himself up, he said, 'Ben, I know what you value most, and I'll take it away.' He did."

I couldn't imagine what he meant. "What did he do?"

Ida answered. "He started the fire all those years ago."

What? "But I thought Clarice's mother started it."

Mr. Roth turned his ice-blue eyes on Ida, silencing her before she answered me. "I'm going back to the hotel. I have phone calls to make."

Mr. Roth planned to return to the hotel after this? "But Mr. Roth, my Uncle Baron—"

He shushed me with a look. "There's a lot to do. You and your sister come back to the hotel with me."

By then my tears were flowing. "What about Zisel, my other sister? She's in New York and has no idea he started that fire."

He patted me on the shoulder. "Call her long distance. Tell her we'll take care of her."

Would he take care of Zisel the same way he had Clarice and Uncle Baron? I had so many questions and things to discover. I'd find out everything, no matter what.

Mr. Roth barked out a final order as I walked out the door. "Mitzi, don't think about that animal."

How could I not?

****

We returned to the Casa the next day with the knowledge Nussbaum had killed Uncle Baron. Since he was on the loose, the threat remained. The hotel's switchboard had attempted to contact Zisel, to no avail. Ida promised to send a telegram, but we were on the telephone to Zisel as soon as we arrived. Tension permeated the living room as we attempted our first coast-to-coast telephone connection. The line crackled with static, the operators failed on the early tries, but after two hours, Leah finally reached Zisel.

"Zisel, it's me, Leah. What? Hang the expense. I'm calling because we've discovered something horrible and I wanted to warn you. Can you believe it? Nussbaum is not really Nussbaum. His name is Jacob Neuberger and he's a murderer."

My eldest sister's scream flew across the wires. Leah winced and moved the receiver away from her ear. "Thank you, Zisel, for making me deaf. Nussbaum started the fire that killed our Baron."

Zisel's voice bellowed from the phone again. "My dear sister, if you don't calm down, I'll need a hearing aid. What? No! You can't talk like that. No, no, no, please, Zisel, you can't."

Leah turned to Omar. "You won't believe the oaths coming from Zisel's lips. She wants to kill Nussbaum."

Then it was Leah's turn to scream into the phone. "Stay away from him, Zisel. No, Zisel, no. You can't deal with it. No, no, no. You won't buy a gun. Mr. Roth is handling it. Stay away from him. How about a nice vacation? We'll pay for a ticket. Huh? You'll come here, of course. No, Zisel, you can't talk like that. What? Oh. Very well, if you won't come here, then it will have to be the Catskills. Uh-huh, uh-huh. Yes, she's in the room. I'll put her on."

She handed the telephone receiver to me. My hands shook since I'd never spoken coast-to-coast. Leah encouraged me with a nod.

"Hello, Zisel."

The connection wasn't the best, but I made out her every word. "Mitzi, please act calm so as not to alarm Leah. I have information on the best authority, namely that fat buttinsky, Mrs. Gorshem. Nussbaum saw one of your movies and talked about you day and night. Nobody's seen Nussbaum for days. It's as if the bastard has disappeared from the planet. I'm sure he's hiding his ugly face in shame. Tell Leah I love you both and not to worry. Goodbye, my darling."

With that, she hung up.

No one said a word at dinner. I kissed Leah goodnight, then went to my room. I had already hit the hay when I heard Leah tiptoeing out the door. I knew Omar awaited her. He'd found love, and maybe I would too if only Chick would wise up.

I thought of that night in Chick's room and how he would have kissed me if only that schmo, David Stein, hadn't stuck his nose in. After tossing and turning, I floated to New York and my last day at Barnard. It had rained overnight, and the floors were sodden with the footprints of a hundred pairs of galoshes. Hundreds of open umbrellas lined up at the entry to Barnard Hall like a grove of monstrous black tulips.

A man came out of the shadows, pulled me into his arms, and held me close. We tangoed in the rain. I looked up into my partner's face and stared into David Stein's green eyes. What the heck was wrong with me? I didn't even know how to tango.

****

When I returned to the Regal lot the next week, folks treated me like a queen. Everyone—grips, extras,

235

and even established actors—waved and smiled at me as if I were somebody.

Kids on the Lam didn't turn out to be the dark tale of the times David had envisioned. He ignored Breen all right, kept the naked girls and the saucy language, but, at Mr. Roth's insistence, added music. Chick played the ukulele, I sang, and Buster did a little shuffle. Sure, the songs may have been sappy, but I loved working with Chick. I pretended it was just the two of us and ignored Willy, Buster, an army of grips, and a battery of lighting technicians, set decorators, sound engineers, and everyone else. Sometimes, Chick looked at me as if he wanted to continue our little chat.

"Uh, Chick, were you going to say something?"

He looked around and shrugged. "Nah, baby, this isn't the time or the place."

Everything was ducky until a certain blonde floozy showed up on set and plopped her ass in a chair next to the script girl. I refused to let her get my goat because I knew everything would work out. The police would apprehend Mr. Nussbaum, Clarice's mother would tell me where she buried Uncle Baron, and Chick would realize that he couldn't live without me.

The final shots went off without a hitch and I thought things were going great until Betty managed to slip away from Jill and snuck into my dressing room after the last shot. "I don't have much time. Miss Carpenter is having lunch with Mr. Hagan and will be screaming for me soon. I wanted to warn you about her. I know she comes off as a high-hat bitch, but she ain't as bad a person as you think. Only thing is, she don't like you because of that Chick fellow. Be careful, miss." She looked toward the commissary. "I better be on my way."

With that, she rushed off.

Ida called me to the publicity department the next week. I moved through the massive chamber, past the drone of worker bees, to Ida's office.

"Mitzi, my little pearl, have you heard the news? You and Chick Hagan are now the uncrowned prince and princess of Regal Pictures. David sat down at a Moviola with one of the negative cutters and whittled out a dandy flick. Adding a couple of songs and a bit of comedy did the trick. The public will flock to it. Look at these. Aren't they fabulous?"

My publicity stills covered her desk, me in the infamous torn camisole, me posed on a chaise in a ripped slip. Me, draped in a fox stole and nothing else. Me, lounging on a polar bear rug in my scanties. Some would call them tawdry and salacious, but if a girl could look glamorous half-naked, I did.

Everything was aces—that is, until…

Ida placed a motherly arm around my shoulder. "Kid, I have to talk to you. There's been a bit of unsavory gossip about Chick's behavior in Carlisle."

Aha! Someone must have spilled the beans about the "Turkish" cigarettes. Still, marijuana was legal, after all, so there shouldn't be a problem.

Ida's demeanor suddenly changed from jolly to grave. "Mitzi, I've got to give it to you straight. Chick may be dashing, but he's not the fellow for you. We can't have an innocent undone by a rogue."

Not her too. Was everyone against me being with Chick? She took my hands in hers. "I'm afraid Ben is concerned, Mitzi dear."

I wanted to run out of the room screaming, *Stay out*

of it. It's my life!

She continued the lecture. "Ben has taken a fatherly interest in you and doesn't want to see you compromised in any way."

"Some father. He didn't seem concerned about me walking around his studio half naked." Once again my future with Chick dissolved before my eyes. "Tell Mr. Roth not to worry. Chick would never give me a tumble."

Ida fiddled with her cigarette holder. "Not according to the grapevine. The guy has expressed, shall we say, an earthy interest in you."

"He has? Honest?"

Her expression told me that my response didn't thrill her. "Watch your step, Mitzi. I know you think I'm an old fuddy-duddy and I don't know a thing about love, but I do. I assure you, you'd rather hear it from me than from Ben."

"Ida, Mr. Roth doesn't own me."

"Oh, yes, he does. You belong to him, body and soul. He's a benign master, and you could do a lot worse, but remember, you are the property of Regal Pictures."

Time to take a powder. "I have to go, Ida."

I had made it halfway out the door when she called out to me. "Mitzi, while you were in Carlisle, a British fellow phoned here from the Hotel Hollywood. He said they found an envelope addressed to a 'Miss Vanderbilt.' The guy didn't know where to locate you until he recognized you from the screen. He assured my secretary you'd be interested."

****

My heart raced like crazy when I reached the Red

Car tracks. A British fellow phoned from the Hotel Hollywood, and I'd discover what old Clyde had found. A trolley heading east toward Hollywood stopped, but before I climbed on board, I heard a horn honking.

"Mitzi, get in."

David sat behind the wheel of his Cadillac. From the way he scowled at me when I slid next to him, you'd think I'd done something wrong. "Dollface, what are you doing on the streetcar?"

Golly, he could be obtuse. "I always take the streetcar. That's how I get around."

He looked at me as if I had three heads. "You have an auto, don't you?"

Honestly, someone needed to set the guy straight. "Yes, I do. It's called the Red Car, it's on a track, and the chauffeur rings the bell, 'ding, ding.' I ride it like everybody else in Los Angeles."

He shook his head. "Well, that won't do, not for an up-and-comer like you. You need a snappy little roadster that will turn heads. You know how to drive, don't you?"

David would bring up a sore spot. "Yes, of course I can drive. Well, sort of. I learned on one of those old tin lizzies, the kind you have to crank up. I almost broke my wrist starting the engine. But, if you must know, I haven't mastered the art of shifting and talking at the same time."

He snorted. I saw a hint of a smile and didn't like it. "If you're going to laugh at me, drop me off at the next corner, please."

The smile disappeared. "No laughing, I promise. I'd be honored to take you wherever you want to go."

Since he already knew about Uncle Baron, I gave

him the lowdown on our way to Hollywood Boulevard. "Well, I'm heading to the Hotel Hollywood. Uncle Baron once lived there. When Leah and I first came to Los Angeles, I went there looking for information."

"I'm impressed, Miss Schector. In addition to being a great singer, musician, and actress, you're also a regular Nancy Drew."

He may have been able to talk and drive at the same time, a real talent as far as I was concerned, but I found his Nancy Drew analogy exasperating. "Thank you for comparing me to a girl sleuth in a children's book, Mr. Stein. It might interest you to know I've read all of Conan Doyle, and I know a thing or two about deductive reasoning."

Not even a flicker of a smile from him, so I continued talking.

"I went to the hotel and met an old fellow who'd worked there since Moses wore short pants. He knew Uncle Baron and had even met Pops. The old guy said the previous owner had hidden some papers before she passed away, and he knew where they were. Then he phoned to say I'd be interested in something he dug up, only—"

He turned onto Hollywood Boulevard, and the Chinese Theater loomed in the distance. "Only what? What, Mitzi?"

Just thinking about Clyde made me want to start bawling. "He was a sick old bird and kicked the bucket before he could give me whatever he'd found. I thought I'd lost everything forever, but now it seems I haven't."

We were fast approaching the hotel, and I remembered my disguise. "There's something else, and it's very important. If the desk clerk calls me Miss

Vanderbilt, don't blink an eye. I was incognito."

The fink started laughing. I chose to ignore him.

****

David and I entered the lobby just as the string quartet ripped into "The Blue Danube Waltz." Two little girls, graceful in organdy summer dresses, danced together. The English desk clerk stood at the front desk, and his face lit up the moment I walked up to him.

"Miss Charles, how wonderful to see you again!"

How fascinating that a modicum of fame had changed his tune. He nearly swooned when we got to the desk. He was still oily, but now he behaved like a fawning toady.

"Miss Charles, or should I say, Miss Vanderbilt? From the moment you walked in that day, I knew you were a young lady of breeding."

He looked up at David and simpered, "And this young gentleman is?"

David smiled, extended his hand, and spoke like a real New York aristocrat. "I'm Miss Vanderbilt's fiancée. The name's Rockefeller."

The desk clerk pumped David's hand so enthusiastically I feared he'd break it.

"Mr. Rockefeller, I am so honored, sir!"

He handed me a large envelope with "Miss Vanderbilt" scrawled on it, and then slid an embossed leather book toward us. "I wonder if you both would be good enough to sign my autograph album."

David and I had great fun playing two goy swells to the hilt. Smiles frozen on our faces, we posed for photographs with the staff. Once we got back to David's motorcar, however, my hands shook so violently that I couldn't open the envelope. I handed it to him.

"I can't. Please, David, tell me what's in it."

He tore it open, pulled out an official-looking document, and I watched as he read it. Minutes went by before he slumped against the running board. "Wow. You have to take a gander at this." David shoved the certificate into my hands.

I'm sure my jaw dropped to the garage floor, but somehow I managed to speak. "It says Clarice Dumont, age nineteen, married Baron Meyer Schector, age nineteen, on the tenth of April 1923. Ben and Samuel Roth were witnesses. Clarice Dumont was my aunt?"

"Yes."

He opened the Caddie's door, and I slipped in next to him. He didn't fire up the engine right away.

"I could use your help, David."

The crumb feigned surprise. "You want my help? Will wonders never cease?"

"Sarcasm is unnecessary and quite unbecoming, Mr. Stein. You can be difficult, but you're a man of the world and you know about these things. Ida took us to the cemetery where they buried Clarice. Her mother brings flowers to her grave on the twenty-fifth of every month, maybe because Clarice died on April twenty-fifth. I want to talk to her. Would you come with me when I do? Carlotta Dumont might have been a witch and Nussbaum's pal, but I've got to find out what happened to my uncle's body."

He shook his head. "Mitzi, I don't know, a woman like that probably wouldn't talk."

"But maybe she'd listen if I told her how much my family has suffered all these years. My bubbe died grieving over Uncle Baron's death. Pops went to his grave wondering where his brother's final resting place was. If I begged her on bended knee, don't you think she might tell me where he's buried?"

I couldn't keep the tears away and bawled like a baby. David pulled out a fancy monogrammed handkerchief and wiped my eyes. At that moment, I knew the Icebox had died.

"Doll, if you ask her like that, she can't turn you away. It would be my honor to come with you. Do we have a date for next month, Mitzi?"

Maybe he could be a cold fish, but I knew he was a man of his word.

"Yes, only don't tell Leah. She'll worry if she knows. Promise you won't."

"I promise, baby, cross my heart and hope to die."

Just hearing him say the words made me feel a million times better.

"Thank you for all you did today, David. Well, I guess we should go home now." For once, he'd been a brick, and I had to make it up to him. "Say, if you don't have plans for this evening, maybe you'd like to break bread with us. Leah is always happy to see you and so is Omar. If we're lucky, he might play his saxophone. He used to play in a jazz band."

He looked me square in the face. "What about you? Would you be happy to see me too?"

"I invited you, didn't I?"

For the first time I noticed the golden flecks in his eyes. David Stein was one handsome fellow.

Chapter Twenty-Seven
The Plot Thickens Even More!

Leah hadn't stopped scrutinizing the marriage certificate from the moment David handed it to her. She examined every inch of the document, threw it down in frustration, then picked it up again. In fact, she became so engrossed she paid no attention to anything else. For the first time since we'd met him, Omar appeared annoyed with her.

"Leah, we have a guest."

She looked up, embarrassed. "David, please excuse my rudeness, but this is so unexpected. Uncle Baron married Clarice Dumont? I'll have to ask Mr. Roth about this."

David reddened. "Leah, I wouldn't do that if I were you."

When Leah gave him the Look, I knew she meant business. "But I have to ask him about it or we'll never know the truth."

He shrugged. "Nobody talks to Ben about Clarice. He'll think you're spying on him and blow his stack. If he does, don't say I didn't warn you."

Leah spoke, but not to anyone in particular. "Maybe we don't have to mention how we found out. If Mr. Roth asks, we can say we discovered it with some of Pops' old papers." She thought about it for a second. "But that would be a lie, wouldn't it?"

Tears of frustration rolled down her cheeks. "You don't understand how important this is, David. It's about our family. I won't let Mr. Roth push us around."

I looked to Omar to intercede, but he walked into the kitchen without a word. Leah had made up her mind, and that ended it. Three hours later, we dined on the world's best chicken paprika, but the conversation centered on Baron's marriage. David was still mulling over the situation when I walked him to his automobile.

"You think we should keep quiet, don't you, David?"

He paused for a moment then nodded. "Yes, I do. You've never seen Ben in a real rage. He's impossible."

Maybe he was right, but as Leah said, it involved our family. "I wish Pops was around. He'd know what to do. I'm so confused."

Perhaps my nerves got the better of me, but for some reason I began playing with David's lapels. It couldn't be called flirting, but a fellow like David Stein didn't take anything lightly. I realized what I was doing and pulled my hands away, but he grabbed them back, and held on for the longest time. We looked at each other without speaking. After what seemed an eternity, he released me, jumped into his automobile, and sped away. I felt the familiar warmth between my legs and walked back to our apartment, confused.

****

Leah and I had been nervous Nellies for most of the week, waiting for Mr. Roth to fit us into his schedule. Finally, we got the call. Since he expected his employees to always look their best, we wore our snazziest outfits. We sat outside his office, listening to him howl at his brother in New York. With his voice, I bet the whole Eastern seaboard got an earful.

"Sam, the next time I'm in New York I'm gonna knock that putz's block off. Huh? Mae West? She's talking to Paramount? About what? Huh? They want her for movies? That broad's forty if she's a day. Besides, Will Hays and his hayseed cronies will blow a gasket over her shenanigans. Oh, is that so? Then you find me another fat-assed blonde who talks dirty."

With Leah's nerves already on edge, Mr. Roth's screaming didn't help. She turned to a secretary with bright red, finger-waved hair. "Excuse me, but why is Mr. Roth in such a foul mood?"

The girl looked at her, confused. "Foul mood? What do you mean? Foul mood is when he throws the telephone out the window. Everything's swell today."

We heard a telephone receiver slammed down, and then Mr. Roth yelled from his office. "Come on in, why don't you? I don't have all day."

Not exactly a warm invitation, but we entered his office anyway. Mr. Roth sat at his desk, smiling, impeccably groomed as usual in a double-breasted suit, his white carnation boutonnière in place. Perhaps his secretary was right. He gestured to two chairs in front of his desk.

"Ladies, take a seat, take a seat."

Leah and I had decided I'd do the talking. We figured since Mr. Roth considered me a kid, he might not yell at me, or at least not as loud.

"Well, Mr. Roth it's like this—"

He interrupted before I could say another word. "Girls, you couldn't have come at a better time. I've got something to talk to you about. I know I said musical pictures stink, and they do, but we've hired some of the sound wizards from Western Electric. Guess what? They tell me that musicals will be the next new thing. If Metro and RKO are planning to make musicals, Regal isn't going to be left out."

Leah gave my hand a squeeze, a signal for me to speak up. "That's wonderful news, Mr. Roth, but you see—"

He glared at me. "Of course I'll have to deduct the cost of your dancing lessons from your salary, but that's fair, isn't it?"

Dancing lessons? "Excuse me, Mr. Roth. I don't dance."

He turned his head from side to side, baffled as if I'd spoken to him in Chinese.

"What do you mean you don't dance? You're a kid, aren't you? Kids are crazy about dancing. I hired this guy, a Broadway hoofer who claims he could teach a bull moose to tap. A little soft shoe, a time step, whatever it takes to get your caboose in gear. Slap a big smile on your kisser while you're at it. I'll give you a couple of months to polish up your dancing. I really believe in you, kid. You're aces. Now scram."

Leah and I glanced at each other. Then she took over. "Mr. Roth, Ben, it's a wonderful offer, but Mitzi is a singer, not a dancer." She threw her shoulders back and went into elegant lady mode. "To be honest, tap dancing is kind of vulgar, especially for such a cultured girl."

Mr. Roth jumped up from his chair. "What do you mean, vulgar? It's the rage. The public pays good money to see it. What is it with you, lady? You think your sister is too hoity-toity to dance for her supper? Ingrate! 'He who eats my bread sings my song.' Now, get out."

I never thought I'd hear Pops' words used against us. I took Leah by the hand and we left.

What a horrible day it turned out to be. Mr. Roth had gone into a rage, we were still in the dark about Uncle Baron's marriage to Clarice Dumont, Nussbaum was on the loose, and now I had to learn to tap dance.

Mr. Roth had so upset Leah she took to her bed with a dreadful headache, and Omar wouldn't be home for hours. Life stunk. Then a light bulb went off in my brain. I had a marvelous idea: potato latkes. I hate to toot my own horn, but even latke connoisseurs considered mine the best: light, crispy, and golden brown. The applesauce and sour cream were cooling in the refrigerator, and I'd put a brisket on to braise that morning. I set to work grating potatoes and chopping onions.

I'd just pulled out the skillet when someone knocked at our door. David stood at the threshold, stroking the brim of his hat. I felt the color rising to my face. He cut a very fine figure in his classy double-breasted suit, terribly suave, a striking fellow indeed. What the heck? Was I mooning over David Stein again? Perish the thought.

"Hello, David. Won't you come in?" I took his fedora and placed it on a chair. "You were right about Mr. Roth. He has a horrible temper. We didn't even get a chance to ask Mr. Roth about Uncle Baron. I might even be out of a job because I don't know how to tap dance."

I hadn't cracked a joke, yet David burst out into laughter.

"Everything's in the crapper and you think it's

funny? Who am I, Fred Allen? I'm so glad my life in ruins amuses you, David Stein. Maybe I should chug-a-lug a little cyanide while I'm at it. I'm sure my convulsions would be a real kick in the head."

He laughed even louder, and I wanted to knock his block off. "Doll, Ben flew off the handle because that's the way he is. He's really very fond of you and Leah."

How confusing. "Fond of us? He sure has a strange way of showing it."

Still David's smile beamed such warmth I felt a million times better. "Yeah, well, that's Ben, all right, and don't say you weren't warned."

Those green eyes sparkled, and his good looks struck me once again. "Listen, we're raising both your salaries and paying for those tap lessons."

"Zowie! Can you image that? Mr. Roth blew his stack, then gave us a raise, all in one afternoon!"

He had an intense expression on his face. "Say, Mitzi, I was wondering if you'd have dinner with me. But don't feel any pressure to say yes."

He wanted to step out with me? He'd probably take me to one of those swell places on the Sunset Strip where he took Miss Vassar.

"Gee, I'd love to, honest I would, but I can't leave Leah alone. And besides, I'm making dinner. I was about to start the latkes."

He moved a bit closer. "Latkes? I haven't had latkes since the last time I was in New York."

I couldn't be rude to the bearer of such good tidings, could I? "You're more than welcome to join us. Latkes are one of my specialties."

"You cook too? Is there no end to your talents? I'd be honored."

I must confess the next few hours were golden. Omar came home and poured chilled "medicinal" wine, David set the dinner table, and by the time Leah joined us, things were quite gay. Our guest dug into the potato pancakes and declared, "Miss Schector, these are the best latkes I've ever eaten."

Of course, I wasn't surprised. People have hailed my latkes far and wide. Leah had a bright grin on her face throughout dinner, and I knew why. I hated to disappoint her, but a ladies' man like David Stein could never be my beau. Still, I have to admit, things had gone quite swimmingly. We talked about everything from Edith Wharton to Franklin Roosevelt, who, I discovered, he grudgingly admired. "Movie folks, at least producers, think the guy's bad for business. I don't."

At the end of the evening, David insisted I walk him to his auto. Someone had parked a bright blue Ford Roadster with a cream-colored top and gleaming chrome wheels in front of the Casa. He stopped at the car, a huge grin on his face.

"Golly, David, that's a beautiful automobile, but I'm sorry that you got rid of your Cadillac."

He pointed across the street. "No, there's my car. This one's for you, Dollface."

"For me? You're kidding. This is mine? Honest?"

I tried to be nonchalant but failed miserably. "I love it, even if Henry Ford hates Jews."

David flicked a bit of invisible dust off the hood. "Ben bought this little honey for his wife, but it wasn't grand enough for her. It's been sitting in his garage for weeks, and I asked him if Regal's new musical star should be seen riding the Red Car. He said, 'Hell, no.'

It's his way of saying he's sorry."

He handed me the keys. "Maybe you'd like to take her for a spin?"

I shook my head. "I know you'll laugh every time I put the car in gear."

"Bet I wouldn't."

Our conversation suddenly stopped. We gazed into each other's faces for a long moment. Yes, David Stein was a very handsome fellow, indeed.

****

"And a five, six, seven, eight, hey, you in the yellow shorts, yeah, you, pick up those feet! You, Mr. Big-Stuff in the second row, you call that dancing? Well, it ain't!"

A colored pianist called Fingers pounded out a tune on an old upright. The metallic cadence of forty pairs of tap shoes kept perfect time as they beat out the rhythm. Like the rest of the budding chorines, I'd dressed for battle in a cotton blouse, shorts, ankle socks, and tap shoes. Next, I mastered dance lingo and tossed around terms like the "wing," the "grapevine," "buffalo," and "Irish." Most importantly, after hours of practice I'd finally managed a decent "flap-ball-change." After a few more hours of torture, I could smile and execute a time step at the same time.

Mr. Roth had one of the older buildings where they used to shoot silent dramas rechristened the Regal Dance Academy. The place had no ventilation, and our skulls baked beneath the glass skylight. But ratty as it was, the plank floors were ideal for dancing. Regal put every female extra with a shapely figure and pretty face in bondage to the dancing master, Rollo Palmer.

Perhaps Rollo didn't use a bullwhip on his dancers,

but he was a slave driver all the same. He preyed on the desperation of the kids, some of whom were as young as thirteen. We all needed jobs, but Mr. Palmer didn't make it any easier on those of us who'd never danced before.

Mr. Palmer showered his wrath on all and sundry but saved his nastiest comments for any dancer who hinted of arrogance. One in particular, a swarthy fellow with brilliantined hair and a sinister air about him, seemed to annoy him no end. I'd heard he'd been a chorus boy in New York who'd come to Los Angeles to make gangster movies.

"You, Vaselino, with the greasy hair, stop looking at your feet! You might have been hot stuff on Broadway, but they'd skin you alive in Harlem."

Imagine thirty sweating dancers, the girls in shorts, the boys in cotton pants and undershirts, all crammed together in an oven. Two girls collapsed from the heat before Rollo finally brought in fans and tubs of ice to cool us off. He bellyached the whole time. "A bunch of softies, that's what you are. None of you would last a day in New York."

Despite the heat, the smell, and the blistering sun, something magical happened when a group of dancers tapped their hearts out. We were all troopers, especially Edna. She'd undergone the Factor treatment and now sported bright red hair and plucked eyebrows. What she lacked in natural gifts she more than made up for with hard work and enthusiasm.

I was one of the lucky ones, light enough on my feet to convince an unsuspecting public I could dance. "Smile, kid, keep smiling."

I'm sure I looked like a yutz, but miracle of

miracles, Rollo approved. "Hey, kid, I like that shoulder thing. I grew up on the Lower East Side and—" He looked around the barn and whispered, "My name is really Reuben Finkelstein, but keep it to yourself. When you've grown up on Yiddish music, the feeling is in you, and there's nothing you can do about it."

Rollo's words inspired me to put those rhythms into my dancing. Funny thing, the more comfortable I got with tap, the faster the time flew. Sometimes I'd pretend to tap through the old neighborhood with all the old grandmothers and grandfathers in rhythm with me. Practicing tap became like practicing the piano and stopped being a chore I hated.

That day I was alone in the dance barn trying a variation on a step when someone called my name.

"Mitzi!"

The voice belonged to Jill Carpenter. Pretending she didn't exist wouldn't work, so I went the polite route.

"Hello, Miss Carpenter. If you're looking for Chick, he left a while ago."

She came over to me, a smile brightening her beautiful puss. "I wasn't looking for Chick. It's you I want, sweetheart. You don't like me any more than I like you, so drop the Alice-in-Wonderland crap. And, by the way, the name's Jill, so you can dump the 'Miss Carpenter,' too."

Without warning, the smile disappeared and we went nose to nose.

"Listen, sister. I'm the big cheese here, and don't you forget it. It doesn't matter to me if you can sing and dance, or even if David Stein is screwy over you. I'm the one who's been slaving in movies since I was four. I helped make this dump, and no one's going to take my place!"

For months Jill Carpenter had treated me like something she scraped off the bottom of her shoe, but she'd gone too far this time. I'd give her an earful all right.

"Listen, Goldilocks. I don't want anything you have. All I'm trying to do is keep my job. Times are lousy—there's a Depression going on, or haven't you noticed?"

Tears welled in her eyes. If it had been anyone else in the world, I would have felt sorry for them, but not her.

"Yeah, I've noticed. Times are always lousy for me. Do you know what it's like to work like a dog so your mother can spend every nickel on booze and fancy men? Thank God for Benny. When I turned eighteen, Ben arranged for Bobby Fayette to marry me, and I threw the bitch out on her ear."

I'd seen the movie magazine photos of Bobby staring at her photo, pining after his foolish young wife. Don't tell me their fairy-tale romance was another big fat lie.

"Didn't you love Bobby?"

She broke out in empty laughter. "You are a dumb cluck, aren't you? Haven't you noticed Bobby is a pansy? Some sailor boy he picked up threatened to spill the beans to the press if Regal didn't pay. Benny couldn't take a chance, so he asked me to marry him. I got a swell mink coat as thanks for getting Bobby out of a jam. Marrying him got me out of one too."

Her face twisted, from frustration or pain, I couldn't really tell. Jill blabbed on, and I kept my lips zipped. "I was Benny's favorite before you came on the scene, but now it's Mitzi this and Mitzi that. Well, I won't have it."

She dropped one final word of wisdom before she turned away. "Oh, and as for Chick, forget about getting your paws on him. He's mine."

With that she walked out. My anger got the best of me, but I didn't cry. I sure would have loved to give her a swift kick in the rump, but what would that accomplish? He's mine. What was he, her hot water bottle?

After that little incident, I made sure I drove my little blue roadster to the lot every single day. Of course, motoring four blocks didn't really make much sense, but I had my reasons. I wanted to improve my driving skills, and learn to shift and talk at the same time. But I had a far more important plan. One fine day I'd run it into Jill Carpenter and bounce the bleached slut to the moon.

Chapter Twenty-Eight
Cinderella at the Ball

Regal's announcement about celebrating its twentieth anniversary on Friday, August 26, 1932, caused a minor sensation. The big shindig would take place three weeks after my twentieth birthday. Everybody in tap class buzzed over the big news that the studio was holding the party at the Cocoanut Grove and would be outfitting the dancers in gowns and tuxes. Everyone who worked for Regal received an invitation, but all I cared about was that Chick, my one and only, would be there.

I lived for the days Chick strutted into class, his glorious smile flashing under the lights as he showed up every dancer in the joint. The guy was a natural hoofer and picked up any step Rollo threw at him. Sometimes Chick would twirl me around in front of everyone as if I were his girl. "Take a gander at those gams! We should step out some time, baby."

If Chick really asked me to step out with him, my tap steps wouldn't go over big on a ballroom floor. I couldn't rumba or tango to save my life. Leah insisted on teaching me a few steps. "What good does it do to have a sister who worked in a dance hall if she can't teach you anything?"

I'd spent part of the afternoon perfecting my box step when David poked his head into the barn.

"Whatcha doing, baby?"

I kept dancing away. "Practicing for the big party at the Cocoanut Grove."

"That's a very good idea. It's going to be sweet. Everyone's coming, and the house band is Eduardo Durant, really hot, so there'll be lots of dancing— rumba, foxtrot, tango—"

I couldn't fib to him. "Pops taught me a smashing waltz when I was eleven, but we never got to other dances. Leah is going to teach me the rumba and tango, but I've been practicing the foxtrot on my own."

He stood in silence, his arms folded while I danced away. His scrutiny got on my nerves. "What are you looking at?"

My expression and clumsy moves must have told him everything. He shook his head and walked over to the Victrola.

"I knew it. You've never really danced with a fellow, only other young ladies, right? I bet you even lead, like those Radcliffe girlies. We'll get your dancing sorted out. Come on, I'll show you."

He went through the stack of records, found one. "Bing Crosby will do."

Then he turned to me, his arms opened wide. I didn't move, and we were at what you might call a standoff.

"Mitzi, how can I teach you how to dance with you standing over there?" He laughed when I shook my head. "Are you afraid I'll get fresh or something? I wouldn't dare after you threatened to buy a gun and shoot me into a piece of Swiss cheese."

I stayed where I was. "My words were just for effect."

"You could've fooled me, baby, especially the part about laughing all the way to the electric chair."

"They don't have the electric chair in California. They hang people."

He broke out into laughter. "Come over here."

I ramped up my courage and walked over to him. We stared at each other. I felt the heat rising to my face and got tingly all over. David smelled of lemon soap and peppermint. When he took me in his arms, my heart started racing. I noticed a dimple when he smiled. I found it easy as pie to follow someone as light on his feet as David. We moved from two-step to rumba. I bet my dancing wasn't nearly as bad as he thought it would be. "All right, sister, now we'll dip."

David placed his hand on the small of my back and nearly lowered me to the floor. It felt like the most graceful dip in the history of ballroom dancing. He pulled me back into his arms, and we glided cheek to cheek as if we'd been doing it all our lives.

Our lesson ended, yet David held me so close I could feel his heart beating. Maybe he wanted to get fresh—maybe I wouldn't have minded too much. But he didn't get amorous. Instead, he bowed and kissed my hand like a real gent.

"Doll, anytime you want a repeat lesson, just let me know."

With that, he walked off, a big grin on his face. Did I have bad breath or something?

****

An hour later, I hurried to Wardrobe, still questioning my encounter with David. Why did I let the guy get under my skin?

"Mitzi, hey, Mitzi!" A voice calling my name

wrenched me out of my reverie. My ticker began pounding like a bass drum when I recognized the voice—not Goldilocks, but Chick, my Chick. Be still my heart. He looked even more dashing than usual, in a white double-breasted suit. He flashed his million-dollar smile and pulled me into an alcove.

"Baby, I've wanted to talk to you alone for the longest time, but with Ben and the Icebox breathing down my neck, I've been scared to talk to anything in a skirt. Boy, did Ben dress me down about my little shindig in Carlisle. I never thought I'd hear the end of it."

Who could have ratted him out? "Did David, I mean Mr. Stein, tip off Mr. Roth?"

He dimpled, and I fell even more in love. "Nah, it wasn't Stein, but he sure gave me a heck of a tongue-lashing about the kids smoking those, uh, Turkish cigarettes with you in the room. The hotel manager bellyached to Ben about the noise and certain young ladies."

He moved a bit closer. "Mitzi, all this time I've been hoping that maybe we could finish our conversation."

I felt the warmth inching up to my face when he whispered, "I saw you tied to the bed in *The Golden Falcon* and thought about the two of us together. Does that shock you?"

Yes, shocked and excited me. "Uh, golly, Chick, I don't know what to say."

He moved closer. "Say you'll step out with me sometime."

Chick wanted me to step out with him? "I'd love to, Chick."

He chortled, then breathed in my ear. I felt the heat moving south toward my private parts. As Mrs. LaRue would say, "It felt wicked good."

"Your sister doesn't like me much, does she? How about this? We'll meet at the big Cocoanut Grove party. Since everybody has to be there, she can't say anything about us spending time together, can she?"

My heart began hammering so hard I thought I might faint on the spot.

"What about Miss Carpenter?"

Chick looked around and moved a bit closer. "Jill? Don't worry about her. We can't let a little fling come between us, can we? I want to finish our conversation, but now, how about a little preview?"

Then he did it. He leaned over and kissed me. I'd imagined his lips would be soft like a baby's tush, but they were chapped. I hadn't prepared myself for his tobacco breath, or the faint smell of whiskey lingering on his tongue. Still, none of it bothered me as much as the undeniable truth, one I found quite confusing: I felt nothing, zero, bubkes. No electricity, no passion, just a pleasant smooch from a handsome guy who needed a Sen-Sen.

Chick ignored my bewilderment, took my hand, kissed it, turned it over, then stared at my palm. "Baby, has anyone ever told you that you've got one heck of a love line?" He began nibbling my fingers. "I think you better go now, Mitzi. I just might take a bite out of something else."

I took off before I embarrassed myself, but something made me look back. Chick lit a cigarette, but his eyes were still on me. Dying would have to wait, I'd faint first. I forgot about his tobacco breath and chapped lips. We'd try it again, and next time would be better.

I'm sure that my feet never touched the ground as I floated toward the Wardrobe Department. My dream would soon come true, and I could barely contain myself. What difference did it make if Chick stank at smooching? We were finally going to finish our conversation.

****

That evening at dinner, I mentioned the celebration to Leah and Omar. "I hear it's going to be a big shindig, and everyone will be there." Leah looked at Omar, then averted her face. "Have fun, Mitzi. I'm not going."

I couldn't believe her. "Leah, everyone is going. It would be unprofessional if you don't show up. You're expected."

She shook her head. "No, everyone is not going. I hear they didn't invite Buster Sweet because colored people aren't welcome in the Cocoanut Grove." She clasped Omar's hand. "What about Omar? I'm not setting foot in that place without him."

How could I have forgotten about Omar? Boy, what a pickle. Leah wouldn't go without him, and despite wanting to meet up with Chick, I couldn't celebrate without my sister. Still, there was one person who had everyone's ear.

The next morning, the disarray in David's office shocked me. He'd tacked sketches of set designs and costumes haphazardly on an easel in the center of the room. Tossed scripts sat willy-nilly on top of his usually well-ordered desk.

"Hello, David. I hope I'm not disturbing you."

He stood, sans jacket and tie, his vest unbuttoned. I hadn't seen him looking so informal since Carlisle.

David didn't smile, just gazed at me intently before pointing to a chair. "To what do I owe this unexpected pleasure?"

The Icebox had returned.

"Well, David, Ida told me I'm expected to attend Mr. Roth's celebration, the one at the Cocoanut Grove. She said everybody has to be there, but, well, Leah won't go, and I don't want to attend without her."

It might have been late July, but when he spoke the temperature in the room dropped by thirty degrees. "Not a problem. She's already on the guest list."

Then, silence. He wasn't making this easy. "It's a bit trickier. You see, well, she won't go without Omar, and the Cocoanut Grove is touchy about serving people of color. She said Buster Sweet won't be there either."

He didn't say a word, just moved to the edge of his desk, his eyes never leaving my face.

"If Leah won't go, then I won't. I know it's silly. I'll turn twenty next week, but Leah's my sister. Since you're such an important fellow, I thought maybe you could smooth things out. I have a swell gown I've been dying to wear."

He leaned back into his chair, his lips twisted into a wry smile. "I assure you, Buster will be there. He helped build this studio, and Ben hasn't forgotten him. You want me to fix it so Omar can get in? No problem, I can do that. I'll speak to Leah, too."

I'm sure folks heard my sigh of relief all the way to Beverly Hills, but with David Stein, you get a dose of vinegar with the honey. He stood and sauntered over to me, his lips spread in a chilly smile, his movements like a panther about to strike. "I know why you want to go, Mitzi. It doesn't have a thing to do with Buster, your sister, that 'swell gown,' or Regal, for that matter, does it? I saw you with Chick yesterday."

"You saw us?"

The way he was glaring at me, you'd think I'd rubbed out his grandmother.

"Yes, I did. You let him kiss you, didn't you? That sappy goy with his sweet talk and ukulele. You're planning to meet him at the Grove. That's it, isn't it?"

I couldn't handle another lecture. "What possible difference could it make to you if Chick shows up? I know you think he's a dolt, and I'm just a dumb kid, but I want to go to that party. I've never been to a nightclub. I've never been anywhere, except summer camp in the Catskills. Just for one night, I don't want to think about Nussbaum, Clarice, or Uncle Baron. Maybe things are looking up for me. Chick told me that his fling with Jill Carpenter is over."

David moved close enough for me to feel his breath on my cheek. My nerves had gotten the better of me, and I started to giggle. Funny, he gave me the creeps, but the feeling thrilled me.

"So you want to go to the party to be with Chick? Well, isn't that ducky? Don't worry. I'll take care of everything."

I stood and turned to go, but he pulled me back to him. "Maybe you and that pill will finish your 'conversation,' maybe not, but if the whole thing blows up in your face, don't blame me."

It took all my strength not to scream, but I managed to control myself. "Why do you hate him so much, David? What did he do to you?"

He released me and sat back on edge of his desk. "He reminds me of every fraternity schmuck I've ever

met, with their boolah-boolah crap. I know the type—
everything comes easy to them. They live off their
charm."

"Yeah, that's something you never have to worry
about."

At that moment I wished I could have taken back
my words. "I'm sorry, David, I shouldn't have said
that."

"Say what you like, doll. I can take whatever you
dish out. I know you get mad at me, but at least we
have things in common, like our roots, the way we
think about life. Guess what—we can talk about all
kinds of things. Tell me, what the hell do you two
converse about? *The Katzenjammer Kids*? Oh, yeah, I
forgot. He likes *Maggie and Jiggs* too. Does that chump
have an opinion on anything other than playing the
ukulele and getting girls in the sack?"

How I hated David at that moment. "So what if
Chick can't discuss great literature and world events?
What does that matter? He doesn't have a mean bone in
his body, unlike others I could name. He has feelings
for me, real feelings, regardless of what you say. Just
when I think you and I are friends, you say something
that ruins it. Good afternoon, David."

David called to me, but I dashed out of his office.
Thankfully, he didn't follow. He remained on my mind
for the rest of the day. I'd circled August the twenty-
fifth on my calendar, a week away. Since the thought of
confronting Carlotta Dumont alone terrified me, we
were supposed to face her together. I depended on
David, and he knew it. How could he be so cruel?

****

The next day I ran down to Wardrobe with Zisel's

crimson gown for Al's inspection. He scrutinized every inch of fabric and every stitch. "I know this cut. It's from Madeleine Vionnet's Paris design house. We all steal from her, but you can't duplicate her work. C'mon, put it on."

When I did as he asked, he shook his head. "Take off your brassiere. You don't need it with that firm young body. I can see the lines of your panties, so forget about wearing any."

I'd worn clinging bias-cut gowns before, but only in front of Rose and her assistant, so it didn't matter. Frolicking around a crowded nightclub with nothing beneath my gown was something else.

My face must have revealed what I couldn't say. The great Alexandre looked at me like I was a potato bug he planned to squash.

"Yeah, how else can I fit a dress on you? What is it? You think I'm gonna try to get you in bed or something? Don't flatter yourself, sister. I've undressed the most beautiful dames in the world and never laid a finger on any of them."

His lip curled in a sneer. "Why am I surrounded by prudes? If you're too ashamed to show off your body, why the hell did you bring me this gown in the first place? You're going to a Hollywood party, not your cousin's bar mitzvah."

I decided to throw caution to the wind. No underwear for this gal. Al put some finishing touches on the gown, and then I pinched a pair of matching silk pumps, a slave bracelet, and some swell gold earrings inset with red glass. I'd wear the frock no matter what. I couldn't wait to laugh in David Stein's fat face when he saw me in it.

****

The next week, my twentieth birthday came and went. Ida arranged a small party on set, and David stayed away. I worked like a pack mule for the next couple of weeks, shooting a short in the morning, dancing all afternoon. For some reason, Chick had skipped most of the dance practices, but I knew by the time we met at the Cocoanut Grove I'd have mastered the rumba and the tango. Most importantly, I'd wear my crimson gown.

Chapter Twenty-Nine
The Cocoanut Grove

Zisel,

You'll never believe what is happening. Regal Pictures is having a huge soiree at the Cocoanut Grove, and I'm going! Leah and her special friend, Omar, are going too. (Omar has hinted about a disguise, and I'll give you the lowdown later.)

I've been polishing my rumba and tango. Can you imagine? I'll finally wear that scrumptious crimson number you sent me. Leah found a sophisticated, très chic gown in Regal's vast wardrobe.

A special someone promised me he'd be there, and I'm keeping my fingers crossed.

Your ever-loving Mitzi

****

Arcs of light crisscrossed the horizon as limousines snaked down Wilshire Boulevard. The Ambassador Hotel loomed in the distance, the gateway to an oasis of enchantment, the Cocoanut Grove.

Our driver parked, opened the passenger door, and bowed slightly when Omar alighted, looking every bit the Turkish diplomat. The get-up was David's idea. Although I still considered him a fink, boy, was it a pip! Omar wore white tie and tails, a brilliant red satin sash slung from his right shoulder to his left hip. He topped it off with a monocle and false mustache, all courtesy of

Regal Pictures Wardrobe and Make-Up. The fez belonged to him.

Omar gave his arm to Leah, resplendent in a black satin gown with a plunging back. The wizards at Factors had primped her, and she wore a fabulous diamond necklace—maybe not really diamonds, but definitely the finest paste.

The chauffeur held the door open, and I stepped into the warm California air. Like Leah, I'd received the glamour treatment, but refused a coating of Mr. Factor's gloss. Tonight a special someone would be sampling my lips. My jacket concealed the daring lines of the gown, but I planned the great unveiling for later in the evening. I couldn't wait to see the expression on David Stein's mug.

The doorman tipped his hat as we walked into the smoke-filled lobby and past the elegant shops selling the most opulent goods imaginable. I heard the explosions of a hundred flashbulbs, and then the air cleared. Suddenly, we were in the receiving line with Ida at its head. For once, she had left her tailored suits at home and dressed in a stylish blue silk gown. She stood next to a chubby, dark-haired matron whom I recognized as Louella Parsons, the Hearst newspaper columnist. Her carmine-caked lips spread in a wide smile when Ida whispered, "Mitzi Charles, debutante and singing ingénue, her sister, Leah, and His Excellency, Councilor Bey of the Turkish embassy."

Ida obviously enjoyed David's ruse as much as Omar and Leah did. We were all imposters, a former Pullman porter, and two once-penniless Jews joining all the rest of the charlatans. It seemed that every studio big shot was making an appearance, perhaps to inspect the new merchandise or to pick up pointers for their own shindigs. The backslapping and boisterous conversations stopped when I passed and everyone gave me the eye. If Mr. Roth threw another tirade, maybe I'd pack up and take my goods somewhere else.

We descended the grand staircase. The flash of teeth, eyes, and diamonds nearly blinded us. The maître d'hôtel led us through a grove of papier-mâché palm trees everyone swore were leftover props from Valentino's *The Sheik*. The scent of perfume mingled with plumes of smoke from a thousand cigarettes. The gods and goddesses deserted Mount Olympus that night—hair coiffed to perfection, skin suntanned, teeth perfect, they had descended into the Cocoanut Grove.

A baritone crooned "Prisoner of Love" and caressed the microphone as if it were his lover, while a throng of extra girls stood at the foot of the bandstand in silent adoration. Mr. Factor had personally supervised the girls' transformations, and watched as an army of cosmetologists plucked, powdered, and rouged them. Hairdressers had lacquered every lock of hair, whether lemonade yellow or flaming red, into submission. They wore gowns of cerise, chartreuse, teal, and pale pink, blossoms of a giant bouquet cast at the singer's feet.

Votive candles illuminated every table, along with the tiny flares from cigarette tips. That night everyone drank "coffee" mixed with ginger ale or Coca-Cola. Omar smiled mischievously. "A cup of joe here is at least a hundred proof."

Stars flickered on the blue ceiling, but I kept my gazing to the celestial bodies crowding the dance floor. I caught sight of Edna across the room—with her new flame-red hair, she was hard to miss.

Bobby Fayette sat at a table with his companion, Helga Nielson, whispering in her ear and nibbling on her fingertips. Once an actor, always an actor, I guess. Buster Sweet wasn't celebrating with us, and though I missed him, the night would be mine, no matter what. My audacious gown fit to perfection, and although the jacket concealed most of it, my daring revelation was imminent.

David had arranged for us to join Mr. Roth at his table. I wasn't looking forward to spending the evening with the Icebox and had planned to be celebrating with the livelier contract players. David's date, Beth Cushing, drew admiring looks in her frock of periwinkle silk, the fabric an exact match of her eyes. Beth's patrician features may have set her apart from the doll faces and kewpies, but all the fellows gawked at me. I couldn't wait to see the look on David Stein's kisser when I strolled off with Chick.

Mr. Roth danced with a zaftig lady so heavily made up her face would have cracked if she'd smiled. She never did. I asked Omar about her.

"Who is the lady dancing with Mr. Roth?"

"That's Mrs. Roth."

Poor Mr. Roth. I sympathized with being stuck with such a gnome, but I remained on pins and needles, waiting for Chick to make his appearance.

Omar guided us to Mr. Roth's table. Although I hate to admit it, David looked dashing in white tie and tails. He rose to make introductions. "May I present His Excellency, Councilor Bey of the Turkish embassy, Miss Mitzi Charles, and her sister, Leah."

David smirked as he seated me between Beth

Cushing and Al. He murmured, "Turkish ambassador" into Miss Vassar's ear, and she extended her hand for Omar to kiss. I barely kept a straight face when Omar obliged.

Miss Vassar immediately regaled everyone with the triumph of her latest society drama. "It's so fabulous. *Variety* insists I'm the blonde Norma Shearer."

She hee-hawed like a donkey in heat, and I wanted to read David the riot act for seating me next to the broad. Al occupied himself with gawking at every girl who sauntered by, but his real interest lay in the lines of her gown. "Whoever put that fat-assed dame in that gown should be shot at dawn."

Eduardo Durant yelled, "Hit it, boys," and the rhythm of the rumba pulsated through the room. Couples moved onto the dance floor. Omar took Leah's arm, and they joined them.

Aha, time for my reveal. I worked with stealth, first unfastening the frog holding my jacket closed, then letting the jacket drop onto the back of my chair. Voila! I sat there for the entire world to see, sans brassiere or panties. Suddenly, all the gents in the room seemed very interested. David looked as if his eyes would bug out of his head. He could be so tedious.

Before David could say a word, the fellow from tap class that Rollo called Vaselino, stepped over to the table. "May I have this dance, beautiful?"

I turned to David with a smile, then gave Vaselino my hand. "Why, certainly."

We moved onto the floor, every eye on me. I placed my hand on Vaselino's shoulder.

"Doll, I've seen you in class, but we never met.

The gals call me Frankie. You don't think I'm a big bad gangster for chasing the most beautiful girl in the room, do you?"

He sure looked like a gangster. "No, Frankie."

I knew calling me 'beautiful' was part of his usual line of baloney, but I didn't care, I only wished David Stein, the worm, could have heard it. Frankie and I did a basic rumba break, what they called "cucarachas," a sensual side step that I made even hotter by slowly moving my hips. Frankie commented, but not just on my dancing skill.

"Never seen a nice girl dance like you or wear a dress like that. You trying to make the Icebox jealous or something? Is he your fellow?"

Before I could answer, he pantomimed moving his hands down the length of my body as I undulated my hips in rhythm with the music. The other dancers burst into applause when we moved into a spot turn. All my practicing with Leah had paid off. I was hot stuff!

"Oh, Frankie, I don't have a boyfriend, and if I did, it wouldn't be David Stein."

He snickered and dipped me so low that my shoulders almost touched the floor—more applause. "Well, he's sure giving me the evil eye."

I glanced over at David. The crumb had the most poisonous look on his face. There he was, wining and dining that braying trollop, but he had the nerve to glare at my partner. The guy was insufferable.

"I have no idea what's wrong with him. Don't pay any attention."

Frankie spun me into three consecutive turns, then whisked me across the floor. He pulled me against his chest and murmured, "I hope to hell the Icebox isn't packing a gat. I'll be a dead man for sure."

Before I could ask Frankie if he carried a gat and could shoot David Stein between the eyes, the band tore into a tango. I moved closer and rubbed against Frankie's leg. I felt the heat of a klieg light burning into my back. The more that nudnik, David Stein, glared at me, the more suggestive my movements.

Frankie placed his hand on my back, and our tango began. I'd practiced the steps with Leah until I could do them blindfolded. Everyone watched. Frankie pulled me closer. "Baby, you're causing quite the commotion. From the way the fellows are looking, Ben Roth should have hired a couple of goons to watch over you."

"Oh, Frankie, you're such a card."

I tossed my head back with the same toothy laugh that Norma Shearer used in all her movies. Life was grand, wasn't it? I'd gotten David Stein's goat, I was tangoing with a fabulous dancer who was probably a real gangster, and the man I loved would soon make an appearance.

The number ended to loud applause, and the orchestra moved on to the opening vamp of the Cab Calloway number "Minnie the Moocher." A bunch of beautiful chorus girls costumed like French Apache dancers glided onto the stage. To my surprise, Buster Sweet, dressed in white tie and tails, followed them. The whole place lit up like a Roman candle when he began dancing with the girls to the accompaniment of the Rumba Boys. So David had figured out a way to get Buster in after all. The number ended to enthusiastic applause. Buster strutted up to the microphone, smiling and bowing to the partygoers, his teeth flashing white under the lights.

"Ladies and gentlemen, it is my honor to present the newest lovebirds in Hollywood, Mr. and Mrs. Chick Hagan! They've just returned from a short honeymoon in Mexico—Hit it, boys!"

The band played a rumba version of "Here Comes the Bride" and my head began to spin. A giant spotlight lit Chick and Jill as they walked onto the stage, arm in arm, smiling as if they were the happiest lovers in the world. The band segued into "My Baby Just Cares for Me." A slaphappy smile on his face, he began serenading his new bride with my song.

I wanted to scream from the rafters, "That fink sang the same song to me!" I kept my mouth shut.

For me, the night was over. I excused myself, "Frankie, forgive me, but I have to visit the powder room."

What a sap I was, the biggest in the world. How could I think Chick and I would ever be together? Jill Carpenter had pegged me right, a dumb cluck who fell for a two-bit chiseler who only knew one song. Luckily, the photographers were long gone by the time I staggered out of the Cocoanut Grove into the corridor. Except for a maid collecting cigarette butts from ash urns, I found the place deserted. I stepped into a small alcove and stood there trying to get my bearings.

I refused to cry. It couldn't help matters, and besides, I'd get mascara all over my face.

My forehead against the wall, I heard soft footsteps padding up to me, and felt warm breath on my neck. Someone had crept behind me, and I recognized the spicy fragrance of David's aftershave.

"Doll, you really took one on the chin tonight. Leah's worried about you."

He hadn't come to gloat, but I wanted to be alone. I knew he thought I was a weak sister, but I wasn't.

"I'm fine. Please tell Leah I'm perfectly all right."

"Mitzi, you should go back in and tell her yourself."

I would rather have died than face Chick and his new spouse. "No, I don't think so. I'm never going back in there, ever. If you don't mind, I'll just wait here."

"Well, how about I wait with you? Need some comfort, baby?"

He moved closer, and let his soft lips roam up and down my spine. I guess I should have been devastated. After all, the man I loved had chosen another—but David's mouth nibbling on my backbone felt so wonderful, I couldn't think about anything else.

He spoke softly against my ear. "It should be against the law to be as beautiful as you are. If I were a cop, I'd lock you up for driving a fellow crazy."

I didn't move when he slipped down the straps of my gown and feathered his lips across my shoulders. By the time his mouth slid upwards to my neck, I couldn't have pulled away even if I wanted to.

His voice droned in my ear. "Don't be mad at Chick. Marrying Jill wasn't his idea. She's in the family way and went to Ben about it."

Who was thinking about Chick, or Jill's impending motherhood? The neck kissing became even more intense. He slowly pivoted me toward him until we were face to face. I thought my heart would stop. We looked at each other as if we were gazing into each other's souls, and I wondered if his heart was racing like mine.

I wouldn't have thought it humanly possible for David to get any closer, but somehow he managed to. He moved his cheek next to mine, his deep baritone vibrating down to my toes.

"Maybe I should have told you about Jill before, but I figured you'd get upset and wouldn't come to the party. That would have been a shame, because I had to see you. I know you thought you'd finish that conversation with Chick, but how about you finish it with me?"

He stopped talking. His lips touched my forehead, moved to each cheek then found their way to my mouth. We finally got back to the kiss. I closed my eyes and felt something as gentle as stroking my lips with rose petals. When David used his tongue to open my lips, the sensation almost knocked me off my feet. His breath smelled of mint and ginger ale, his skin spicy from aftershave. His tongue slowly ravaged my mouth, the sensation sweeter than the finest honey. We kissed for an eternity—mouths, lips, tongues entwined. His hand moved up to my bodice and released one of my breasts from the confines of my gown. He pressed his lips to it with a moan, suckling it like a babe.

****

I couldn't stop myself from rubbing up against him like a sex-crazed trollop, a common slut. Something hard throbbed against my thigh, and I moved my hand to feel his excitement. I didn't want to stop, but he pulled up my bodice before fleeing to the men's room. As he raced off, he yelled, "Don't move and don't talk to any men."

Wow, I finally knew what kissing was all about, a kiss to end all kisses, a million times better than Chick with his chapped lips and tobacco breath. It seemed like forever before David returned. When he did, I threw my arms around his neck and turned my face to his. Something must have happened, because he took hold of my arms, pulled them away, and backed away from me as though I were poison. Perhaps I'd been too forward, but everyone said fellows liked girls who were fast. He'd turned on the deep freeze. "What's wrong, David? What did I do?"

"You didn't do anything. I'm taking you home."

"But I don't want to go home. I want to stay and dance with you, just you, and drink champagne from a coffee cup. Please!"

He put his arm around me and led me away.

David didn't say a word on the drive home. His silence was much worse than the news about Chick. We'd kissed with such passion at the Cocoanut Grove, but on the way to the Casa, he acted as if I had the plague.

We arrived at the Casa de Monte and walked into the courtyard. Night-blooming jasmine and freesia perfumed the air, and the wind chimes tinkled in the evening breeze. Everything screamed romance, but David looked glum and wasn't talking. My Romeo had transformed into a block of ice.

David kept up the silent treatment all the way to the front door. I guessed he'd pegged me for a wanton hussy. How mortifying.

"I can't imagine what you must think of me for allowing so much familiarity. Please forgive me. I don't know what came over me—"

I never finished my sentence because he pulled me into his arms. The lovemaking began all over again, only even better. He held me, dropped my bodice, his lips moving over my bosoms while his hand moved south. Maybe a stronger girl would have stopped him, but who said I was strong? Then he touched me on that special place where only husbands tread. It was the most wonderful experience of my life. I guess I was one of those hot-assed mamas that fellows snicker about after all. He whispered naughty things when he touched me. I should have been shocked, but, slut that I was, I loved every trashy word.

"Does it feel good when I touch your honey pot, baby?"

The sensation was so intense that I moaned. It was the moan that did it. He pulled his hand away as if it was on fire.

"I can't do this! I'm sorry. I can't take advantage of an innocent kid."

What? He called me an innocent kid? I threw my arms around his neck. "David, I'm a woman. Don't you want me?"

David shook his head as if he were punch drunk. "Yes, I want you, but not like this. I want you to be as screwy about me as you were about Chick. I want you to wake up thinking about me, not him, and when you go to sleep, I want you to dream about me, only me." He pulled away. "Their marriage won't last. Chick will be free again, and believe me, it'll be soon. Which one of us will you choose? I won't be played for a chump."

He stepped toward me and took my face in his hands. He planted a chaste kiss on my forehead as if he were my brother. We gazed into each other's eyes for an eternity. I knew then and there that, despite his flaws, David Stein was the fellow for me. "I think I love you, David."

He kissed me on the forehead and looked at me for a long, sad moment. "Baby, when you really love someone, you say, 'I love you,' not 'I think I love you.' "

David walked away, and my tears began.

Chapter Thirty
After the Ball

After my tears dried, I went inside our flat and scrubbed the makeup from my face. After I changed into a nightgown, I sat on my bed, pondering my predicament. It took a while, but I realized I didn't have a predicament to ponder. The guy loved me and I was nuts about him. Why should I worry?

Despite my schoolgirl crush on Chick, I wasn't a flippant girl. I'd always known that when I found my special someone, come hell or high water, I'd be with him forever. David didn't know that, so I'd have to tell him.

The next morning, my jacket hung next to the infamous gown, and my handbag sat on my dresser. I heard Leah puttering around the kitchen and knew I would have to face the music about last night.

When I strolled into the kitchen, I'd prepared myself for Leah to hit the roof about me running away, but she didn't blow up. Instead, she tormented me by saying, oh so sweetly, "I made my bubala her oatmeal the way she likes it, with a sliced banana and strawberries on the side. Here's some orange juice to wash it down."

Leah called me "bubala," her term of endearment since we were children. Maybe she'd smother me with kindness before launching into the lecture.

"Thank you, Leah."

She sat across from me, a beatific smile lighting up her face.

"Last night was magical. Everyone said you were the most beautiful girl in the place, and everyone commented on your gown."

I'm sure they did.

She took my hand. "How are you, darling?"

Perhaps it was best if I played the wounded dove. "Oh, I'm better, but everything was such a shock, it devastated me."

I didn't mention that David had kissed and fondled me and I'd dreamed of him all night, that I hungered for his touch, that I had rubbed against him like an alley cat in heat and, most of all, that I didn't care if the world knew I was a sex-crazed hussy; however, it wasn't the type of information most girls shared with their older sisters. I didn't say a word when she brought up Chick, figuring I'd play the sympathy angle. She'd feel sorry for me and wouldn't comment about my torrid dance with Frankie or me behaving like a chippie.

"I'm sorry about Mr. Hagan. I never liked him, but I hate the thought of him being trapped into marriage like that."

Golly, did the entire world know that he'd knocked up Jill Carpenter? Still, as long as Leah didn't bring up the dress, the tango, or me running out on her, everything was copacetic.

"Darling Mitzi, now that you have David, you must know that Chick was just a schoolgirl infatuation. Your David is such a lovely fellow."

"Your David?" I almost choked on my oatmeal. "How did you know?"

She took my hand in hers. "By the time David came back to the Grove, he'd managed to wipe off most of your lipstick, but some still remained on his neck. I didn't say a word, and that phony-baloney girl he's been seeing never noticed. Too busy telling anyone who'd listen about her newest movies. David came back and spoke to me from his heart. He's a very intense young fellow."

What an understatement. "Yes, he is, Leah."

She clasped my hand. "Of course, I'm thrilled about the two of you, but there are things that concern me. He's older."

"You said yourself, only by four years. Isn't Omar four years older than you?"

Leah paused for a moment. "Yes, and I'm nuts about him. But, there are, uh, things we've never discussed. David is already a man of the world, yet you, you're my Mitzi. Are you sure about your feelings for him?"

This wasn't kid stuff, and I knew it. "Yes, Leah."

She glanced down at her hands. "He's been married, had affairs, and you're so innocent."

If she knew about the shenanigans we'd gotten into last night, she might have second thoughts about me being "so innocent."

Leah stood up to clear the table. "David sent over a messenger this morning. I left everything in the living room."

I rushed into the room and found an envelope embossed with the Chateau Marmont watermark attached to a narrow box that looked like it held a fountain pen set.

I opened the note. Typed, not one mistake, truly

from my David.

Doll,

I thought about you all night. I wanted to stay with you, but you're so young, so willing, and I'm no saint. Just know I'm a regular guy who is crazy about you and finds it hard to keep his hands to himself. I told Ben last night just how I feel, and he wants us to hold our horses.

"Hold our horses?" What was I supposed to do in the meantime? Age like a wheel of Cheddar cheese? I bet Mr. Roth never told David to hold his horses with Miss Vassar. Did he expect me to twiddle my thumbs while he stayed chummy with that braying idiot? If he did, he had another think coming. I remembered how much I loved him and decided if necessary I'd wait for him until my hair turned white.

There are others to think about, namely Beth. I didn't bring you back to the ballroom because she was there, and, frankly, I didn't want a scene. I can't hide the way I feel about you any longer. I have to be careful with her. I know she's self-centered and puts on airs, but in her way she cares for me. Please, darling, let me handle her. I've trampled on one heart already, and I don't want to make the same mistake again.

Then, of course, there is Chick. Regardless of what I think, I can't underestimate your fondness for him and his attraction to you. This thing with Jill is already a disaster, and I'm sure Chick will want a shoulder to cry on.

Why did he bring up Chick? He was old news.

Lastly, the box. Maybe you'll think it presumptuous, but I'd ordered it after the evening you made the latkes. I promise to make up for us not

*dancing together at the Grove. I hope one day you'll
wear a dress like your red one just for me. Think of
what happened last night as a preview of coming
attractions.*

*Call me if you need me for anything. I'll be waiting
by the telephone. I'm close by at the Chateau Marmont.*

David

I realized everything I'd done in the past weeks,
including wearing the infamous gown, was for him.
Every time I looked at it, I thought about his reaction to
seeing me in it. He'd been all I'd been thinking about,
and I hadn't even realized it. Gosh, I loved the guy.

I opened the narrow box and found a gorgeous
jumble of baguette diamonds in a platinum setting
which nearly blinded me. How could anything be so
beautiful? Every stone looked perfect to me, but what
did I know about diamonds? The inscription engraved
on the underside read, "To my Mitzi, from David." I
heard Leah's footstep and handed the bracelet to her.

"He sent this diamond bracelet as a thank you for
my latkes."

Leah responded with a whistle. "Wow." She
chuckled as she walked away. "Such a thoughtful guy.
Feel free to wear your diamonds when you wash the
dishes."

I had a diamond bracelet and the man I loved
waited for my call. What a lucky girl I was!

****

Before I entered the barn that morning, I heard the
low murmur of chuckles and whispers. My watch said
10:00 a.m., but gossip whispered sotto voce from the
corners.

"I hear she's in the family way and that's why they

did it."

"Mr. Roth must be fit to be tied, his big star knocked up."

"Well, at least Chick made an honest woman of her."

Chick? Honest woman? Finally, Edna clarified it. "Hey, Mitzi, want to know why Chick and Jill Carpenter got hitched in Mexico?"

She looked about the room then whispered in pig Latin. "Everyoneway ayssay Ickchay ockedknay upway illJay Arpentercay. Eshay ouldn'tway etgay idray ofway itway osay Istermay Othray ademay imhay arrymay erhay. Everyone says Chick knocked up Jill Carpenter. She wouldn't get rid of it, so Mr. Roth made him marry her."

Jill Carpenter had pegged me for a sap, the biggest in the world. How could I think Chick and I would ever be together? Yes, I was a dumb cluck who had a crush on a two-timing Casanova with tobacco breath. Imagine, whispering sweet nothings in my ear while he and Jill Carpenter were doing the ultimate.

After two years of adoring a smiling dime-story Romeo from afar, I felt nothing but relief. I couldn't stop myself from smiling. Fingers and Rollo showed up, and I spent the rest of the day tapping my heart out.

"Okay, kids, playtime's over."

Gods of tap dance, thank you. We tapped our hearts out and called it quits after an arduous six hours. I emerged a sweaty mess.

I was making my way toward Hair and Make-Up for a shower and shampoo when I heard a voice calling my name. "Miss Charles, it's me, Betty. Come over here." She signaled to me, a morose look on her usually sunny face.

"I guess you heard about Miss Carpenter and Mr. Hagan."

When I nodded, she moved closer and whispered in my ear. "Well, forget it. She ain't having no baby." I pulled away from her, unable to believe her. Betty moved closer. "It's part of my job to make sure she's always ready for that time of the month. She ain't missed her monthlies, so I know she ain't knocked up. Mr. Chick Hagan was too dumb to figure out that gal pulled the wool over his eyes."

I couldn't think of a worse fate than being stuck living with Jill Carpenter, except for getting cozy with Beth Cushing. Perish the thought.

By the time I'd showered, dried, and fluffed my hair, I found the lot practically deserted. Despite the twilight heat, my temperature dropped. I walked past empty doorways and darkened alcoves without a sign of life. Something felt off and the hair on the nape of my neck rose. Before I could mount the front office steps, I heard a voice whisper my name. The speaker was male, definitely not Betty.

"Mitzi."

My eyes searched my surroundings. Nothing. I must have been going screwy. The events of the last weeks would unhinge anyone and send them straight to the loony bin. The late August heat had stifled my breathing most of the day, but I suddenly felt a chill. I dashed into the front office lobby and up the elevator.

I found David's office door ajar. David sat in his shirtsleeves, engrossed with a stack of screenplays, blue pencil in hand, while Duke Ellington played on the Victrola.

I tapped on the door and walked in. "Hello. I hope I'm not disturbing you."

He sat back in his chair and looked me up and down. "You always disturb me, baby."

"Uh, is that Duke Ellington? I love his music. I know that one. 'It Don't Mean a Thing if it Ain't Got That Swing.' It's a great song."

David sat back in his chair, a sly smile on his lips, his eyes on me. "Yes, it is."

He wasn't helping. The bouncy music ended, but we still weren't talking. I felt the heat rising to my face and looked away. My eyes lit on the silver picture frame with my photo from so long ago, my hands trembling. Someone had smashed the glass, and I knew who.

He took it from me. "I'll have it replaced, and it'll be good as new. Things have been cool with Beth for quite a while, and seeing that picture confirmed her fears. I thank God her aim was bad."

"It looks like she stomped on it too. I don't know why she got so sore. She doesn't love you like I do. Besides, I look twelve years old in that picture. Rose has taken so many great photographs of me, why do you want this one?'

"I like looking at that nervy kid from back home." He smirked. "So, you love me?"

Caught in the act. "Yeah, a whole lot."

We stopped talking and just stared at each other in the unbearable silence. I found it torturous to want to fly into someone's arms and know he wouldn't let me. The Victrola kept spinning. David walked over to it and put on another record. A trumpet knocked out a bluesy refrain and Louis Armstrong started singing.

"We never did get our dance, did we?"

David swept me into his arms. I rested my head on his chest, and he held me tight. Not only was he the handsomest man on the face of the globe, he was the smoothest dancer, too. The record ended, but we just kept on swaying in each other's arms.

The man I loved tilted my face to his, and I went weak at the knees.

Suddenly, the door swung open. Nussbaum stood on the threshold, looking horrible. To be honest, he wasn't such a nice-looking fellow to begin with, but in the last two years, he'd aged badly. His hair had grayed, and I could have packed my whole wardrobe in the bags under his eyes.

The moment I looked at his demonic mug, I knew he'd gone nuts.

I screamed bloody murder. Nussbaum fled, slamming the door. David sped after him. The thought of David tangling with a crazed maniac unnerved me, and I collapsed against the desk. It seemed like forever before I heard his footsteps. I threw my arms around him—no matter how tough I pretended to be, I was just a big cream puff—and started wailing like a baby.

"He could have killed you, and then what would I have done?"

David held me close and stroked my hair. "Don't cry, baby. If that monster planned to hurt us, he would have done it when he opened the door. Got to admit, the guy was fast on his feet. We'd better leave. He might still be around."

I shook my head. "He's gone. Don't ask how I know, I just do. He's playing with us, David."

"Yeah, maybe you're right. I'll call Ben. The

lunatic must have flown in from New York on an aeroplane, but how the heck did he get on the lot?"

****

David and I reached the Casa a few minutes later. Leah and Omar sat in the living room, listening to Rudy Vallée on the radio. She jumped up from the sofa and gave David a sisterly embrace. "David, what a wonderful surprise. I kept dinner warm for Mitzi. Why don't you join us?"

I opened my mouth to reply, but no words tumbled out. David squeezed my hand. "I'd love to, Leah, but we have a problem. Nussbaum is in Los Angeles. Mitzi and I saw him on the studio lot."

Leah gasped, then exchanged a look with Omar and sat heavily on the sofa. "This is horrible news. I should have known something was up when Zisel said he'd left New York."

Omar placed a comforting arm around her shoulders. "Don't worry, my darling. You and Mitzi have nothing to fear with David and me protecting you."

David took a step forward. "Omar is right, Leah. I called Ben after we saw Nussbaum. He'll arrange for a guard to watch over the Casa, and we'll get extra security on the lot. I'll pick Mitzi up tomorrow morning and make sure she's looked after."

Leah gave him a nod of her head, but I saw the fear in her face. "Leah, let me walk David to his car. I'll be back in a minute."

David halted me. "You're staying inside." He turned to Omar. "I'm relying on you to watch her every movement."

He gave me a sweet buss on the forehead and left.

Later, I picked at my dinner, then crawled into bed. I dreamed of dancing the tango in the Cocoanut Grove with a handsome, dark-haired fellow. Around midnight, I woke in pitch dark to the sound of muffled footsteps coming from the living room. My bedroom door opened, and I heard someone padding toward my bed. I whispered into the darkness, "Leah, is that you?"

Leah didn't answer. Instead, a deep baritone spoke, barely above a whisper. "You thought you could get away from me. Silly little girl."

Nussbaum's voice was as soft and menacing as I remembered. I saw him moving close. I wanted to jump out of the bed and run away, but something held me fast. I opened my mouth to scream, but I froze.

"You'll never get away from me."

Nussbaum held a gun to my temple, and I felt cold steel. I gasped, and he laughed in my face.

"No. If I shot you, it would be too quick."

His hands encircled my neck, and he began to squeeze, slowly choking the life out of me. Suddenly, I found my voice and screamed like there was no tomorrow.

The lights flashed on. Omar and Leah rushed to my side. Leah took me in her arms. "My poor darling, you're shaking."

"Nussbaum was here. He was going to kill me."

She looked up at Omar. He nodded to her, and she climbed into bed with me.

"No, it was just a bad dream. Now go back to sleep. I'll be here."

I heard the worry in her voice, but somehow I managed to fall asleep anyway.

Chapter Thirty-One
The Turn of the Screwy

David arrived at the Casa the next morning and brought the Icebox with him. I took a seat next to him, vowing I wouldn't bring up my horrific nightmare. The key went into the ignition, the motor buzzed, but instead of immediately driving off to Regal, he turned to me and took my chin in his hands. The kiss started gently, but heated up. "Look, baby, we'll get through this thing with Nussbaum. Don't you worry."

Easier said than done.

When David turned onto Santa Monica Boulevard, he could barely maneuver his Caddie onto the Regal lot. Half the hoofers in Los Angeles had queued at the front gate, all of them auditioning for parts in the dance-marathon movie. They were youthful and good-looking, so I figured Joseph Nussbaum would surely stand out among them. Extra guards were on hand, but for some reason, I couldn't shake the feeling something wasn't right.

On my way to the barn, I noticed the piano tuners in their battered jalopy heading to the front office. They were probably on their way to work on Mr. Roth's old upright. I hoped the big man wouldn't give them the bum's rush for driving their piece of junk onto his pristine lot. Still, I had other things to worry about than Ben Roth losing his temper. I'd soon be facing Chick and didn't relish it.

By the time I reached the barn, a few of the principal dancers were having a smoke before work began. It would be another long, smelly day. Learning the intricate marathon routines wasn't going to be easy. Rollo wasn't in a jolly mood with all the desperate dancers on the lot. Edna and the twins were there, and luckily, Chick wasn't. The happy newlyweds were shooting a pictorial for *Silver Screen Magazine*.

Rollo partnered me in the Lindy hop, insisting we dance with a rhythmical Charleston step, the way they did in Harlem.

"And a five, a six, seven, eight—" We were in the midst of practicing our turns when the scar-faced guard ran into the barn screaming.

"Stop, everyone! Some fellow just shot Mr. Roth and took Mr. Stein prisoner!"

I felt my heart pound wildly like a bass drum. My pulse soared so rapidly that I braced myself to avoid falling to the floor in a dead swoon.

Sweat rolled down the guard's face, and the poor fellow could barely catch his breath. I feared he would collapse before telling us what happened.

"Mr. Roth and Mr. Stein, uh, were talking when— oh, my God—this guy barges into Mr. Roth's office holding a gun. Mr. Roth's secretary said the guy was— dear Lord—babbling on about how Mr. Roth had ruined his life and—uh—took something he owned. They'd warned us, said a maniac was on the loose…but no one figured…he could get on the lot…Mr. Roth was expecting the piano tuners…for that clunker of his…the crazy fellow waylaid them…shot one dead…stole the truck…the other one is lucky to be alive."

The guard turned to me. "The guy that shot Mr. Roth was screaming about you, Miss Charles. Lots of fellows go wacky for a face they've seen on the screen, and try to storm the front gate. None of 'em ever brought a gun before. Lord, help us!"

The room went silent. Edna put a reassuring arm around my shoulder. I'm sure she silently prayed to Jesus, but her entreaties didn't comfort me. Rollo finally spoke.

"Kids, go on home. I'll make sure they pay you for the day. I don't know what else to say except I want you here tomorrow. Mr. Roth would expect the show to go on no matter what."

With that, everyone left, except me.

****

I tried to speak to some of the deputies from the Sheriff's Department, but only got a pat on the head and empty assurances.

"We're handling it, little lady."

Nuts to them. I wasn't going to cool my heels waiting for Nussbaum to kill David. I knew what I had to do. With sirens blaring and coppers crawling all over the lot, no one noticed me heading to Wardrobe.

The hum of sewing machines greeted me. Nussbaum had shot Mr. Roth and kidnapped David, yet nothing interrupted the business of creating the costumes that made the movies glamorous. The seamstresses and tailors were so engrossed in their work they didn't notice when I grabbed a jacket, a pair of slacks, and a boy's shirt.

I had already buttoned up when Al walked in. "What the hell do you think you're doing, girlie?"

Before I answered, I looked around the shop, then

moved closer. "Al, if I ask you to keep your mouth shut, will you?"

He rolled his eyes then snorted a response. "No. Why the hell are you dressed like that?"

"I'm in disguise."

His mouth twisted in disgust. "For what?"

Of all the times for him to act like a hard-nosed putz. "Look, Al, I can't stay around and schmooze. The flatfoots are crawling all over, looking in the wrong places. I'm sure the crazy bastard is holding Mr. Stein in the building where they store the old film stock. The guy used to work at Regal and probably knows the place from the old days. I'm betting he has Mr. Stein hostage there."

"Swell. Tell the sheriff and go home. You're not needed here, cupcake!"

"Golly, you really know how to hurt a girl's feelings. I tried to talk to them, but they won't listen. Don't you care that a maniac shot Mr. Roth, and he might kill Mr. Stein?"

He made a grab at my jacket, but I slipped out of his reach. I turned to see the tears welling in his eyes. "Of course I care. Ben and I were boys together. I've known David since before he could walk, but you can't do anything for either of them. I once pegged you as a smart girl, but after that boxcar stunt, I knew you were as dumb at the rest of these bozos."

I ignored his comment about my intelligence. "Please listen to me. The fellow who took Mr. Stein hasn't been on the lot in years. That old storehouse has to be the only place he knows. The sheriffs are searching the sound stages, but the maniac wouldn't set foot on any of them, would he?"

Al shook his head. "So little Mitzi's got it all figured out, huh?"

Jeez, the guy could be really annoying. "Yes, I do. In this heat, with that nitrate stock, if the cops storm the place they could start a fire. If I can get in there, maybe I can talk that animal into letting Mr. Stein go."

Al sneered, unconvinced. "And just how do you think you can do that?"

How the heck did I know? "It's a long story. I've got to go now."

He took me by the arm. "How do you know David's not dead already?"

My eyes began to well, and I wiped them on my sleeve. I didn't want to start blubbering in front of Al. "Because I can feel him." He looked deep into my face without saying a word. "Al, if anything happens, if I'm not back in an hour, tell the sheriff where I went."

"Kid, you have no idea what Ben went through nine years ago. If something happens—" His voice trailed off. "I need my head examined. Okay, I'll give you an hour, but that's all. Be careful, honey."

I didn't look back. "I will."

With everyone rushing around the lot like a flock of decapitated chickens, no one noticed a boy walking toward the old gate and the abandoned storage building. Although I couldn't hear the buzz of human activity around the building, and the place looked empty, I knew David was inside somewhere. The scar-faced guard had abandoned the place. When he got a second wind, he'd probably joined the flatfoots racing around the studio and led them up one blind alley and down another.

Regal buzzed with the gossip. A secretary swore

Nussbaum shot Mr. Roth in the shoulder. Mr. Roth must have been preoccupied with the doctor digging out the bullet or he would have figured out where Nussbaum had hidden himself. The second-floor window remained ajar. If I could pry it open, getting into the building would be a snap. An old wooden ladder looked like it could reach the second floor window, and there was that abandoned scaffolding. I tried to move the ladder, but the darn thing wouldn't budge. The old scaffolding reached all the way to the roof.

Back when I was a Girl Scout, our leader taught us that young ladies must always be prepared. I'd readied myself. In the hunt for Nussbaum, some of the grips had abandoned their toolboxes. I lifted a flashlight, a screwdriver, and some flares, which I vowed to return after the ordeal ended. Although nitrate stock could flame spontaneously, I'd pinched a box of matches, too.

I began climbing the wooden scaffold, a rickety mess that creaked and swayed with my every step, but I figured if it could support a grown man, it would hold me. I'd just started my ascent when I felt a tug on my trousers. I looked down. Omar, garbed in a denim work shirt, overalls, and a cap, stared back at me.

"Omar? What are you doing here?"

"I might ask you the same thing. Where the hell do you think you're going? Come down right now!"

I lowered my voice in case Nussbaum was listening. "I'm not coming down, and you can't make me. If David is in there, I have to get him out."

For the first time since I'd known him, Omar shot me the evil eye.

"Tell me, miss, just how do you plan to get inside?

That scaffolding is on its last legs, and I doubt it'll hold anyone, even someone as small as you. If you don't break your fool neck, how are you going to find your way through that old firetrap? I've been in there. They've got everything but Judge Crater stored in that dump. Now, come down, or I'll climb up and get you."

I did as I was told, not because of the wisdom of his words, but because the scaffolding moaned like an old yenta. By the time I'd climbed down, Omar had moved the ladder into place.

"Mitzi, I won't let that son of a bitch wreck your life and your sister's any more than he already has. Go on home."

"Omar, I'm going in there with you, and that's the end of it!"

He tried staring me down, but I stood my ground. "You're a stubborn little thing, aren't you, Mitzi? Okay, I'll go up first, look around, and you follow, understand? What's in that sack?"

I showed him the tools I'd nabbed. He took the knapsack and hung it around his neck. "Good stuff, but I've got something that trumps all of it."

He pulled a small caliber revolver from beneath the overalls.

"Where did you get that?"

He caressed it before putting it back in his pocket. "You don't think a fellow like me could survive without one of these, do you? I figure this Nussbaum, or whoever he's calling himself these days, probably dragged David through the rear door, the one we'll use when we leave."

I had no idea about another entrance. "What? There's another door?"

"Yes, but the minute it opens, David is a dead man. Now listen. I've worked it out. We'll take the scenic route and surprise Nussbaum. If you're coming, let's go."

Maybe I acted tough, but Nussbaum scared me out of my wits. Still, I wouldn't let my fear stop me. Omar ascended the ladder and reached the partly open window. He used the screwdriver to pry it all the way open. After he climbed in, I waited for his signal. Nothing. My stomach knotted at the thought Nussbaum had laid in wait and ambushed him. Suppose the monster had murdered both Omar and David? I almost started bawling, but finally, a hand poked out of the window and gave me a wave. By the time I clambered half way up the ladder, Omar reached out and steadied it.

When I climbed through the second-floor window, slivers of light from the open window cut through the blackness. The place felt like an oven, surely as hot as the Black Hole of Calcutta and a million times smellier. Then, as if things weren't bad enough, I felt something crawl over my shoe.

"Omar, we have a guest—the hairy, four-legged kind!"

He flicked on the flashlight and the little long-tailed critter scampered away. Growing up in New York, I'd become acquainted with rats, and the only one I feared went by the name "Nussbaum." The flashlight's glow revealed a graveyard of the grotesque and the ornate. Regal had been making films since 1912, and I imagined their entire history was in this room. Ancient Bell & Howell cameras, relics from the days of silent dramas, were stacked against each other.

Tiffany lamps leaned against velvet divans and lacquered coromandel screens. They were discarded set pieces from the racy divorce dramas and high society melodramas that brought the studio fame in the old days.

Omar grabbed my hand and guided me to the stairwell. "When we were in Carlisle, Mr. Roth told me that Nussbaum and his cronies used to play poker in the basement. Now, it's like a bank vault, reinforced with steel in case of a nitrate fire. There's a door at the rear. If he's down there with David, that's how he got in."

He poked around in his pockets and dragged out a skeleton key. "I swiped it from the guard shack. It'll open the storage room."

I started down the stairs, but he stopped me. "It's hotter than blazes down here, Mitzi. It's too dangerous. Maybe I better go it alone."

I shook my head. "To heck with that. We're in this together, Omar. Besides, the nitrate in that cracker box could ignite at any moment, so it really doesn't matter if I stay or go, does it?"

At that moment, we both knew there was no turning back. Making our way down the stairs was no joy ride. The flashlight only lit part of the staircase, and the heat and stench added to our discomfort. Suddenly, a tiger with blood-covered fangs leaped at us out of the darkness. Our goose was cooked—we were goners. Omar's hand over my mouth stifled my scream.

"Button it, Mitzi! This is where they stored the stuffed animals from old jungle movies."

Omar swung the flashlight. The place resembled a taxidermist's studio and gave me the heebie-jeebies. He removed his hand, then guided me back to the stairs.

We started our descent in earnest.

"When we find David, don't try to act like Joan of Arc. Let me do the talking, and you make sure you stand behind me. You got that?"

I nodded, and we traveled through the dark to the basement. When we reached our destination, we didn't make a sound. The smell of deteriorating nitrate nearly overpowered us. They used the place as a morgue of forgotten movies, and I feared it might be ours too. Omar played the flashlight over reels of film stock. Some of it had disintegrated into brown powder. Nussbaum wouldn't have picked such a dangerous hiding place if he knew how volatile nitrate stock was. Or would he?

Omar and I walked through the smelly void without knowing which way to turn. We edged our way through the darkness and stopped dead. David was somewhere in this chamber of horrors.

Suddenly, we heard voices, one low and muffled— and the other belonged to David. He tried to reason with Nussbaum. "I asked politely the first time, even said 'please.' The place is a firetrap. Put out your cigarette and douse the lamp."

I almost sobbed with relief, but Omar gripped my arm. Now wasn't the time to get sappy. We moved toward David's voice.

"Look, Nussbaum or whatever your name is, if you don't incinerate us and manage to escape, even if you dream up another alias and leave the country, you won't get away. Ben will hunt you down to the ends of the earth."

I heard the cold fury in Nussbaum's voice. "That schmuck will never lay a finger on me. As soon as I finish here, I'll be on my way, flying off to points unknown. Tell me, Mr. Hot Shot, did you enjoy despoiling Mitzi?"

I turned and could barely make out Omar in the darkness. "Omar, I'll go and talk to Nussbaum. When I get him into the light, wing him with your gun."

He tried to grab me by the sleeve. "Are you crazy? Suppose he shoots you?"

"Nussbaum won't shoot me, but he might kill David. I've got to get in there."

I darted toward the voices before Omar could stop me, shouting at the top of my lungs so David would know I was near, "Mr. Nussbaum, Mr. Nussbaum, where are you?"

David screamed out, "Is that you, Mitzi? Go away!"

The light from Nussbaum's lantern illuminated a room lined with metal plating and cement all the way to the ceiling. If the nitrate ignited, this bunker would contain it—hopefully.

Nussbaum sat behind a dilapidated metal desk, pointing a gun at David, who sat upright in a chair. Nussbaum's cigarette glowed, and in the dim light, I could see bruises on David's face. The coward had roughed him up. I looked around for Omar but couldn't see him, so I took a step forward and pulled off my cap.

"Hello, Mr. Nussbaum. It's Mitzi."

I moved farther into the light so Nussbaum could see me. He stared at me for a long time and then spoke in a voice so low I could barely hear him.

"So you came for him, little Mitzi. Here you are to plead for your lover. A whore, that's what you are. There you were, chained to a bed in that filthy movie, and that's where you belong. I'm sure you spread your legs for him and Ben Roth."

Of all the films I'd made, *The Golden Falcon* had to be the one that maniac saw. It didn't matter if the lunatic said nasty things about me, but I didn't relish having a gun pointed at the man I loved. I looked around once again and still didn't see Omar.

"Mr. Nussbaum, it's not true. I'll go anywhere with you, but please let David go. He hasn't done anything to you."

Nussbaum's voice cracked. "Oh, he's done a lot. I saw the two of you together in his office. I knew right away he'd ruined you. Where is the virgin I wanted to marry? She's gone. Now you're just a tart, a cheap whore going from one man to the next."

How could someone wise up a moron who was straight from the sixteenth century? "Not that it's any of your business, but I'm still a virgin, if that's what you're worried about. I swear on the grave of my poor Uncle Baron. Do you even remember Baron Schector? You murdered him."

Nussbaum shrugged. "I made a mistake with the boy. I made up for it. I gave your family cheap rent for years."

"Cheap rent? That sure takes the cake. You think cheap rent makes up for killing my uncle and destroying my family? Do you?"

He answered by cocking the gun. "You're coming with me, Mitzi. Say goodbye to your lover."

I darted in front of David. "You'll have to shoot me first!" Without warning, I heard a gun blast, then a scream. I fell back into David's arms.

Omar stepped out of the shadows, smoke circling

the barrel of his revolver. I made a dash for Nussbaum's gun while Omar leveled his at Nussbaum's prone figure. In my haste, I tipped over the lantern. Kerosene dripped onto the floor, mingling with the blood spurting from Nussbaum's knee. I looked from the bleeding man to Omar.

"With that leg, how are we going get Nussbaum out of here?"

The look on Omar's face didn't bode well for Nussbaum. "Get him out of here? I can't help him and David too. We have to shove off. Let the sheriff handle him. Come on."

David struggled to his feet. Omar put a supporting arm over one shoulder, I took the other side, and the three of us made for the door. Before we left, Omar glanced back at Nussbaum.

"Whatever your name is, I'll leave the place unlocked," he told him. "You'll have a sporting chance, more than you ever gave anyone else."

Nussbaum screamed out, "Help me! Take me with you!"

Omar turned his back on him. "Sorry, brother. Where you're concerned, the milk of human kindness dried up a long time ago."

I heard no rancor in Omar's voice, only disgust. David found his footing and pushed me out the door. It took a moment for our eyes to adjust to the searing sunlight. We all took deep breaths of clean air and then hightailed it away from the building as if demons were chasing us.

We were across the lot by the time we found a sheriff who would listen to us. Omar pointed at the storage building. Smoke billowed from the chimney. I guess Nussi regretted not putting out his cigarette. A stench wafted across the lot, burning nitrate, and probably Nussbaum too.

David glared at me. "Mitzi, whatever possessed you to do such a fool thing? What were you thinking? You could have been killed."

"But I wasn't thinking. I did it because he wouldn't have kidnapped you if it weren't for me. Besides, I love you."

His jaw dropped, but before he could say anything, a crowd of gaffers, electricians, and carpenters jostled me aside. All the little guys David had once dismissed in his arrogance surrounded him. "Gosh, Mr. Stein, we thought you were done for. How are you, sir?"

David attempted to speak. "I'm fine, thank you. Thanks to all of you, I, well, I—" When he broke into tears, a roar of goodwill cheers went up. David continued sobbing.

Omar took me by the arm and helped me up into the ambulance. "Mitzi, I would go with you, but I'm off to make sure your sister knows everything is A-OK. I'll see you later. Stay with David. He needs you."

He gave me a brotherly buss on the cheek and walked away. At that moment, it would have taken a regiment of Marines to keep me from the man I loved.

Chapter Thirty-Two
The Morning After

The Los Angeles Herald Examiner
August 22, 1932
The Los Angeles County Sheriff's Department
made a concerted effort yesterday and contained the
disturbance on the Regal Pictures lot in West
Hollywood. A deranged man wandered into the studio's
front office and attacked Benjamin Roth, President, and
David Lincoln Stein, Vice President and Head of
Production at Regal Pictures.

The assailant wounded Mr. Roth during the assault
and held Mr. Stein hostage for a short period of time.
Studio Security alerted the Sheriff's Department after
spotting the unnamed culprit. Once the authorities were
on hand, the alleged desperado freed Mr. Stein. The
mysterious intruder later died by his own hand.

****

On the afternoon of August 25th, 1932, my hands
trembled when I fired up the engine of my roadster. The
gorgeous jumble of baguette diamonds and platinum
flashed from my wrist. Since David and I were a
couple, I wore the diamond bracelet to seal our pact.
Just as he'd promised, David accompanied me to the
meeting with Carlotta Dumont.

With our troubles finally behind us, I questioned
the wisdom of confronting her.

"Nussbaum is dead. He can't take another life, David. Are you sure I should do this?"

"You can't go soft on me now, baby. Your uncle's death is what brought you to Los Angeles in the first place, isn't it? You have to ask her what happened to Baron's body."

I couldn't deny his words. I shifted the roadster from neutral to first gear, and we took off down Santa Monica Boulevard. I still couldn't talk much when I was behind the wheel, but I was getting better at it. David smiled as he always did when I sat behind the wheel. "Baby, you'll get the hang of it one day."

We arrived at the cemetery, and I parked at the main gate. "She comes around two in the afternoon."

I tried to remain calm, but my heart pounded double time. At six minutes past two, a limousine drove up, and I followed. Since the cemetery remained deserted except for the limo and my blue roadster, the driver must have known we were behind him. We followed the automobile up the winding path until it finally stopped at Clarice's grave. The chauffeur hopped out and opened the rear door. Carlotta Dumont didn't step out. Ben Roth did.

David and I exchanged a look. A few seconds later, a pudgy lady in a veiled cloche hat emerged, and Ben extended his arm. She carried a spray of white roses and made her way to the grave. Here was Nussbaum's confederate, the woman who helped murder my uncle, her own daughter, and old Mr. Roth, yet Ben Roth had helped her out of the limo. I leapt from my automobile and ran over to the woman I hated more than anything on earth.

"Carlotta! Carlotta Dumont!"

She turned, dropped the roses and lifted her veil. "Mitzi, my darling girl, I know you from your movies. I'm your Aunt Clarice."

Chapter Thirty-Three
Coda

The earth stopped rotating on its axis. I gazed at the woman's face for a long moment and finally saw Clarice Dumont. She possessed the same luminous smile as in her movies, but her fabled golden curls were gone, replaced by an auburn marcel. Folds of pink flesh enveloped her once-slim body. Still, even zaftig, Clarice remained lovely.

"You must be confused, my dear. Where do I begin? Mother was soused for days. She became a monster when she drank, but Baron protected me. He told her never to bother us again, and she swore he'd pay for his words."

Mr. Roth guided us to a little Jewish cemetery tucked behind the larger, gentile one. Enameled portraits of the dead embellished many of the gravestones, many of older people, but the images of handsome swains and solemn beauties most affected me. The death pictures captured their youthful likenesses for eternity.

Clarice made her way down a well-worn path past rows of gravestones inscribed with Hebrew letters, almost every one with a stone perched on top.

"That horrid man, Nussbaum, was the one who decided fire would be the best revenge. Mother was vicious, but not a murderess. The monster locked the both of us in the dressing caravan and set it on fire. Baron pulled me out to safety and went back for Mother. She was so drunk she couldn't move. He tried to save her even after all the pain she caused, but the fire was too fast."

She stopped walking and leaned on Ben, sobbing, her grief revived. "So many young fellows these days aren't worth a dime, but your uncle was a prince, my prince. His last words to me were, 'Clarice, you have to live for our baby.' "

If David hadn't been holding me, I would have fainted.

Mr. Roth finished the story for her. "Clarice and Baron came to my father when they found out she was pregnant. They were determined to have that kid even if it meant curtains for her career. Pops said, 'Okay, let them get them married. We'll work out the details later.' After the fire, I knew Nussbaum still roamed the streets. I lied to protect her from him."

Clarice opened her pocketbook, pulled out a photo, and handed it to me. The child was the spitting image of Uncle Baron. My tiny family was growing by the minute.

"You and your sister must come to see our little boy, handsome devil that he is. He's the joy of my life, my son, Baron, Baron Sachs. I married the physician who treated me. I've gained weight since they starved me for the screen. Thank goodness, my Melvin likes his ladies on the plump side. We live in a place where no one remembers Clarice Dumont. She's long gone, but everyone knows Mrs. Clara Sachs. You, your young man, and your sister shall come for a visit."

I finally asked the question that had bothered me

since I learned she was Clarice. "Your mother destroyed so many lives. Why do you apologize when you visit her grave?"

A streak of sunlight fell on the side of her cheek, and I glimpsed the young beauty my uncle had loved.

"My husband said it would help with my anger. I hated her so much it nearly destroyed me." She pointed to an ornate gravestone accented with jet and onyx and surrounded by a bronze-and-wrought-iron gate. "Baron is there."

An enameled portrait of Uncle Baron's smiling face, his Panama hat tipped at a rakish angle, sat under a bubble of glass. He looked as debonair as any leading man in the movies. We huddled together, quietly grieving for the unnecessary deaths and pain. Ben uttered the words everyone was thinking: "What a star that kid would have made."

Birds chirped, and the sun streamed over the green oasis. David placed an arm around me. Finally, after all our tribulations, I knew everything would be fine.

A word about the author…

Lee René is a jazz-loving author of erotic romances, and of Young Adult and New Adult novels. She had the good fortune of being born in one the most diverse cities in the world, sun-kissed Los Angeles. The City of the Angels is more than just palm trees, toned bodies, movie stars, and beaches; it's a fusion of people, languages, and cultures.

In her past literary life, Lee worked as a lifestyle writer for magazines in Los Angeles, San Francisco, New York and Vancouver as well as entertainment journalist and movie reviewer in print, on-line, and on radio in the Los Angeles area. She is a student of American history and her works are usually set in the past.

When Lee is not writing, she spends her time watching movies from the golden era on TCM, delving into history, enjoying classical music and jazz, and reading gothic literature.

Lee says: I'm thrilled to meet other writers, bloggers, reviewers, editors, and those involved in publishing. I write dark Young Adult fiction with strong female protagonists.

I'd love a follow on my Amazon author page: http://www.amazon.com/Lee-Rene/e/B00S37AJWG

I am on LinkedIn: https://www.linkedin.com/in/francescamiller?trk=hp-identity-name

My website is located at: https://leerene.com/

I always follow back on those who follow me on Twitter at: https://twitter.com/gothicimp

I am on Facebook:
https://www.facebook.com/francesca.e.miller
I have three Facebook fan pages:
https://www.facebook.com/TheDivaAndDoctorGod
https://www.facebook.com/The-Gothic-Imp-Francesca-
Elizabeth-Miller-Author-346017262153233/timeline/
https://www.facebook.com/AuthorLeeRene
I also have boards on Pinterest:
http://pinterest.com/gothicimp/boards/
Please connect with me on Goodreads at:
https://www.goodreads.com/user/show/1414244-
francesca-miller
My romance name is Lee René and I have a page:
https://www.goodreads.com/author/show/
11363327.Lee_Rene

Thank you for purchasing
this publication of The Wild Rose Press, Inc.

For questions or more information
contact us at
info@thewildrosepress.com.

The Wild Rose Press, Inc.
www.thewildrosepress.com

www.ingramcontent.com/pod-product-compliance
Lightning Source LLC
Chambersburg PA
CBHW070047030726
47506CB00002B/386